LAST DANCE

Novels By Sheldon Siegel

Mike Daley/Rosie Fernandez Novels
Special Circumstances
Incriminating Evidence
Criminal Intent
Final Verdict
The Confession
Judgment Day
Perfect Alibi
Felony Murder Rule
Serve and Protect
Hot Shot
The Dreamer
Final Out
Last Call
Double Jeopardy
Dead Coin
Last Dance

David Gold/A.C. Battle Novels
The Terrorist Next Door

LAST DANCE

A MIKE DALEY/ROSIE FERNANDEZ THRILLER

SHELDON SIEGEL

This is a work of fiction. Names, characters, places, and incidents either are the product of the author's imagination or are used fictitiously, and any resemblance to actual persons, living or dead, businesses, companies, events, or locales is entirely coincidental.

Sheldon M. Siegel, Inc.

Copyright © 2024 Sheldon M. Siegel, Inc.

ALL RIGHTS RESERVED

No part of this book may be reproduced, scanned, or printed or electronic form without permission. Please do not participate in or encourage piracy of copyrighted materials in violation of the author's rights. Purchase only authorized editions.

Cover Design by Linda Siegel

ISBN: 978-1-952612-18-3 E-Book

ISBN: 978-1-952612-19-0 Paperback

ISBN: 978-1-952612-20-6 Hardcover

In loving memory of Erica and Rabbi Neil Brief.

"Every San Francisco block is a short story, and each of its hills a novel."

— William Saroyan

1
"I DISTRACTED HIM"

The Honorable Robert J. Stumpf Jr. flashed a wry grin and invoked a commanding baritone. "I didn't expect to see the co-head of the Felony Division of the Public Defender's Office at a preliminary hearing on a traffic case, Mr. Daley."

I returned his smile. "One of my associates is on vacation, Your Honor. I didn't expect to see the Presiding Judge of the San Francisco Superior Court this morning, either."

"One of my colleagues was called away on an emergency."

"Nothing serious, I hope."

"The situation has been resolved."

"Good to hear."

It was ten AM on Monday, May eighth, 2023. I had first appeared before Bob Stumpf when I was a rookie Public Defender shortly after he was promoted to Presiding Judge. Thirty years later, I'm still representing criminals, and Bob is still running Department Twelve on the first floor of our decaying Hall of Justice, which was condemned because of earthquake safety issues, asbestos-laden walls, faulty plumbing, and an overwhelmed electrical system. The courts and SFPD's Homicide Detail are still here, but the District Attorney, the Public Defender, the Southern Police Station, and the Medical Examiner have moved to buildings with functional bathrooms. The old jail on the sixth and seventh floors was replaced by a newer building next door, and the cafeteria in the basement is now used for storage.

Judge Stumpf was appointed to the bench by Governor Jerry Brown during his first term. The native of Southern Indiana and onetime backup center on the USF basketball team was a thoughtful jurist with a keen legal mind and an incisive wit that turned acerbic if you weren't prepared. At seventy-five, he showed no signs of slowing down, and he still ran the grueling Dipsea Race from Mill Valley to Stinson Beach every year.

He looked at the prosecution table. "Good morning, Mr. Paolini."

The young ADA sprang to his feet and spoke too loudly in an ingratiating voice. "Good morning, Your Honor."

Ernie Paolini was a third-generation native of the City. His great-grandfather, Luigi, immigrated from Palermo and opened a deli in North Beach. Seven of Luigi's eight sons became police officers. The black sheep was a firefighter. The following generation included a judge, two ADAs, a union organizer, and a member of the Board of Supervisors. Ernie's parents moved to a house in the foggy Sunset District, a few blocks from where I grew up. He attended St. Ignatius High School (also my alma mater), USF, and USF Law School. He's been a baby ADA for about nine months. He's a nice kid who will probably be a competent prosecutor when he grows up.

Judge Stumpf nodded at his bailiff. "Please call our case."

"The People versus Javier Morales. Preliminary hearing."

Paolini was still standing. "The defendant is guilty of violating California Vehicle Code Section 23105."

In English, this means that he's charged my client with felony reckless driving.

Showtime. "Your Honor, I would remind Mr. Paolini that Mr. Morales is innocent until proven guilty. It is therefore presumptuous and legally incorrect to state that he is guilty."

"Duly noted, Mr. Daley." Judge Stumpf glanced at the gallery, which was half-full of ADAs, Deputy PDs, and a handful of private defense lawyers waiting for a few moments of assembly-line justice. They were joined by our regular contingent of courtroom junkies, homeless people, law students, and other hangers-on who passed the time watching the wheels of justice grind ever-so-slowly in San Francisco's crumbling bazaar of criminal law.

Judge Stumpf inhaled the eighty-five-degree air that smelled of mildew. "The purpose of a preliminary hearing is to determine whether there is a reasonable basis to conclude that the defendant committed the crime for which he is charged. The prosecution is not required to prove its case beyond a reasonable doubt as it would at trial. By law, I am obliged to evaluate the evidence and give the benefit of the doubt to the DA. The defense may call witnesses and present evidence, but it is not required to do so. Everybody understands why we are here?"

Paolini and I responded in unison. "Yes, Your Honor."

"Please proceed with your presentation, Mr. Paolini."

"Thank you, Your Honor. We will be brief."

We'll see. And for future reference, it's okay for the judge to invoke the "royal we." It isn't a good look for a rookie ADA.

I gave a reassuring nod to the nervous young man sitting next to me at the defense table. Javier Morales was a slender man of twenty. In his ill-fitting navy suit, he could have passed for a sophomore in high school. The graduate of Mission High worked at his uncle's produce market on Twenty-fourth Street. He had no criminal record, although he was picked up for shoplifting once, and he had two speeding tickets.

Paolini buttoned his charcoal Men's Wearhouse suit jacket, walked to the lectern, and placed his laptop in front of him. "Your Honor, the facts of this case are not in dispute."

Come on. "With respect to Mr. Paolini, we dispute his contention that the facts are not in dispute."

"Noted, Mr. Daley. Please continue, Mr. Paolini."

"On Monday, May first, at seven-seventeen in the evening, the defendant was driving his 2013 Honda Civic northbound on Mission Street between Twenty-fifth and Twenty-fourth. The defendant suddenly accelerated, lost control of his vehicle, and slammed into an Amazon delivery van parked in front of La Taqueria."

"I've eaten there on several occasions," the judge said.

So have I. The no-frills Mission District classic has been serving award-winning burritos since 1973. The overstuffed carnitas burrito was once voted the best in the U.S.

Paolini introduced the police reports and a dozen photos into evidence, then he scrunched his face into a melodramatic frown. "The defendant's recklessness resulted in ten thousand dollars' worth of damage to the Amazon truck. The defendant's car was totaled. The driver of the truck briefly lost consciousness. Fortunately, he did not sustain life-threatening injuries."

"Good to hear," the judge observed.

Paolini surmised that it was a good idea to agree with him. "Indeed."

Indeed. "Your Honor," I said, "as noted in the police reports and in our papers, the driver acknowledged that he may have lost consciousness because he had taken a large amount of over-the-counter cold medicine. It is therefore likely that my client's actions did not cause him to lose consciousness. Moreover, my client and Amazon are fully insured, and the costs are being worked out between their respective carriers. Neither Amazon nor my client will incur any out-of-pocket expenses except for modest deductibles."

"Good to hear, Mr. Daley. Anything else, Mr. Paolini?"

"Based upon the police reports, photos, and eyewitness accounts, there is sufficient evidence that the defendant committed the crime for which he is charged. As a result, he should be bound over for trial." He closed his laptop and returned to the prosecution table.

The judge turned my way. "Does your client dispute anything that Mr. Paolini just said?"

Not really. "There are extenuating circumstances, Your Honor."

"That seems to be the case whenever you appear in my courtroom, Mr. Daley. Do you wish to present any evidence or witnesses to support your assertion?"

"I do." I glanced at the anxious young woman sitting next to her mother in the front row of the gallery. "The defense calls Ms. Anita Gutierrez."

She looked at her mother, whose expression combined maternal support and profound irritation. Anita adjusted the lapel of her gray jacket and walked tentatively to the front of the courtroom, where the bailiff swore her in. Per my request, she had dressed conservatively and wore no makeup. She took her seat in the box, gulped two cups of water, and looked up at me.

"Good morning, Ms. Gutierrez," I said.

"Good morning, Mr. Daley."

"May I ask how old you are?"

"Nineteen."

"Are you employed?"

"I work part-time at my parents' restaurant in the Mission. I am a freshman at City College."

"What are you studying?"

"Nursing."

"Good for you." I had instructed Anita to follow my lead and keep her answers short. I asked the judge for permission to approach the box, which he granted. "Ms. Gutierrez, do you know the defendant, Mr. Morales?"

"Yes. We have known each other since we were in kindergarten at St. Peter's."

It's the school in the century-old Catholic Church in the Mission where my parents were baptized and later married.

"He's your boyfriend, isn't he?" I asked.

An overanxious Paolini jumped to his feet. "Objection. Mr. Daley is leading the witness."

Yes, I am. "I'll rephrase. Is Javier your boyfriend?"

"Yes. We've been together for almost two years."

Paolini was still standing. "Your Honor, I fail to see the relevance."

I invoked a patient tone. "I'm getting there, Your Honor."

"Quickly, Mr. Daley."

I moved a little closer to Anita. "You were with Javier on Monday, May first, when his car accidentally collided with an Amazon truck?"

The hyperactive Paolini was up again. "Objection to the use of the term 'accidentally.'"

"I'll rephrase," I said. "You were in the car when it collided with the Amazon truck?"

"Yes. I was in the passenger seat."

"Were you or Javier hurt?"

"Thankfully, no."

"Was Javier driving fast?"

"No. He was going the speed limit."

"Were you concerned about your safety?"

She glanced at her boyfriend. "No. Javier is very careful."

"In your opinion, was he driving recklessly?"

"Absolutely not."

Just the way we rehearsed it. "But he did, in fact, run into the Amazon truck, didn't he?"

"Yes, but it wasn't his fault."

"Could you please explain?"

Anita looked at her mother. She took a sip of water. She glanced at Javier. She cleared her throat. "I distracted him." She added, "I didn't mean to."

"How did you distract him?"

Another glance at her mother. "We were joking around, and I, uh, accidentally touched him in a sensitive place."

I suspect that it wasn't entirely accidental, but I had assured Anita that I wouldn't ask her to provide details. "Could you please describe what happened next?"

"Javier was startled. He inadvertently hit the accelerator, and we ran into the Amazon truck. It happened very fast."

"Did he do it on purpose?"

"Of course not. It was an accident." She looked over at Javier, tears streaming down her cheeks. "It wasn't his fault. Javier didn't mean to hit the truck. If anything, it was my fault."

I trust that Javier appreciates the fact that you are a wonderful girlfriend. "Thank you, Ms. Gutierrez. No further questions."

"Cross-exam, Mr. Paolini?"

The young ADA correctly decided that it would not enhance his case by going after a nineteen-year-old who was crying. "Nothing for this witness, Your Honor."

Good call, Ernie.

The judge looked my way. "Any additional witnesses, Mr. Daley?"

"No, Your Honor. I would, however, like to make a motion to have the charges dismissed as a matter of law."

"On what grounds?"

Here goes. "It is a violation of Section 23105 of the Vehicle Code if you drive recklessly and cause great bodily injury, which includes a loss of consciousness. However, as we previously noted, it is likely that my client's actions did not cause the driver of the Amazon truck to lose consciousness. In addition, Section 23103 of the Vehicle Code defines reckless driving as a 'willful or wanton disregard for the safety of other people or property.'" I shot a disdainful glance at Paolini. "Based on Ms. Gutierrez's testimony, Javier did not act willfully or with wanton disregard for the safety of other people or property. He was startled and inadvertently depressed the accelerator. The result was unfortunate, but it was also an accident. As a result, he did not violate the statute, and the charges should be dismissed."

Paolini pogoed to his feet. "He rear-ended a truck, Your Honor. It was only through the grace of God that nobody was seriously injured."

That much is probably true. It's also bad form to whine. "It doesn't rise to the level of reckless driving."

Judge Stumpf rested his chin in his palm and listened as Paolini and I volleyed back and forth. Finally, he spoke with measured authority. "Gentlemen, I find both of your arguments to be well-researched and thoughtful. In the spirit of justice and cooperation, I would like to think that we can resolve this matter without taking the time and resources to empanel a jury and go to trial."

That's my cue. "I have a suggestion for what I believe would be a fair resolution of this matter, Your Honor." *I would never think of suggesting anything that isn't fair.*

"I'm listening, Mr. Daley. So is Mr. Paolini."

The rookie ADA forced a smile.

I invoked a tone of reason. "Mr. Morales will be issued a speeding citation which he will not contest. He will pay the fine, get a point added to his insurance, have his license suspended for three months, and attend traffic school. He will reimburse Amazon for the deductible and for the cost of any repairs on the van not otherwise covered by insurance. He will apologize to the driver. In exchange, Mr. Paolini will dismiss the reckless driving charge."

The judge looked at Paolini. "That seems reasonable to me."

"I need to check with my boss."

"Fine. Please inform her that Judge Stumpf finds this to be an equitable solution."

"But, Your Honor—,"

"*Very* equitable."

"I think we can work it out, Your Honor."

"Good to hear. I will leave it to you and Mr. Daley to agree on final terms and complete any necessary documentation."

"Yes, Your Honor."

I gave Javier a subtle nod. It was a victory, but you never want to spike the ball until you're outside the courtroom.

The judge looked at Javier. "Please drive more carefully next time." He nodded at Anita. "And please be sure to thank Ms. Gutierrez for her testimony."

"I will, Your Honor."

"Next case."

My suit jacket was drenched in perspiration as I stopped at the workstation in the sauna-like corridor of the PD's Office at eleven-ten that same morning. "Any word on when they might send somebody over to fix the air conditioner?" I asked.

My new assistant looked up from her computer. "Maybe next week."

Great. Twenty years ago, the PD's Office moved into a repurposed auto repair shop on Seventh Street, a half block south of the Hall of Justice. At the time, it was a substantial upgrade from our ratty old digs where the heater worked sporadically, the asbestos-laden walls were covered in lead-based paint, and the plumbing worked when it was in the mood. Two decades of deferred maintenance later, our no-longer-state-of-the-art facility needed a tune-up.

I grinned. "Any chance you might be able to use your charms to persuade them to come over a little sooner?"

"Let me see what I can do, Mike."

"Thanks, Dazz."

Debra "Dazzle" Diamond was a Daly City native, a single mother, and a San Francisco State alum. After she was laid off from her job as a paralegal for a corporate law firm during the economic downturn in 2008, she started dancing at the Gold Club, an upscale strip joint down the street from Moscone Center which caters to the tech bros who work in the nearby office towers. I represented her several times after she pilfered cash from her customers while they were entranced by her dancing skills. To her credit, she's an excellent assistant and an outstanding dancer. Unfortunately, she wasn't a very good thief.

"Have you heard from Terrence?" I asked.

"He'll be back later this week. He's having fun in San Diego. He said that his new granddaughter is a beauty."

My onetime client, long-time assistant, and former small-time professional boxer, Terrence "The Terminator" Love, had planned to retire at the end of last year. I persuaded him to stick around and work a reduced schedule. Around the same time, Dazzle was looking to supplement her income to help pay for her daughter's tuition at UC Santa Cruz. I worked out a Solomon-like arrangement where Terrence and Dazzle each work two days a week and every other Friday. I got both of them just enough hours to qualify for health insurance. As far as I know, I am the only Public Defender in California who employs two of his former clients. In addition to my other responsibilities, I'm a one-person rehabilitation program.

Dazzle's blue eyes sparkled. "Did you get the charges against Javier dropped?"

"I got him off with a speeding ticket, a suspended license, and traffic school."

"Not bad. And Anita?"

"She wasn't charged, but she has to answer to a higher authority: her mother."

"I trust you informed Javier that Anita just won a gold medal for being the Supportive Girlfriend of the Year?"

"I did. And I told Anita to keep her hands to herself when he's driving."

"Good advice." Dazzle flashed the grin that captivated tech entrepreneurs at two shows five nights a week. "You sure it was just her hands?"

"No comment."

Her smile broadened. "Did you ever have a similar experience when you were their age?"

"Afraid not."

"Either you were a goody-goody, or you needed to get out more."

"My dad was a cop. I was an altar boy at St. Anne's. If I misbehaved, I heard about it at home and at church."

"Did you have a girlfriend in high school?"

"As a matter of fact, I did. She was an honors student at Mercy High who is now a Superior Court judge. She never grabbed me by my, uh, magical parts while I was driving."

"What about when you weren't driving?"

"No comment."

"And when you were a priest?"

"Absolutely not."

"Good to hear."

I decided to become a priest after my older brother died in Vietnam. I liked the spirituality and intellectual rigor, but I wasn't good at saving souls. I gave up after three years and went to law school.

She winked. "I trust that Javier didn't incur any serious injuries."

I grinned. "Let's just say that there was nothing reproductively catastrophic. Are you working tonight?"

"I have to pay Wendy's tuition, Mike. You should come to the show."

"No, thanks, Dazz."

"Don't be such a prude. Have you ever gone to a club to watch women dance?"

"It's been a long time." I pointed at the closed door of the office next to mine. "The boss is running for re-election. It wouldn't be a good look if somebody takes a photo of the co-head of the Felony Division giving you a gratuity during your finale."

"It isn't a big deal."

"It would be if the photo goes viral on Facebook, Instagram, and TikTok."

"Probably true. On the other hand, you're not the only lawyer who patronizes the club."

I can't resist. "Ever seen anybody from the DA's Office?"

Her smile broadened. "All the time."

"Care to mention any names?"

"I don't dance and tell." Her expression turned serious. "The boss wants to see you. You heard about the dancer who was stabbed to death in the alley behind For Gentlemen Only?"

"Yes." For Gentlemen Only is an upscale strip club in North Beach.

"They arrested the doorman. He's about to be charged with murder, and our office is getting the case."

2
"I OWE HIM ONE"

The Public Defender of the City and County of San Francisco flashed the incandescent smile that I still found irresistible three decades after we'd met in the file room of the old PD's Office, twenty-eight years after we'd gotten married, twenty-seven years after our daughter, Grace, was born, twenty-six years after we'd gotten divorced, and three years after she'd won her second term as PD. Rosita Carmela Fernandez mouthed the words, "One sec."

I sat down in the chair opposite the mahogany desk that she had bought on her own dime. Her window was caked in dirt. The walls were covered with photos of Rosie posing with local politicians. Her bookcases held dusty case reporters. If she needed a citation, she looked it up online. A wedding photo of Grace and her husband, Chuck, sat on the credenza next to a picture of our son, Tommy, who was born after Rosie and I got divorced. Old habits. Grace and Chuck worked as production supervisors at Pixar. Tommy was a junior at UC Berkeley.

I nodded at my younger brother, Pete, who was sitting on the windowsill. The former SFPD cop now worked as a private investigator. At fifty-eight, he was two years younger, a couple of inches shorter, and twenty muscular pounds heavier than I was. His full head of hair and bushy mustache used to be a half-shade darker than mine, but now they were silver.

"Are Donna and Margaret okay?" I whispered.

He absent-mindedly played with the zipper of the bomber jacket that he always wore even though it was eighty degrees in the office. "Everybody's fine."

Good. His wife, Donna Andrews, was the CFO of a big law firm downtown. His daughter, Margaret, was a sophomore at UC Santa Barbara.

"Why are you here?" I asked.

His mustache twitched as he pointed at Rosie. "I'll let her explain."

Rosie ended her call and gave me a conspiratorial grin. "I heard you got Javier off with a ticket, a suspended license, and traffic school. Nice work."

Word travels fast. "Just doing my part to improve our statistics."

She tugged at the sleeve of her Anne Fontaine blouse. The days when she wore faded jeans to work were a distant memory. At fifty-six, her olive skin was still flawless, but the crow's feet were entrenched, and her coiffed shoulder-length hair required artificial assistance to keep its jet-black color. Rosie went to spin class three mornings a week to maintain her perfect physique. She was running for her third and (she swears) final term against one of our former colleagues who had the audacity to challenge her. She had mastered the dark art of San Francisco politics after two successful election campaigns. I would bet a year's salary that she will annihilate her opponent in what promises to be the political equivalent of a knife fight in the Tenderloin.

First things first. "Kids okay?"

"Status quo. Mama is fine, too."

"Good."

Rosie and I are members of what the pundits have dubbed the "sandwich generation." Her mom, Sylvia, is eighty-seven. She's as sharp and opinionated as ever, but she refuses to acknowledge that two artificial hips and an artificial knee have slowed her down. She still lives in the two-bedroom bungalow in the Mission that she and her late husband, Eduardo, bought almost sixty years ago.

"You okay?" I asked.

"Fine."

As if you would ever admit that you're anything but "fine."

"Anything new on the election?"

"The latest polling looks solid. I made some calls over the weekend and raised almost thirty grand. My war chest is ten times bigger than my opponent's."

She never mentions her challenger's name. "You're going to beat her."

"I'm going to crush her."

I stand corrected. Rosie and I had met when I was a rookie PD, and she had just been promoted to the Felony Division. She had spun out of a brief and unsatisfying marriage. Grace was born less than a year after we got married. The demands of a baby, our jobs, and a new marriage overwhelmed us, and Rosie and I called things off when Grace was one. I took a job at a big law firm to pay the bills, alimony, and child support. Rosie started her own criminal defense practice and took me in after I was fired for not bringing in enough clients. We've been working together ever since—first at our two-person firm around the corner from the old Transbay Bus Terminal, and, more recently, back here at the PD's Office. We were co-heads of the Felony Division for a few years before our old boss retired and Rosie ran for PD.

Time for business. "Dazzle said that you wanted to see me."

Her expression turned serious. "How's your time?"

"I can tear myself away from my administrative responsibilities if you need help."

As co-head of the Felony Division, I spend most of my time budgeting, assigning cases, supervising younger lawyers, and handling bureaucratic matters. Once or twice a year, I step in and work on a trial.

She glanced at Pete, then she turned back to me. "Since you did such a fine job keeping Javier out of jail, I need you to handle something more challenging. You heard about the dancer who was stabbed to death behind For Gentlemen Only over the weekend?"

"Yes."

"Her name is Chloe Carson. Twenty-two. Single. Never married. Grew up in Fremont. Dropped out of San Jose State. Her mother raised her. Her father is deceased."

"And the defendant?"

Pete finally spoke up. "It's César."

I stopped cold. "Seriously?"

He nodded.

César Ochoa was Pete's onetime training officer, partner, mentor, and friend. A native of the Mission, César joined SFPD after he graduated from Archbishop Riordan High School. He was a tough cop who had a propensity for roughing up suspects. He and Pete got into hot water when they allegedly broke up a gang fight with a little too much exuberance. The instigator ended up with a concussion, a broken arm, and four cracked ribs. It turned out that he was the nephew of a member of the Board of Supervisors. After the inevitable lawsuit was filed, the City caved, the kid received a seven-figure settlement, and Pete and César got fired. They steadfastly maintained that they had done everything by the book, although Pete later confided to me that they might have been able to defuse the situation with a little more finesse. Pete became a PI. César became an alcoholic.

I looked at my brother. "When was the last time that you talked to César?"

"A couple of years ago."

César's life went off the rails after he was fired. He spent a few years in private security until his drinking became problematic. He developed high blood pressure and diabetes. His wife left him. His son stopped talking to him. He ended up living in a studio apartment in the Mission and working as a doorman at a series of strip clubs.

Rosie cleared her throat. "Pete has offered to help us *pro bono.*"

I would ordinarily be delighted to accept free assistance from one of San Francisco's most tenacious PIs, but I was perplexed by my brother's motivation.

"Why do you want to help the guy who got you fired?" I asked.

"I owe him one. César looked out for me when I joined SFPD. He stood up for me when we got into trouble. It's my turn to stand up for him."

"César gave that kid a concussion."

"Heat of battle, Mick."

"You haven't even talked to him in a couple of years."

"He got really angry. I didn't have the patience or the energy to deal with him. Besides, I didn't think I could fix his problems."

"But you still think you owe him?"

"There's no statute of limitations on paybacks."

I looked over at Rosie. "You're okay with this arrangement?"

"When one of San Francisco's best private investigators offers to donate his services, I'm inclined to accept."

Me, too. I turned back to Pete. "Did César have any connection to the decedent?"

"Other than the fact that they both worked at For Gentlemen Only, I don't know."

"Do you know anything about what happened?"

"I have a couple of calls in to my sources at SFPD."

I looked my brother in the eye. "Do you think that César is capable of killing someone?"

His mustache twitched. "César had a temper, but he never lost control. He wasn't a killer when I knew him."

His instincts were excellent. I turned to Rosie. "I may need a little help."

"Rolanda did César's intake interview. She has some time."

"Great."

Rolanda Fernandez was the co-head of the Felony Division. She was also Rosie's niece and, I suppose, my ex-niece. Like Rosie, Rolanda graduated from Mercy High, San Francisco State, and what was then known as Hastings Law School, and is now known as UC Law San Francisco. She and her husband, Zach, yet another lawyer, were the proud parents of a three-year-old daughter and a six-month old son. Rolanda had recently returned from maternity leave.

Rosie looked at Pete. "I don't want you and Mike playing cops-and-robbers."

"We'll be careful."

She turned to me. "When can you start?"

"I'll go see Rolanda right now."

3
"I ALWAYS HAVE TIME FOR YOU"

I knocked on the open door of the office across the hall from mine. "Got a sec?"

Rolanda Fernandez's face transformed into a radiant smile that was almost identical to Rosie's. "I always have time for you, Mike."

I sat down in the creaky swivel chair opposite her metal desk in the windowless office with just enough room for a dented credenza and an IKEA bookcase. The only personal items were framed photos of her two children: Maria Sylvia Teresa Fernandez Epstein and Antonio Eduardo Fernandez Epstein. The only hints that she was closer to forty than thirty were the flecks of gray in her long black hair—souvenirs from a dozen years as a Deputy Public Defender and three years as a mom.

"Kids okay?" I asked.

"Great."

"You and Zach getting any sleep?"

"Not much."

"Comes with the territory."

An eternity ago, Rosie and I babysat Rolanda when she was in grammar school. By the time she was in high school, she was an all-conference softball player and an all-state debater. Even then, it seemed inevitable that she would end up in law school. While Rosie wouldn't acknowledge it to anybody but me, she was discreetly setting the stage for Rolanda to succeed her. Rosie's master plan was delayed after Rolanda's son was born. Rolanda decided that running for office while dealing with two kids in diapers was more than she wanted to take on. As a result, Rosie was running for one more term.

I pointed at the silver-and-black Keeshond sleeping in the corner. "Is Luna okay?"

"Fine. Two more days and I hand her off to her next babysitter."

Luna was the most beloved character in the PD's Office and, perhaps, San Francisco. The impeccably-trained dog belonged to our colleague, Nadezhda "Nady" Nikonova, a talented attorney whom I had liberated from a big firm downtown a few years ago. If Rosie's plans come to fruition, Nady will take my spot as head of the Felony Division when Rolanda becomes PD.

I walked over to Luna, who opened her eyes, looked up hopefully, wagged her tail, and scrambled to her feet. I pulled out a treat, held it above her nose, and then dropped it into her mouth. She devoured it enthusiastically, licked her chops, smiled, and slunk back to the floor.

"Good girl," I said. I turned back to Rolanda. "Have you heard from Nady?"

"She and Max are hiking somewhere in Peru."

Nady's husband, Max, was an overworked partner at Story, Short, and Thompson, a megafirm in Embarcadero Center. When I persuaded Nady to come to work for us, Luna was part of the package. I convinced my bureaucratic masters at City Hall to make the PD's Office a dog-friendly space after I agreed to indemnify the City if Luna ever bit somebody. When Nady and Max are out of town, the rest of us take turns looking after Luna. She could have stayed with one of Nady's neighbors, but we didn't want to disrupt our favorite canine's routine.

Rolanda's eyes twinkled. "I heard that you got Javier off with a speeding ticket, a suspended license, an apology, and traffic school. Not bad."

"Thanks." I lowered my voice. "Rosie asked me to handle César Ochoa's arraignment tomorrow. She said that you did his intake interview."

"I did. The police say that he stabbed a dancer named Chloe Carson in the alley behind For Gentlemen Only in North Beach. César says that he didn't."

"Any idea why San Francisco's finest have the misconception that he did?"

"They found a bloody steak knife in the Dumpster next to Ms. Carson's body. They expedited forensics. The blood matched the decedent's. Our client's fingerprints were on the handle."

Uh-oh. "Not helpful facts for our defense. Any other prints?"

"One that didn't match César. Another one was smudged."

"Maybe the real killer—assuming that it isn't our new client—wore gloves."

"As far as I know, they didn't find any gloves in the Dumpster."

"Maybe the real killer tossed the knife into the Dumpster and kept the gloves."

"Maybe."

"Did César offer any explanation as to how his prints found their way onto the knife?"

"He had a burger at the club shortly before closing time. He cut it with a steak knife."

"He thinks that somebody picked up the same knife and stabbed Chloe Carson?"

"That's all I have so far, Mike."

"Did they find any blood on our client's hands, clothes, or car?"

"No, but they didn't arrest him until early this morning. He could have gotten rid of his clothes and washed his hands."

"Motive?"

"Witnesses saw César and the decedent arguing on Friday night. César said Ms. Carson and the guy running the sound system got into an argument after the show. Evidently, it wasn't the first time he had screwed up. César claimed that he told Ms. Carson to let it go. She didn't appreciate his advice. Either way, the police found his explanation to be less than credible."

"Got a name for the sound guy?"

"Jerry Henderson."

Pete will find him. "What time did César leave the club?"

"Right after last dance at one AM. Ms. Carson left a few minutes later. Her body was discovered at seven AM by a man walking his dog."

"Police reports?" I asked.

"Not yet. We don't have a preliminary autopsy report or toxicology yet."

"Evidence of a struggle?"

"I don't know, Mike."

"Who is the homicide inspector?"

"Melinda Wong."

Game on. Wong was a native of the Sunset and a graduate of Lowell High School and UC Davis. Her father was a captain at Taraval Station. The twenty-year SFPD veteran didn't arrest people without substantial evidence.

"She's good," I said.

"She's a pain."

That, too. "Have they assigned an ADA?"

"You aren't going to like that, either. It's Catherine O'Neal."

This is going to be hand-to-hand combat. Catherine "No Deal" O'Neal was one of a half-dozen young prosecutors recently hired by our new DA, Vanessa Turner, a law-and-order zealot who was appointed by her friend and political ally, Mayor Nicole Ward, after our last DA, a former colleague of mine at the PD's Office, was recalled for allegedly being soft on drug dealers. He took the brunt of the blame for San Francisco's well-documented problems ranging from homelessness to drug dealing to shoplifting. A year after the recall, the homeless are still on the streets, the drug dealers are still in the Tenderloin, and the shoplifters are still breaking into stores. The mayor and the DA talk a good game, but the only thing that's changed is that they're getting the heat now.

I opted for diplomacy. "She's good, too."

"She's an even bigger pain than Melinda," Rolanda said. "I understand that Pete is going to help with the investigation."

"He is." I explained that Pete was César's partner at Mission Station. "He says that César isn't a killer."

"We'll see. Are you heading back to court this afternoon?"

"No, I'm going to meet our new client."

4
"I DIDN'T DO IT"

César Ochoa paced like a caged tiger in the cramped attorney-client consultation room that smelled of Lysol. "I didn't do it."

"We'll get to what happened in a minute," I said.

He spoke in a gravelly cop staccato. "We'll get to it right now. Nothing happened." He adjusted the sleeve of his orange jumpsuit that looked two sizes too large for his wiry frame. "I didn't do it," he repeated.

"Good to know. First, I need to explain a few things to you."

"Fine."

At one-fifteen on Monday afternoon, César and I were meeting in an airless room on the ground floor of County Jail #2, the plexiglass-covered seven-story building that was shoehorned between the Hall of Justice and the I-80 Freeway in the nineties. At the time, it was a huge upgrade over the overcrowded and outdated jail on the sixth and seventh floors of the Hall, and the cops dubbed it the "Glamour Slammer." Three decades of deferred maintenance later, the plumbing was spotty, the walls were chipped, the lights flickered, and the linoleum floors had faded to an unnatural shade of yellow. Given the state of the City's finances, it is unlikely that the no-longer-glamorous Glamour Slammer will get even a modest upgrade before I retire.

"You okay?" I asked.

He took a seat in the white plastic chair. "Been better."

At five-eight and a hundred and seventy pounds, "Little César" was a tightly wound man of sixty with narrow eyes, a pockmarked face with the wisp of a gray goatee, and a shaved head glistening with sweat. His marriage had ended badly a few years after he and Pete were dismissed from SFPD. His ex-wife, Selena, got custody of their son, Jesus, who became a firefighter. According to Pete, César and Jesus were estranged for years, but resumed occasional communications after Jesus and his wife had their first child.

"Have you eaten anything?" I asked.

"A little. How soon can you get me out of here?"

That's always the first question. "You know the process. Your arraignment is tomorrow morning. You'll plead not guilty. The DA still has a policy of not asking for cash bail, but she'll request no-bail detention. It's up to the judge to grant pretrial release."

"I'll wear a monitor, surrender my passport, and have regular check-ins."

"We'll ask for pretrial release." *But we probably won't get it.*

I needed to manage his expectations. Our previous DA adopted a guideline against cash bail because he believed that it discriminated against those of limited means, and it (arguably) complied with a California Supreme Court ruling. Our new DA has retained the policy for now. As a result, judges must consider a variety of factors to determine whether a defendant should be released pending trial. This holistic approach is more of an art than a science, and judges legitimately err on the side of caution.

I added, "The judge isn't likely to release you if the charge is murder."

The bravado disappeared. "You have to get me out of here."

"I'll do everything that I can."

"How soon can we go to trial?"

"We can ask for a preliminary hearing in ten days. By law, you have the right to a trial within sixty days after that."

"That's what I want to do."

No, you don't. "That's a bad idea, César. We'll need time to investigate, interview witnesses, and prepare."

"I'm not going to rot in here for two years."

"We'll talk about it after the arraignment."

"We'll talk about it now. I used to be a cop. I already have a target on my back."

"I'll ask them to house you in 'Ad Seg.'"

Administrative segregation, or "Ad Seg," meant that César would have his own cell. It didn't guarantee his safety, but it enhanced his odds of avoiding trouble.

"Are you going to handle my case?" he asked.

"Yes. Pete has agreed to help with the investigation—free of charge."

"That's very generous of him."

"Yes, it is." *First things first.* "I trust that Rolanda explained that we have only one hard-and-fast rule: you need to tell us the absolute unvarnished truth, and you can't leave out anything important."

"She did. I'm good with that."

"Everything you told her was true?"

"Of course."

"Anything you'd like to add or reconsider?"

"No."

Good. "Is there anybody that I should call?"

"No."

"What about Selena?"

"No." His lips turned down. "I left her a message. If she wants to get in touch, she will."

"You want me to call Jesus?"

"He knows that I'm here, too."

"How long were you working at For Gentlemen Only?"

"Almost two years. I didn't kill Chloe."

"The DA thinks you did."

"She's wrong."

"What happened on Friday night?"

"Nothing happened."

For defense lawyers, it's sometimes a positive sign when your client issues a forceful denial. Guilty people tend to massage their stories. Innocent people get mad. From a legal standpoint, however, it was a mixed bag. The California Rules of Professional Conduct prohibit attorneys from letting clients lie on the stand. If I find out that he did, in fact, kill Chloe Carson, I can't let him testify to the contrary. We defense lawyers come up with all sorts of creative justifications to get around this rule, but I prefer to avoid the issue if I can.

I kept my voice even. "You knew Chloe Carson?"

"Of course."

"How well?"

"Not well. She had been working at the club for just a few months."

"Did she ever give you any trouble?"

"No."

"When was the last time that you saw her?"

"Shortly after last dance on Saturday morning. I left at closing time at one AM." He said that he left via the back door leading to the alley.

"Was she still there when you left?"

"As far as I know."

"Did you see her outside?"

"I didn't see anybody."

I asked if there was a security camera in the alley.

"Yes, but it was broken."

I eyed him. "Is there any chance that the DA has video of you in the alley?"

"If she does, it isn't from the club's security camera. And even if I'm on video, it won't show me stabbing Chloe because I didn't. The alley dead-ends into a retaining wall at the foot of Telegraph Hill. I suppose it's possible that there is security footage from one of the apartment buildings up the hill, but it seems unlikely."

I'll check the police reports. "Where did you go after you left?"

"Home." He said that he walked to his car, which was parked a few blocks away near the Embarcadero. "I drove straight to my apartment." He confirmed that he lived by himself.

"Did the cops find any blood in your car?"

"There wasn't any to find."

"I take it that they searched your apartment when they arrested you?"

"Of course. They didn't find any bloody clothes, either."

"Did they find anything else that might be of concern?"

"My Glock was in my nightstand. I told them about it as soon as they showed up. They confiscated it."

Not surprising.

He added, "I purchased it legally, and I have a license. When this is over, I expect to get it back."

"You will. What time did you get to work on Friday night?"

"Four PM." He said that he helped with setup and worked the front door. "It wasn't very busy. We cater to an upscale crowd: frat boys, tech bros, neighborhood regulars, and out-of-town businessmen looking for a good time."

"Did anybody give you any trouble?"

"No."

"Did anybody give Chloe any trouble?"

"Not that I saw."

"Was she well-liked at the club?"

"As far as I know."

"Anybody mad at her?"

"A couple of the more experienced dancers were upset when Chloe solicited their regulars. They worked it out."

"The DA told Rolanda that a witness said that you and Chloe got into an argument on the night she died."

"I would call it a conversation. She got mad at the tech guy because the sound went out a couple of times during her routine. I told her to let it go. She didn't take crap from anybody, and she didn't appreciate my advice."

"That would be Jerry Henderson?"

"Yes."

"How well did you know him?"

"Not well. He worked once or twice a month."

"Any idea where we can find him?"

"He lives in North Beach and plays in a band."

"A guy who was walking his dog found Chloe's body in the alley behind the club. The police found a bloody steak knife in the Dumpster. The blood matched Chloe's. Your prints were on the knife."

He hesitated. "I'll tell you the same thing that I told Rolanda. I had a burger shortly before I went home. I cut it with a steak knife which I left on the plate."

"You think somebody picked it up and took it outside?"

"That's the only possible explanation."

Unless you used it to stab Chloe Carson. "Inspector Melinda Wong believes you used it to stab Chloe."

"I didn't."

"She has a good reputation."

"She's a good cop, but it doesn't mean that she's right this time."

5
"RIGHT HERE"

I handed Pete a paper cup of scalding Peet's coffee. "The homicide inspector on César's case is Melinda Wong."

He took a sip of coffee. "She's good."

"Good cops make mistakes."

"It would make our case easier if we can find some hard evidence that she did."

"That's where you come in."

At four o'clock on Monday afternoon, Pete and I were standing on the sidewalk on the northwest corner of Broadway and Montgomery, the approximate dividing line between the upscale boutiques and offices housed in the Earthquake-era buildings of Jackson Square and the densely packed two- and three-story apartment buildings in North Beach and Telegraph Hill. The wind was picking up, and the afternoon fog was creeping toward us over Russian Hill. The air was filled with the aroma of salt and pepper calamari from Little Szechuan down the street, wood-fired pizzas from Tommaso's around the corner, and cheeseburgers from Sam's just past Columbus Avenue. A steady stream of cars crawled from the Embarcadero toward the Broadway Tunnel on their way to Van Ness Avenue. I turned to the east and had a postcard-quality view of the Bay Bridge above the shimmering water of San Francisco Bay. It was a vast improvement over the days when the view was obstructed by the unsightly Embarcadero Freeway, a double-deck monstrosity that was built in the fifties and torn down after it was damaged in the 1989 Loma Prieta Earthquake.

I looked at the strip clubs, restaurants, smoke shops, and bars lining San Francisco's no-longer-so-notorious red-light district. The Hungry I nightclub where Lenny Bruce and Mort Sahl once played was now an upscale bar. The beat hangout, Enrico's, remained closed after multiple ownership changes. The neon sign above the Condor Club at Broadway and Columbus still displayed a picture of the late Carol Doda, the first topless dancer on the West Coast. The female impersonators at Finocchio's departed after the club went out of business in 1999. The space that once housed Vanessi's, my parents' favorite special occasion restaurant which launched a thousand exhibition kitchens and fed tender osso buco and foamy zabaglione to generations of San Franciscans, was empty.

"Is he coming?" I asked Pete.

"He's on his way, Mick."

A police unit drove up Montgomery, crossed Broadway, and parked in front of a fire hydrant. A muscular officer emerged from the car, put on his hat over his closely-cropped hair, placed his nightstick into its holder, and marched across the street to meet us.

Officer Jeff Roth smiled beneath a bushy mustache, extended a meaty hand, and spoke to Pete. "Family okay?"

"Fine." Pete grasped his hand. "Yours?"

"All good. My daughter is in law school."

"Mine is in college." Pete pointed at me. "You remember Mike?"

"Of course. Good to see you."

"Same here, Jeff."

I waited patiently as Pete and Roth exchanged police gossip. Roth was about Pete's age. The native of the Excelsior started his career at Mission Station. The SFPD nomad rotated through Taraval, Northern, and Park Stations. For the last decade or so, he had worked out of Central Station, a six-story cement bunker on Vallejo between Stockton and Powell, about six blocks from where we were standing. Roth was a conscientious cop who played by the rules, knew how to work the system, and kept his nose clean.

Pete turned to business. "Mike picked up César's case. Helluva thing."

"Helluva thing," Roth repeated.

"I understand that you were the first officer at the scene."

"I was." He turned to me. "I know why you're here: you don't get to pick your clients." He pivoted back to Pete. "I don't understand why you're here."

"César needs help."

"He's needed it for a long time."

"We go back a long way."

"He got you fired."

"It was complicated."

"Not that complicated."

"I was hoping that I could persuade you to show us the scene."

Roth scowled. "The DA's Office doesn't want me to talk to you."

"Ten minutes."

"You can read my report when you get it from the DA."

"Five minutes."

Roth responded with a grudging, "Five minutes. Off the record."

We followed him up the sidewalk and into the alley behind For Gentlemen Only, which was housed in a post-Earthquake-era two-story brick building. He led us into the urine-soaked alley between the rear entrance to the club and a retaining wall at the base of Telegraph Hill. An overflowing Dumpster was next to the wall. I had expected to see yellow police tape, but there was no evidence that this had been a crime scene two days earlier.

Pete's voice was even. "What time did you get here?"

Roth sounded as if he was quoting his police report. "I got the call from dispatch at seven o'clock on Saturday morning. I was working the overnight shift at Central Station. I got here at seven-oh-nine."

"Who called 9-1-1?"

"A retired lawyer named Stewart Baird who lives on Telegraph Hill. He was walking his dog." A half smile. "He has a beautiful golden retriever named Archie."

"Security cameras?"

Roth pointed at a camera mounted above the back door of For Gentlemen Only. "Just one, but it wasn't working." He said that there was also a camera above the front door. "One inside by the bar."

Pete looked down the alley. "Footage from other businesses or residences?"

"Not as far as I know."

If Roth was telling us the truth—and I had no reason to disbelieve him—the police didn't have video of César stabbing Carson. It wasn't an ironclad alibi, but it would give us a little wiggle room if we moved forward to trial.

"Where did Mr. Baird find the body?" Pete asked.

Roth pointed at the ground next to the Dumpster. "Right here." He said that Baird attempted to administer CPR, but he was unsuccessful. So were the EMTs who arrived a few minutes after he did. "Mr. Baird didn't see anybody else in the alley."

Roth said that he called for backup and assisted the EMTs. "Ms. Carson was officially pronounced at the scene at seven-forty AM. We secured the area in accordance with standard procedure. We canvassed for witnesses, but nobody was around. We contacted the manager of the club, who came over and was cooperative. We interviewed him along with the employees who were working on the night that Ms. Carson was killed. Nobody saw anything suspicious in the alley. I handed the scene over to Inspector Wong at eight-ten AM. An Assistant Medical Examiner arrived about an hour later. She performed the autopsy on Saturday afternoon."

"Cause of death?"

"You'll need to ask the ME."

"Any evidence that the decedent knew her assailant?"

"You'll need to ask the ME."

"Any alcohol or drugs in Ms. Carson's system?"

"You'll need to ask the ME."

Pete pointed at the Dumpster. "I understand that you found a bloody knife."

"I did." Roth confirmed that he handled it with care, bagged and tagged it in accordance with SFPD procedure, and entered it into evidence. "Inspector Wong had it tested for prints and DNA. I was told that the prints matched your client's, and the blood matched the decedent's."

"That's quick turnaround on DNA."

"Inspector Wong pulled strings."

Contrary to what you see on TV, you can get a DNA test within hours.

Pete eyed him. "Did you find any bloody clothes in the Dumpster?"

"No."

"You arrested César?"

"Inspector Wong arrested him after consulting with Catherine O'Neal at the DA's Office."

"Did you talk to Jerry Henderson, the sound guy at the club?"

"Yes."

"We were told that he got into an argument with Ms. Carson shortly before she left."

"He didn't mention it."

I'm not surprised. I asked if the manager of the club provided any useful information.

"He didn't see anything out of the ordinary."

"Got a name?"

"Dave Callaghan."

6
"HE WAS VERY PROFESSIONAL"

The stocky young man with the wide forehead, black turtleneck, and tattoo of a snake on his neck, spoke in a guttural voice from his spot behind the podium inside the door at For Gentlemen Only. "We open at six."

Pete stepped in front of me. "We're looking for Dave Callaghan."

"You found him."

"Pete Daley. I was César Ochoa's partner with SFPD. Nowadays, I'm a PI. This is my brother, Mike, who is with the Public Defender's Office. He's representing César. We're trying to figure out what happened on Saturday morning, and we need to ask you a few questions. We won't take up much of your time."

Callaghan froze. "Uh, sure."

At four-forty on Monday afternoon, the houselights were illuminated as the staff of For Gentlemen Only prepared for the evening. The brick exterior of the building was a hundred years old, but the remodeled interior was Twenty-first Century. With its black walls, leather chairs, chrome-trimmed tables, brass wall sconces, and purple neon lighting, it resembled a lounge at a Las Vegas hotel. Bottles of high-end liquor lined shelves extending from the back of the bar to the ceiling. Three dozen tables surrounded an unadorned stage with a dance pole. A man with magenta hair was testing the sound and lighting systems. A sign at the podium asked patrons to respect the dancers and invited them to see the maître d' to arrange for bachelor parties.

Callaghan led us to a table in the back. "I gave my statement to the police," he said.

"This won't take long," Pete assured him. "How long have you worked here?"

"About five years."

"You from around here?"

"Redding." He said that he and a couple of college buddies moved to the City after they graduated from Chico State. He worked retail and drove for Uber. "One of my roommates was tending bar here. He recommended me to the manager. I worked my way up."

Admirable industriousness. "Are you also the owner?" I asked.

"I wish. We're owned by a private equity firm that also operates clubs in L.A. and Phoenix. They're planning to expand to other cities."

An upscale strip club is still a strip club.

Pete leaned forward. "You were here on Friday night?"

"Yes." Callaghan glanced at his watch. "I'll tell you what I told the police: Chloe's death is a tragedy. I don't know what happened in the alley on Saturday morning."

"You knew Ms. Carson?"

"I hired her. She was a nice kid and an excellent dancer. She went by the stage name 'Athena.' She worked hard. The customers liked her." Callaghan confirmed that Carson had worked at the club for about six months. She was twenty-two, grew up in Fremont, and attended San Jose State for a couple of years. "She lived in Daly City by herself."

"Boyfriend?"

"Not as far as I know."

"Ex-boyfriends?"

"Probably. I try not to ask personal questions."

"You know a guy named Jerry Henderson?"

"He's our backup sound guy. He comes in when I need him once or twice a month."

"What does he do the rest of the time?"

"He works for a moving company and plays in a band."

"Good guy?"

"Yes."

"He was working on Friday night?"

"Yes."

"We understand that he and Chloe got into an argument after the show."

"I didn't see anything."

"Do you remember what time Henderson left?"

"Shortly after we closed." Callaghan promised to get us Henderson's address. "He lives in North Beach."

"Did Chloe have any family in the area?"

"Her mother lives in Fremont. She never mentioned anybody else."

And you didn't ask too many questions.

Pete asked if Carson had any friends at the club.

"She got along with everybody."

Not exactly the answer to the question.

Pete tried again. "Did she get along with the other dancers?"

"Most of the time." Henderson cleared his throat. "A couple of the girls thought Chloe was a little too friendly with some of their regulars. It's a competitive business. They worked it out."

"Did she ever give you any trouble?"

"All of our dancers give me a little trouble from time to time. She came in late a few times. We also have a policy against freelancing. On a couple of occasions I had to remind her not to solicit customers for private arrangements outside the club."

But you were more than happy if she solicited lap dances inside the club where you got the majority of the proceeds.

"Did she get along with César?"

"Everybody got along with César."

"You hired him?"

"I did."

Pete interjected, "He was fired by SFPD."

"He was upfront about it. I believe in second chances."

"Was he good at his job?"

"Yes. He was very professional. He was respectful to our guests. We don't need our security people to break up fights very often. Most of our customers are upscale. Our biggest issue is when people drink too much. Sometimes they do stupid stuff, or they get a little handsy with the girls. If somebody gets out of line, we ask them to leave. Most of the time they do."

"Did César ever give you any trouble?"

"He got a little rough with some drunk kids a few times."

"Did he ever hit anybody?"

"He shoved people once or twice."

"How was his mood on Friday night?"

"Nothing out of the ordinary."

"Did César have any interactions with Chloe on Friday night?"

"They got into an argument shortly before closing time. I don't know what it was about."

"Do you know what time César left?"

"One AM." He said that Chloe left a few minutes later.

"Did she seem upset?"

"Not as far as I could tell."

"Was anybody still here?"

"Our bartender, the janitor, and a couple of girls." He confirmed that he had provided security footage to the police. "The camera outside the rear door wasn't working."

"What time did you leave?"

"One-thirty." He said that he exited via the front door and walked to his apartment a few blocks away. "I didn't go into the alley, and I didn't see or hear anything outside." He gave Inspector Wong a list of employees along with a printout of the names and credit card receipts of the customers who were present on Friday night.

Pete nodded. "We'll get the info from her. Thanks, Dave."

"You're welcome." His tone turned thoughtful. "I hope you find whoever did this—assuming that it isn't César."

Pete eyed him. "You think César is the kind of guy who would have killed somebody?"

"A few days ago, I wouldn't have thought so. Now I'm not so sure."

"Did you hear from the DA's Office?" I asked.

Rolanda looked up from her laptop. "Catherine O'Neal is going to handle César's arraignment tomorrow. The case is generating buzz because César is an ex-cop. I wouldn't be surprised if our distinguished DA shows up in a display of solidarity."

"And to get some media time," I said.

"That, too."

Rolanda, Pete, and I were sitting around the table in the conference room at the PD's Office at six-forty on Monday night. Luna was sleeping in the corner.

"Did O'Neal provide anything?" I asked.

Rolanda nodded. "Not yet. She promised to send over a list of employees and customers who were at the club on Friday night. We'll check everybody out. We should also request expedited discovery."

"We will."

Under California law, the DA must disclose any evidence that might tend to exonerate César before trial. Notwithstanding what you see on TV, there are few genuine surprises in court. On the other hand, the DA is not required to provide any information prior to the arraignment or the preliminary hearing.

"Has O'Neal decided on a charge?" I asked.

"First-degree murder," Rolanda said. "No enhancements so far."

"She thinks she can prove premeditation?"

"So it seems."

I summarized our conversation with Callaghan, then I turned to Pete. "I need you to talk to everybody who was at For Gentlemen Only on Friday. And I want you to find Jerry Henderson."

"Already working on it, Mick."

Dazzle knocked on the open door. "You need anything else from me?"

"Not at the moment, Dazz. Are you working at the club tonight?"

"I have to pay the bills."

"You know anybody who works at For Gentlemen Only?"

"I'll ask around."

"We talked to Dave Callaghan. Ever met him?"

"No, but I've heard that he's a dick." She gave me a knowing smile. "If you want to find out what's going on at a club like For Gentlemen Only, you don't talk to the manager. You talk to the dancers."

7
"HOW DO YOU WISH TO PLEAD?"

The veteran bailiff spoke in a world-weary voice. "All rise."

At ten o'clock sharp the following morning, a Tuesday, César stood between Rolanda and me at the defense table. We watched Judge Ignatius Tsang stride to the bench and sit down in his tall leather chair. The windowless courtroom over which he had presided for a quarter of a century smelled of cleaning solvent and mold.

He turned on his computer, moved his reading glasses to the top of his head, and held up a hand. "Please be seated."

We did as we were told.

From the perfect Windsor knot in his striped necktie to the Cross pen in his breast pocket to his coiffed silver hair, Ignatius Tsang embodied precision. The native of Taiwan had been brought to San Francisco by his mother and father when he was a baby. His parents worked multiple jobs in Chinatown so that he could focus on school. He graduated at the top of his class at Lowell High, raced through UC Berkeley in three years, and placed first in his class at Berkeley Law. He clerked for Justice Byron White before joining the San Francisco DA's office, where he distinguished himself for two decades while writing law review articles and teaching criminal procedure. He brought the same intellectual rigor to the bench.

He scanned the full gallery, then his eyes moved from the prosecution table to the defense table. Finally, he turned to his bailiff. "Please call our first case."

"The People versus César Ochoa. Arraignment. The defendant is present."

César tensed. Dressed in his ill-fitting orange jumpsuit, he looked as if he wanted to leap over the table and argue his case himself.

I looked at the prosecution table where Catherine "No Deal" O'Neal was seated, arms at her sides, unblinking eyes locked onto the judge. Her black pantsuit matched her hair, which she wore in a layered bob. Her small mouth was rolled into a tight ball. Except for a perfunctory nod when she entered the courtroom, she hadn't acknowledged my presence.

I turned and whispered to César. "Remember what I told you. When the judge asks for your plea, say 'Not guilty' in a firm and respectful tone."

He nodded.

César had no rooting section in the gallery. I had spoken briefly with his ex-wife and son, but they declined to attend the arraignment. Our DA, Vanessa Turner, sat behind O'Neal along with Chloe Carson's mother. Dressed in black and wearing sunglasses, Virginia Carson stared straight ahead. Reporters from local media filled the row behind them. Cable news outlets were absent for now. Pete was in the back row pretending to read the *Chronicle*.

Judge Tsang tapped his microphone. "Counsel will state their names for the record."

"Catherine O'Neal for the People, Your Honor."

"Michael Daley and Rolanda Fernandez for the defense."

The judge addressed César. "Your attorneys have explained why we are here?"

"Yes, Your Honor."

"Good." Judge Tsang spoke quickly. "This is an arraignment. We will have a recitation of the charges, and the defendant will enter a plea."

He might have added, "If all goes well, we'll be finished in five minutes."

He looked at O'Neal. "Charge?"

She stood up. "First-degree murder under California Penal Code Section 187."

It carries a minimum sentence of twenty-five years.

As required by law, the judge quickly read the murder complaint aloud.

After he was finished, I spoke up in an even voice. "The facts do not support a murder charge, Your Honor. It is too early to determine whether there is sufficient evidence to support any charge."

"Ms. O'Neal disagrees with you, Mr. Daley, and it's her call."

True.

O'Neal was still standing. "We are also considering a special circumstance."

It's the California euphemism for a death penalty case. Penal Code Section 190.2 lists twelve "special circumstances" including a killing for financial gain, killing a police officer or a witness, lying in wait, torture or poison, multiple murders, and murder by a gang member. As a practical matter, even if convicted, it was unlikely that César would ever be executed. California's last execution was in 2006, and the state subsequently imposed a moratorium. There are almost eight hundred inmates on Death Row at San Quentin. The vast majority, if not all of them, will die from causes other than execution.

"On what grounds?" the judge asked O'Neal.

"Lying in wait."

Come on. "Ms. O'Neal has provided no evidence to support her claim."

O'Neal's voice remained even. "We will provide such evidence in due course."

"Your Honor," I said, "the facts simply do not justify it."

Judge Tsang's stoic expression didn't change. "That is also Ms. O'Neal's call. We will have time to discuss this in the future." He put on his glasses and speed-read the complaint aloud—a required part of the process. "Do you understand the charge, Mr. Ochoa?"

"Yes, Your Honor."

"How do you wish to plead?"

"One hundred percent not guilty. I did not kill Chloe Carson."

"Thank you."

I had asked César to simply say, "Not guilty," without embellishment. Short denials are more convincing than speeches.

The judge looked at me. "I presume that you will want to schedule a prelim?"

"Yes, Your Honor."

The next step would be a preliminary hearing, or "prelim." The ground rules would be the same as yesterday's prelim for Javier Morales. The odds that I would be able to get a similar result were slim.

Judge Tsang studied his calendar. "I trust that you are willing to waive time?"

"No, Your Honor. We are prepared to proceed within the statutorily mandated period of no more than ten calendar days from today."

His eyes showed a hint of surprise. Contrary to my advice, César insisted that we move forward ASAP.

The judge pointed at O'Neal. "How many court days?"

"One."

"Mr. Daley?"

"At least a week. We are planning to put on a full defense." *Well, maybe.*

"You're in luck. Judge Elizabeth McDaniel is returning from vacation and is available a week from tomorrow on Wednesday, May seventeenth."

It was a tight time frame, but it wasn't a bad draw. Betsy McDaniel was a Superior Court veteran who had gone on senior status a few years earlier. She used to be a colleague of Judge Tsang's at the DA's Office. She was smart, thoughtful, and didn't take any crap. I had tried several cases before her. I liked her, and she seemed to like me. She *really* liked Rosie, with whom she attended Pilates classes. I didn't always get what I wanted from her, but I usually got a fair shake.

The judge looked at O'Neal. "Will that work for you?"

"Yes, Your Honor."

"Mr. Daley?"

Since I requested the expedited schedule, I can't complain. "Yes, Your Honor."

"Good. Please contact Judge McDaniel's clerk to schedule submissions of motions and other logistics. If there's nothing else—,"

"We have a couple of items," I said. "First, we ask you to order Ms. O'Neal to provide copies of all police reports, the autopsy report, security videos, and all other evidence on an expedited basis."

O'Neal spoke from her seat. "Your Honor is well aware that we are under no obligation to provide discovery prior to a prelim."

True. "In the interests of fundamental fairness, we should have an opportunity to view the evidence as soon as possible." *She can't be against fundamental fairness, right?*

Judge Tsang didn't hesitate. "I am ordering the production of police reports, the autopsy report, and security videos as soon as possible."

"Thank you." *It's the best that I can do.* "Second, we request that you issue a gag order on all parties and counsel."

"So ordered."

"Third, we ask that Mr. Ochoa be housed in Administrative Segregation for his own safety. He is a former police officer who is likely to be targeted."

"I have no control over the Sheriff's Department's protocols, but I will have no objection if you wish to make the request to them."

Now the hard one. "Finally, we have submitted our motion for pretrial release subject to the conditions that Mr. Ochoa will wear an ankle monitor, surrender his passport, and have regular check-ins. He will remain in his apartment except to come to court."

O'Neal shook her head. "We have submitted our motion for pretrial detention. Given the gravity of the crime, we oppose release."

"Alleged crime," I said. "Mr. Ochoa has no criminal record and has significant family and community ties. He isn't a flight risk."

"Yes, he is," O'Neal said. "The defendant has an automobile and the ability to leave town."

"Your Honor has discretion. Mr. Ochoa is a San Francisco native. His ex-wife, son, and grandson live in the City. He has been a member of St. Peter's Parish since he was a child. He is a former SFPD Officer who understands the gravity of the situation."

O'Neal got to her feet. "Notwithstanding the defendant's community ties, he is charged with a very serious crime, and he represents a threat to our community. It would be highly unusual to grant pretrial release in a first-degree murder case, especially when we are considering the addition of a special circumstance."

Yes, it would.

Judge Tsang listened as O'Neal and I went back and forth. Finally, he made the call. "I am not going to authorize release of the defendant at this time."

No surprise. "We will file another OR/Bail motion with two days' notice."

"Fine. Anything else, Mr. Daley?"

Not today. "No, Your Honor."

"We're finished."

I saw fear in César's eyes. "What happens next?" he asked.

"I'll come see you later today and we'll talk about it."

As the deputy was leading César out of the courtroom, Pete came up behind me. "That didn't go very well," he whispered.

"About what I expected. Where are you headed?"

"North Beach. You?"

"The DA's Office. I'm going to see if I can get a few minutes with O'Neal."

8

"YOU'LL NEVER MAKE MURDER"

"Thank you for seeing me," I said.

Assistant District Attorney Catherine "No Deal" O'Neal nodded. "We always try to cooperate with the PD's Office."

Right.

At two-fifteen on Tuesday afternoon, O'Neal sat behind a metal desk in her utilitarian office on the third floor of a refurbished industrial building at the base of Potrero Hill, about a mile south of the Hall. Unlike the old DA's Office, the plumbing and air conditioning worked, and she didn't have to share an office. O'Neal's ten-by-ten-foot space had just enough room to squeeze in a desk, two chairs, a credenza, and a file cabinet. Her window looked into another refurbished building across the alley. Her "ego wall" was modest: her Stanford law diploma, a few bar association citations, and a photo with her boss. The only personal item was a picture of her husband, a staff attorney with the California Supreme Court.

She cut right to business. "You wanted to discuss César Ochoa's case?"

"Yes."

At thirty-five, her brown eyes sat above high cheekbones. The native of Palo Alto was the daughter of a tech executive and a law professor. She began her career at the Contra Costa County DA's Office, moved into a supervisory position in Alameda County, and was hired by her friend and former colleague, Vanessa Turner, after she was appointed as San Francisco DA. Turner brought in a half-dozen aggressive prosecutors, including O'Neal, to put the bad guys away and to close the revolving door that seemed to allow drug dealers, car thieves, and shoplifters back on the street shortly after the cops arrested them. O'Neal wasn't going to win any popularity contests among defense attorneys and the more liberal members of the Board of Supervisors, but she was implementing Turner's mandate.

She played with her hoop-style earrings. "The charge is first-degree murder. The prelim starts a week from tomorrow before Judge McDaniel. We informed her clerk that we are prepared to file motions by the end of this week. That's all that I have for you."

You have more. "I was hoping that you might provide a little more information. You have a legal obligation to turn over evidence that would tend to exonerate my client."

"In due course. You are not entitled to discovery before a prelim."

"My client says he's innocent."

"They all do."

"Melinda made the arrest very quickly."

"Inspector Wong doesn't arrest people without evidence."

"What makes you think César stabbed Chloe Carson?"

"Your client had words with Ms. Carson shortly before he left. We found a bloody knife in the Dumpster next to Ms. Carson's body. The blood matched Ms. Carson's. Your client's fingerprints were on the knife."

"César had a burger shortly before closing time. Somebody else must have picked up the knife and used it to kill Ms. Carson."

"You can make that argument to the jury unless your client changes his plea to guilty."

"Did you find any blood on César's hands or clothes?"

"No comment."

"What about in his car or inside his apartment?"

"No comment."

"Come on, Catherine."

Her eyes narrowed. "He's an ex-cop, Mike. He knows how to get rid of evidence. He dumped his bloody clothes. He washed his hands. He cleaned his car."

"First-degree murder requires premeditation."

"We have witnesses who saw your client and Ms. Carson arguing shortly before closing."

"César told us that it was just a conversation."

"Then you can put him on the stand to explain it."

That isn't going to happen unless we're desperate. "You'll never make murder."

"I disagree. So does Vanessa. We are seriously considering a special circumstance. He left the club shortly before the victim. He was lying in wait."

"That's way out of bounds," I said. "You know how difficult it is to seat a death-penalty-qualified jury."

"Vanessa promised to enforce the law. We are sending a message to the law-abiding citizens of San Francisco that we are going to clean up the streets and put the criminals away."

"Nobody is questioning your toughness, Catherine."

"They question it every day, Mike. We've been getting an insane amount of heat because of the homeless situation and the fentanyl crisis."

"You inherited both."

"They're ours now."

True. "You're over-charging. You'll never prove first-degree or even second-degree murder. You're going to have a hard time proving manslaughter."

"I disagree."

"Are you prepared to discuss any sort of reasonable resolution?"

"If you're talking about a deal, the answer is no. You and Rosie are straight shooters. I like to think that I operate the same way."

Sure. "And?"

"This is one of our first big cases since Vanessa was appointed. She isn't going to authorize a plea bargain. Talk to your client and insist that he tell you the truth. When he does, come see me and I'll try to persuade Vanessa to work something out."

Rolanda was standing in the hallway when I returned to the office. "Did you get anything useful out of O'Neal?" she asked.

"No." I described my conversation. "Did she send anything over?"

"Inspector Wong's preliminary report. The knife that they found in the Dumpster is probably enough to get them through the prelim and on to trial."

I told her that O'Neal wasn't likely to offer a plea bargain. "She's called 'No Deal' O'Neal for a reason. Her boss isn't in a dealing mood, either."

"Have you heard from Pete?"

"He's in North Beach trying to track down some potential witnesses."

"Are you going to join him?"

"I'm going to see if I can talk to Inspector Wong first."

9
"READ MY REPORT"

Inspector Melinda Wong looked up from her laptop. "How did you get in here?"

I smiled. "I asked Jane nicely and brought her some See's Candies. She loves the Nuts and Chews."

Wong feigned irritation. "I need to talk to her again."

Jane Gorsi had been the gatekeeper at the front desk of the Homicide Detail on the third floor of the Hall for almost forty years. To the untrained eye, she was just another gruff City employee. To those of us who knew her, she was a doting great-grandmother.

"It won't do any good," I said.

The corner of Wong's mouth turned up. "Probably not."

At three-forty-five on Tuesday afternoon, I was standing next to Wong's desk in the drab bullpen housing San Francisco's two dozen homicide inspectors. Her colleagues were out of the office tracking down evidence and witnesses, and the only noise came from the standing fan pushing the heavy air from one side of the room to the other. The circulation would have been better if the windows opened, but they had been painted shut in the eighties.

Wong was mid-forties with expressive features and an empathetic manner that made her especially effective at interviewing suspects. The twenty-year veteran came from an SFPD family and was one of the first lesbians in Homicide. She had worked alone after her last partner, Inspector Ken Lee, took early retirement. Coincidentally, Lee was trained by the legendary Roosevelt Johnson, San Francisco's most decorated homicide inspector. A half-century earlier, Roosevelt had walked the beat in the Tenderloin with my father.

"You heard from Ken?" I asked.

"He got his hip replaced. He has a regular tee time at Harding Park. His daughters are out of college."

"Good to hear." I smiled. "Pam ruled against me on a motion last week."

"She said your argument was creative, but you were wrong on the law."

"I know."

Her wife, Judge Pamela Chen, was a Superior Court judge.

I wanted to keep her talking. "That was a nice feature about you and Pam in *San Francisco Magazine* last month. It's impressive to be included on the list of power couples."

"Thank you." She feigned impatience. "You didn't come here to congratulate me about a puff piece in a magazine."

No, I didn't. "Mind if I sit for a moment?"

She rolled her eyes. "Fine."

I sat down in the card chair opposite her desk. "I'm representing César Ochoa."

"I know."

"Catherine O'Neal has charged him with first-degree murder."

"I know that, too."

"You must be very confident that you have sufficient evidence."

"I am."

"Mind sharing the highlights with me?"

She pointed a finger at me. "You ought to cut a deal."

"Catherine isn't in a dealing mood. Neither is her boss."

"Give them time."

"César says that he didn't stab Chloe Carson. Do you have any evidence proving that he did?"

"This is where I tell you to read my report."

"I did. I was hoping that you might provide some context."

"The context is in my report."

No, it isn't. "You didn't list any witnesses who saw César stab Carson."

"No comment."

"I didn't see any mention of video of the stabbing."

"No comment."

"Please, Melinda."

She feigned irritation. "Your client and Ms. Carson argued before closing time. He left shortly before she did. We found a bloody knife in the Dumpster next to Ms. Carson's body. The blood matched hers. The fingerprints matched your client's."

"Did you find any bloody clothes when you arrested César?"

"No comment."

I'm going to take that as a no. "Blood on his hands?"

"It was the next day, Mike. He could have washed his hands a dozen times."

I'm going to take that as a no, too. "Blood in his apartment or his car?"

"No comment."

"So your case is based on the fingerprints on the knife?"

"It's more than enough."

"Not necessarily. Besides, Catherine will never prove premeditation."

"No comment."

I probed for a few more minutes, but the default response of every experienced homicide inspector is to refer to her report or to say, "No comment."

She looked at her watch. "I need to meet with a witness. I'll show you out."

"I know the way. Did you get the autopsy report yet?"

"You'll have to talk to the Medical Examiner."

10
"SHE HAD NO CHANCE"

"Thank you for seeing me on short notice," I said.

The Assistant Medical Examiner of the City and County of San Francisco fingered the top button of her white lab coat. "You're welcome."

Dr. Ilene Leung was a protégé of Dr. Joy Siu, our long-time and highly respected CME. A Berkeley native, Dr. Leung graduated at the top of her class at UC Davis and studied under Dr. Siu at UCSF. Brilliant, thorough, and meticulous, she is on the short list to succeed her mentor if and when Dr. Siu decides to move back into academia.

"Is Dr. Siu in town?" I asked.

"She's consulting on an autopsy in Berlin, Mr. Daley."

"Mike."

"Mike," she repeated grudgingly. "Ilene."

"Ilene. Any truth to the rumor that Dr. Siu is thinking of taking a teaching position at Johns Hopkins?"

"No comment."

We were sitting on opposite sides of a glass-topped table in a windowless conference room in the ME's new facility in India Basin, about halfway between downtown and Candlestick Point. The location isn't as convenient as the old ME's Office in the bowels of the Hall, but the state-of-the-art examination rooms and expanded morgue are a substantial upgrade.

Time for business. "I'm representing César Ochoa. I understand that you handled the autopsy of Chloe Carson."

"I did." She folded her hands and placed them on the table in front of her—a gesture that mimicked Dr. Siu. She wore her black hair in a pixie cut. Her makeup was exact, her voice precise. "I will make my report available to the police as soon as I receive the toxicology results. I presume that they will forward it to you in due course."

"Any preliminary results on toxicology?"

"There was a small amount of alcohol in her system—below the legal limit. I found traces of cocaine. Enough to create a buzz, but not enough to kill her."

"Preliminary cause of death?"

"Massive blood loss from a stab wound to the neck."

I grimaced. "Was it painful?"

"Briefly. She would have lost consciousness almost immediately. She had no chance."

"Time of death?"

"Between one-oh-five and four AM on Saturday, May sixth."

Medical Examiners always give themselves a little wiggle room. "Will you be able to narrow it down a bit?"

"Doubtful. The manager of For Gentlemen Only told me that the decedent left the club at one-oh-five AM." She estimated the window based upon the usual markers: state of digestion of food in Carson's stomach, rigor mortis, body temperature, etc. "The body wasn't discovered until seven AM. The EMTs pronounced her at the scene at seven-forty. I didn't perform the autopsy until two-thirty the same afternoon. Because of the time gap, it will be difficult to provide a tighter window."

Not surprising. "Evidence of a struggle or defensive wounds?"

"None."

"You're saying that she was killed by someone that she knew?"

"It's possible that someone surprised her or approached her from behind."

"Any other signs of trauma?"

"No." She pushed out a sigh. "It was a quick hit."

I asked her about the alleged murder weapon.

"The fatal wound was consistent with a stabbing inflicted by a serrated knife like the one covered in Ms. Carson's blood that the police found in the Dumpster next to the body."

"Photos?"

"They will be included in my final report." Her lips turned down. "It was gruesome. The force of the stabbing practically decapitated Ms. Carson."

Got it. "There would have been a lot of blood, right?"

"Right."

"Did you find any traces of my client's blood or DNA on the body?"

"No."

"Given the nature of the wounds and the close quarters of a stabbing, some of Ms. Carson's blood would have found its way onto the killer's hands and clothing, right?"

"Probably."

"Does it strike you as odd that the police didn't find Ms. Carson's blood on my client's hands or clothing?"

"That's a question for Inspector Wong and the evidence technicians."

Rolanda looked up from her laptop. "Did you get anything useful from Dr. Leung?"

"Not much."

She listened as I summarized my conversation with Leung. Then she issued her clear-eyed verdict. "Mostly bad facts. A few that might work slightly in our favor if we're trying to get to reasonable doubt. Nothing that will get the charges dropped at the prelim or a slam-dunk acquittal at trial."

"Sounds about right."

Rolanda, Pete, and I were meeting in the conference room at the PD's Office at five o'clock on Tuesday afternoon. The office was buzzing with activity. Rosie's predecessor and our long-time mentor, the legendary Robert Kidd, always said that the only way to survive as a PD is to focus on completing just enough work each day to get to tomorrow.

"Did you get anything else from the DA?" I asked.

Rolanda nodded. "A preliminary list of people who were at For Gentlemen Only on the night that Chloe Carson died. Additional police reports should arrive tomorrow."

"It's a start. Security video?"

Pete spoke up. "There's footage from the camera in the front, but none from the back. The late show ended at twelve-forty-five AM. People cleared out quickly. It was almost empty when they closed at one. Witnesses confirmed that César left through the back door at one AM. Chloe followed him about five minutes later."

"Any evidence that he stayed in the alley and waited for her?"

"There's no video from the alley, Mick."

"Did you get anything from your sources at SFPD?"

"Not yet." He said that he was working his contacts in North Beach.

Dazzle knocked on the open door. "I need to get over to the club. Do you need anything from me?"

"We're good," I said. "Did you have any luck chasing down any connections at For Gentlemen Only?"

"Yes, I did." She handed me a piece of paper with a phone number. "Sheema Smith used to work at the Gold Club. She moved over to For Gentlemen Only a couple of years ago. She's a terrific dancer, a straight shooter, and a nice person. Tell her that I sent you."

11

"SHE WAS A NICE PERSON"

The willowy African American woman with the chiseled cheekbones and braided black hair glanced at her watch as she nibbled at a baby kale salad. "I need to get to work."

"We won't take up much of your time," I said. "Thank you for seeing us."

Sheema Smith flashed a photogenic smile. "Thank you for buying me dinner."

Sheema, Pete, and I were sitting at a corner table in the Old Ship Saloon, an upscale watering hole and restaurant that opened at the corner of Battery and Pacific in 1851 when San Francisco Bay extended all the way to Montgomery Street. The original inn was built from the wreckage of a Gold Rush ship called the Arkansas, which ran aground at Alcatraz. It was replaced by a boarding house which was destroyed by the 1906 Earthquake. The current red-brick building was erected shortly thereafter and now stands among swanky condos, high-end restaurants, trendy boutiques, and law and architecture firms. The walls are adorned with black-and-white photos of the historic landmark, the crowd is professional, and the food is hearty.

Sheema took a sip of her iced tea. "I heard that Dazzle is working at the PD's Office. Does she like it?"

"She likes the regular paychecks, health insurance, paid vacation, and retirement plan," I said.

She let out a full-throated laugh. "Sounds pretty good to me." She said that she was an Oakland native, divorced twice, no kids. She had done some modeling, worked on and off as a dancer, and did short stints at advertising agencies. "Are there any openings at the PD's Office? It might be a nice change of pace."

I handed her a business card. "Email me your resume."

I wasn't sure how Rosie would react if I hired another dancer.

Pete spoke up. "Mike is representing César. How well did you know him?"

"Not that well. He works the front of the house. I work the stage. He's always been professional to me."

"Did he have many interactions with Chloe Carson?"

Her tone turned thoughtful. "He and Chloe talked from time to time. I think César was trying to help her avoid some of his mistakes. He encouraged her to stay away from coke and go back to school."

Pete scowled. "How much coke was she doing?"

"Enough."

"Do you know where she got it?"

"It isn't hard to find."

"Somebody at the club?"

"A lot of people pass through the club."

Not a very enlightening answer.

Pete took a sip of coffee. "How well did you know Chloe?"

"Not that well. She worked at the club for about six months, and she kept to herself. She was a nice person and an excellent dancer."

"Was she well-liked?"

"For the most part." A pause. "We're all competing for the same customers. Some of the girls thought that Chloe was a little aggressive in pursuing their regulars."

"The police told us that Chloe and César got into an argument on Friday night."

"They did. It lasted only a few seconds. I don't know what it was about."

"We talked to Dave Callaghan. He said that Chloe gave him some trouble."

"Dave is hard on everybody. Chloe showed up late a few times. He told her that if she did it again, she would regret it."

"He threatened her?"

"He threatened to fire her."

"Do you think there was more to it?"

A shrug. "Dave has a temper, but I've never seen him make physical contact with anybody."

"Did Chloe have many friends?"

"She used to hang out with another dancer named Kelly Ryan, who started around the same time that she did. Kelly is also very good. And she's a nice person, too."

"Is she working tonight?"

"I think so."

We'll find her.

Pete looked my way, and I picked up the cue. "We heard that Chloe had an argument with the sound guy on Friday night."

"She did. Jerry Henderson isn't as good as our regular guy. The sound went out a couple of times during Chloe's set. She was pretty upset about it."

"Is he working tonight?"

"He works once or twice a month. He probably won't be in for a couple of weeks."

"Any idea where we can find him?"

"He lives in North Beach and plays in a band. If you can find where the band is playing, you can find him."

Good advice. I reached over and picked up the check. "We've talked to Callaghan. We'll track down Henderson and Ms. Ryan. We're also trying to talk to others who were at the club on Friday night, especially the regulars. Is there anybody you would suggest?"

She thought about it for a moment. "Tim Volpe was there on Friday night."

Pete's eyes opened wide. "The cop?"

"Yes."

"On duty?"

"No. He comes in all the time. He's a sweetie and an excellent tipper." She picked up her gym bag. "I need to get to work."

12

"IT ISN'T ILLEGAL"

Sergeant Tim Volpe adjusted the collar of his SFPD windbreaker and took a draw of his Lagunitas IPA. "Thanks for the beer."

"Thanks for seeing us," Pete said.

Pete, Volpe, and I were sitting at a table next to the window in the narrow balcony of Vesuvio, an unpretentious watering hole on Columbus Avenue across Jack Kerouac Alley from Lawrence Ferlinghetti's legendary City Lights Bookshop. In 1948, an art lover named Henri Lenoir opened a bohemian gathering spot in a two-story 1913 Italian Renaissance Revival building on the border between the financial district, Chinatown, Jackson Square, and North Beach. It looks like a pirate ship filled with bounty: mismatched tables, Tiffany chandeliers, a giant wicker chair where the poets used to read, stained glass windows, and Fifties artwork. The Beats are long gone, but the walls are still lined with photos of Kerouac, Dylan Thomas, and Allen Ginsberg. The current owners pay homage to the neighborhood's heritage by sponsoring poetry readings and art exhibitions. In a modest nod to Twenty-first Century tastes, the updated menu includes organic wines, beers, and spirits.

"How old is your daughter?" Pete asked.

"Middle school," Volpe said.

Pete grinned. "Watch out. The girls are light-years ahead of the boys."

"My daughter saves most of her drama for my ex-wife."

Pete gave him a reassuring nod. "Our daughter was the same way with Donna."

Volpe was in his mid-forties with a muscular frame, angular features, and basset hound eyes. He was a steady cop who grew up a few blocks from Kezar Stadium and graduated from S.I. and State. His parents ran a bar on Stanyan Street. His now-ex-wife was an executive at Wells Fargo who got a little too cozy with one of her colleagues while Tim was working nights at Park Station. It caught him off guard, and he was still hurting from the divorce.

He looked at Pete. "Did César kill Chloe Carson?"

"He says that he didn't. You think he did?"

"I barely know him."

"A dancer named Sheema Smith told us that you were at For Gentlemen Only on Friday night."

"I was."

"You go there often?"

"On occasion. It isn't illegal."

Pete arched an eyebrow. "You ever see any of my former SFPD colleagues there?"

"Sometimes." Volpe turned my way and smirked. "I see more people who work at the DA's Office and the PD's Office."

I'm not surprised. "Care to mention any names?"

"Uh, no."

Pete put his hand over his coffee cup—a reminder that I should let him do the talking. "Did you see anything out of the ordinary on Friday night?"

"No. Usual stuff. A bachelor party. Frat boys. Businessmen. A few older guys." He said that he arrived at the club at eleven PM and stayed for the late show. "I left right after it ended around twelve-forty-five."

"Did you see Chloe Carson?"

"You couldn't miss her. She was a terrific dancer."

"Did you know her?"

"Only as an appreciative audience member."

"The manager told us that Chloe and César got into an argument shortly before closing time."

"They did."

"Do you know what they were talking about?"

"Afraid not." He said that Chloe appeared to be pretty upset.

"We heard that she also got into it with the sound guy."

"She did. The sound went off for a few minutes during her set. Chloe told him to get his act together." Volpe smiled. "She may have used a slightly more colloquial term."

"How did he take it?"

"Not well."

"You know him?"

"Afraid not."

"Any hints that he might have been the type of guy who would have taken out his frustrations on her?"

A shrug. "Like I said, I don't know him."

"Is there anybody else that we should talk to who might have some information about what happened on Friday night?"

"I'm sorry, Pete. I don't know."

Pete pressed his phone against his ear as we stood on Columbus Avenue outside the door of Vesuvio. He ended his call and looked at me. "I have somebody looking for Jerry Henderson." He looked at his watch. "You got a little time?"

Not really. "Sure."

"Let's go for a walk over to For Gentlemen Only." He grinned. "I've been a little stressed lately. I think it would be good if we had a drink and went to a show."

"Anybody in particular you'd like to watch?"

"One of my operatives informed me that Chloe Carson's friend, Kelly Ryan, is headlining the late show."

13
"SHE WAS AFRAID OF HIM"

"We enjoyed your performance," Pete said.

Kelly Ryan took a sip of San Pellegrino and flashed a practiced smile. "Thank you."

Pete, Kelly, and I were sitting at a table against the wall at For Gentlemen Only at twelve-ten on Wednesday morning. The club was closed, but Dave Callaghan said that we could stick around for a few minutes. The room smelled of stale beer, leftover steaks, and cleaning solvent. The houselights were up, the custodian was mopping the floor, a server was counting her tips, and Callaghan was at the bar adding up the night's receipts.

"How long have you worked here?" Pete asked, already knowing the answer.

"About six months," Ryan said.

"You like it?"

She darted a glance at Callaghan. "It's fine."

"Where do you live?"

"Vallejo."

"Long commute."

"Yes."

Ryan was twenty-four, but she could have passed for a teenager. The waif-thin dancer had changed into a navy windbreaker bearing the logo of the U.S. Women's National Soccer Team. Her bleached-blonde hair was cut into a Megan Rapinoe pixie cut. Her eyes were crystal blue, cheekbones high, features soft. Offstage, her makeup was modest—a little rouge, lip gloss, and eyeliner. She had wiped the sparkle from her cheeks.

"We're representing César," I said. "Did you know him pretty well?"

"Not really."

"Did he ever give you any trouble?"

"He was always nice to me."

Good. "You were here on Friday night?"

"Yes."

"We heard that César and Chloe got into an argument."

"They did. It didn't last long. I don't know what it was about."

"Any guesses?"

She shrugged. "César liked to give advice. Chloe didn't like to take it."

Pete hadn't taken his eyes off Ryan. "We talked to Sheema. She said that you and Chloe were friends."

"We started working here around the same time, so we got to know each other a little. We didn't socialize outside of work."

"What was she like?"

"Great dancer. Always working. Always hustling." She took a deep breath. "Chloe had it rough growing up. Her mother is an alcoholic. She barely knew her father. She couldn't afford to finish college. She made enough money from dancing to pay for her apartment. She was thinking about going back to school."

"We understand that she may have had some drug issues."

"Coke."

"Bad?"

"Pretty bad."

"Anything else?"

"I don't know."

"Do you know who was supplying her?"

A hesitation. "No."

"Somebody here at the club?"

"I don't know."

"Did she have many regular customers here at the club?"

"A few."

I sensed that she knew more than she was telling us. "Did she ever talk about her regulars?" I asked.

Another hesitation. "She used to see a lawyer named John Foreman outside the club. He lives here in North Beach."

I recognized the name. He was a hotshot litigator at the big firm where Nady's husband worked. "I seem to recall that he's married."

"Three times. He and his latest wife have an open marriage. Chloe told me that he was a good tipper. He was also into some exotic stuff. John wanted her to do a threesome, but Chloe said no. She said that John was pretty upset about it. He doesn't like to be told what to do."

Especially when he's paying.

Pete kept his voice even. "Was he here on Friday night?"

"Yes." She said that Foreman stayed until closing time.

"Did he say anything to Chloe?"

"They talked for a few minutes after the show ended."

"Do you have any idea what they talked about?"

"No, but Chloe seemed upset." She added, "So did John."

We'll look into it. "How do you like working for Dave Callaghan?" I asked.

"It's fine."

"Is he a nice guy?"

"He's okay."

"Did he get along okay with Chloe?"

"As far as I know. Chloe didn't complain."

"He told us that he had to talk to Chloe about showing up on time."

"He did. Chloe wasn't happy about it."

I leaned forward. "How did you and Chloe get along?"

"Fine."

"How did she get along with the other dancers?"

"Fine."

It's your default nonanswer. "We understand that Chloe also had a disagreement with Jerry Henderson on Friday night."

"The sound went out a couple of times during her set. Chloe was upset."

"Did he ever mess up while you were dancing?"

"Once or twice." She shrugged. "He apologized."

"Is he a nice guy?"

She scrunched her face. "He was always nice to me."

Not exactly the answer to my question. "Anything else you can tell us about him?"

She lowered her voice. "Chloe and Jerry went out for a few months. Nothing serious. She broke up with him. She told me that there wasn't any chemistry."

"Any idea where we can find him?"

"He's a drummer in a band called Twisted Metal. If you find the band, you can find him."

Callaghan came over to our table. "We're closed."

"We were just finishing," I said. I turned back to Ryan. "Anything else we should know about Chloe's relationship with Jerry?"

She lowered her voice to a whisper. "She told me that she was afraid of him."

Traffic on Broadway was light as I took a breath of the cool breeze. "We need to talk to John Foreman," I said to Pete.

He looked up from his phone. "He won't be hard to find."

I read a text from Rolanda to Pete. "Henderson has three arrests for shoplifting and one for assault. The assault charge was dismissed when the woman that he allegedly was stalking decided not to testify against him. Another woman obtained a restraining order against him for alleged physical and emotional abuse. Also suspicions of drug dealing."

"Busy guy," Pete said.

"I need your people to find him."

He smiled triumphantly. "Already did."

"When were you planning to mention it?"

"Now. You got time to listen to a little music?"

"It's one AM, Pete."

"Henderson's band is playing at Neck of the Woods in the Richmond. If we hustle, we can catch the end of the show."

14
"IT DIDN'T WORK OUT"

"We enjoyed your show," Pete lied.

"Thank you." The burly man bore a striking resemblance to Hagrid in the *Harry Potter* books. He smiled through his scraggly beard and spoke softly. "How did you hear about us?"

"Instagram."

Another lie. Pete avoids social media except to track cheating husbands.

At twelve-forty on Wednesday morning, Pete, Jerry Henderson, and I were standing in the alley behind Neck of the Woods, a bar and music venue on Clement between Fifth and Sixth Avenues in the foggy Richmond District north of Golden Gate Park. Housed in a two-story wooden building painted red, the neighborhood watering hole has been hosting musicians since 1973. Located between a Chinese grocery and a chiropractor's office on a modest business strip in an otherwise quiet residential neighborhood, it was an unlikely spot for a late-night club.

Pete pointed at Henderson's drum set. "Can we help you load up?"

"I've got it." He hoisted the drums into the back of his beat-up Jeep Cherokee.

Pete extended a hand. "Pete Daley. This is my brother Mike."

"Jerry Henderson." He shook Pete's hand. Then he turned to me. "Nice to meet you."

"Same here," I said. "Can we buy you a beer?"

"I'm exhausted."

"Just one?" I pointed at the back door of the club. "They just announced last call."

The hulking musician tossed another drum into the Jeep. "Just one."

We followed him inside the club, where a few stragglers were paying their tabs. The street-level bar is made of dark wood accented by neon lighting. It has a homey feel with four flat screen TVs and a tiny stage for up-and-coming musical acts and comics. The larger room upstairs has a state-of-the-art sound system and a dance floor. The first time I came to Neck of the Woods, the featured act was a Marin County bar band called Huey Lewis and the News.

We took seats at one of the black tables against the wall opposite the bar. Wednesday is open mic night downstairs, and a half-dozen of the performers had gathered at the bar to celebrate/commiserate. I went up to the bar and brought back three mugs of Pliny the Elder, the flagship ale of the trendy Russian River Brewing Company. I'm more of a Guinness guy, but Henderson asked for a Pliny, so Pete and I joined him.

"How long you been playing with Twisted Metal?" Pete asked.

"On and off for about five years."

Henderson must have started when he was in college. A background check revealed that the native of Crescent City was twenty-five, single, and a graduate of Humboldt State. He lived by himself in a studio apartment under a dry cleaner's on Vallejo Street in North Beach. During the day, he worked for a moving company. At night, he played with the band and occasionally worked the soundboard at For Gentlemen Only.

Pete took a sip of his beer. "It must have been tough getting gigs during Covid."

"We didn't have any live dates for two years. We wrote a lot of new material and put it up on YouTube. The good news is that we built up a pretty big online following. The bad news is that it isn't enough to make ends meet."

Pete feigned empathy. "I played bass in a band for a few years after I got out of college."

Technically, this was true. Pete and a couple of his classmates formed a band that played in public only once at the saloon operated by our uncle.

Pete added, "It's insanely competitive. I take it that you still have a day job?"

"Everybody in the band does." Henderson stretched his fingers. "I work for Shannon Moving and Storage. So does our guitarist. I'd rather be playing music than lifting furniture."

So would I. I nursed my beer as Pete and Henderson exchanged information about their favorite metal bands. Despite the difference in their respective ages, they shared an abiding respect for Black Sabbath, Guns N' Roses, Mötley Crue, and Motorhead.

Pete took a long draw of his beer, placed his mug on the table, and got to business. "In addition to hearing you play, we came to see you because we need your help. Mike is with the Public Defender's Office. He's representing César Ochoa. I'm a private investigator, and I'm helping him. We're trying to find out what happened on Friday night at For Gentlemen Only. We understand that you were working the soundboard."

"I was." Henderson's brown eyes shifted from Pete to me and back to Pete. "I feel terrible about Chloe. She was a nice person and a terrific dancer. I don't know what was going on between her and César. And I don't know what happened in the alley."

Pete's voice remained even. "What time did you get to work?"

"Four-thirty. Dave Callaghan calls me when the regular sound guy is out."

"You like it?"

"It's a paying gig." He said that the dancers bring their own recorded playlists. "I run it through the system and improvise the lighting. It isn't exactly a Taylor Swift concert."

Pete asked him if he talked to Chloe on Friday night.

"Briefly."

"How was her mood?"

"Nothing out of the ordinary. She seemed a little disappointed by the size of the crowd."

"How did her performance go?"

"Fine."

"Dave Callaghan told us that you and Chloe got into an argument on Friday night."

He waited a beat. "The sound went out twice, but it wasn't my fault. She was upset, and I apologized." He added, a little too emphatically, "We were cool."

Pete kept his voice even. "We understand that you and Chloe went out for a while."

He took a sip of his beer. "Just a couple of times. It didn't work out."

"You broke up with her?"

"It was mutual."

Not according to Kelly Ryan.

Pete switched subjects. "How well did you know César?"

"Not that well. He never gave me any trouble."

"Did he ever give Chloe any trouble?"

"César said something to her after she finished her set on Friday. She seemed pretty upset, and she snapped at him."

"Was that the first time you saw them argue?"

"No, there was one other occasion. It happened a few weeks ago. I don't know what it was about."

Pete glanced my way.

"Jerry," I said, "did Chloe get along with Dave Callaghan?"

"As far as I know."

"And the other dancers?"

"As far as I know."

"Was there anybody at the club on Friday night who didn't get along with Chloe?"

He thought about it. "A lawyer named John Foreman came up to talk to her after her set. I think he asked her out, but she didn't like him, and she tried to avoid him. And there was an obnoxious tech guy who approached her, too. I've seen him before. He wanted a private session, but she turned him down. He was pretty upset about it."

"Got a name?"

"Tyler Benson. You've probably heard of him."

"I have." Benson had made and lost successive fortunes during the crypto era. "What time did he leave the club?"

"Shortly after he talked to Chloe."

"Did you happen to notice which way he left?"

"Through the back door, I think."

"Thanks for your time, Jerry."

"Henderson knows more than he told us," Pete said.

"Agreed. I want you to have somebody watch him."

"Already in process, Mick."

We were driving north on the Golden Gate Bridge at one-ten AM. Pete was at the wheel. I was in the passenger seat. Traffic was light. I could barely see the north tower through the fog.

"We need to talk to John Foreman," I said.

"He works at a big law firm, Mick. He won't be hard to find."

"Can you find Tyler Benson?"

"Of course."

"You know him?"

"I was at his wedding. It was a lovely affair on the lawn at Pebble Beach." He smirked. "The wedding ceremony lasted longer than the marriage."

"How did you get invited?"

"I didn't. One of the bridesmaids hired me to see if her husband was cheating."

"Was he?"

"Yes."

"At the wedding?"

"At the reception."

"With whom?"

"The maid of honor."

I glanced at Pete to see if there was any chance that he was joking, but my brother never jokes. "You really should write a memoir," I said.

He chuckled. "Nobody would believe it."

15

"YOU'RE UP LATE"

Rosie took a sip of Cab Franc. "You're up late."

I glanced at my watch. One-forty AM. "Actually, it's early."

"I told you that I didn't want you and Pete taking unnecessary chances."

"We didn't. I texted you that I would be home late. You didn't have to wait up for me."

"Yes, I did. Where have you been?"

"Listening to a heavy metal band at Neck of the Woods."

"At one o'clock on a Wednesday morning?"

"The drummer was the sound guy at For Gentlemen Only on Friday night."

Her eyes reflected the light from the fireplace. "Is he a good drummer?"

"He isn't Mick Fleetwood. He was Chloe Carson's ex-boyfriend. They got into an argument at the club on Friday night. He has a criminal record and a history of domestic abuse. It might provide some possibilities that will help us with César's case."

"Sounds like it was a productive evening."

We were sitting on the sofa in the living room of Rosie's post-Earthquake bungalow in Larkspur, a leafy suburb about ten miles north of the Golden Gate Bridge. Rosie rented the house after we split up, and I moved into an apartment a couple of blocks away. Since the Public Defender is required to have an "official" residence in San Francisco, Rosie also leases a studio apartment a few doors from her mother's house in the Mission. Rosie and I became the proud owners of the Larkspur house when a well-heeled client bought it for us after we got his murder conviction overturned. It wasn't quite as good as winning the lottery, but it was pretty close. We could sell our twelve-hundred-square-foot piece of the American Dream for somewhere close to two million dollars, but it would cost more to buy a replacement. When Rosie won her first election as PD, she remodeled the tiny kitchen and the antiquated bathrooms. When she won re-election, she added an office that doubles as a guest bedroom. I spend most nights here with Rosie, but I keep the apartment for those occasions when we need a little space. It also became our de facto quarantine location during Covid.

I reached over and squeezed her hand. "You worry too much."

Her expression softened. "I'm Sylvia Fernandez's daughter."

Yes, you are. Notwithstanding her stoic public demeanor and her fierce determination never to let anybody see her lose her composure, Rosie was wound tighter than she appeared. Her mother and I were among the few people who knew when she was angry.

She pointed at me. "Your heart okay?"

"Fine."

"I don't want you to overdo it, Mike."

"I'm fine, Rosie," I insisted.

Two years ago, my doctor discovered that I had developed an extra heartbeat called a ventricular bigeminy. It's fairly common even among those of us who aren't overweight, have low cholesterol, exercise pretty regularly, and don't smoke. My cardiologist did a high-tech procedure called an ablation where she inserted a tiny probe into my heart, did a detailed map, and zapped the spot causing the extra beat. I was in and out of the hospital the same day, and I didn't feel a thing. Thankfully, the procedure was successful, and my heart was back to normal.

"Did you get anything else that might be useful for César's case?" she asked.

"Do we really need to talk about this at one AM?"

"It's my responsibility to remain fully apprised of the status of the cases of my subordinates."

"Fine." She listened intently as I summarized our conversation with Henderson. "One of Chloe Carson's fellow dancers told us that Chloe was afraid of him."

"Evidence connecting him to her death?"

"Not yet."

"It isn't enough."

"It's a start. Henderson also pointed us toward a couple of other people who were at the club on Friday night who had connections to Chloe Carson."

"Evidence connecting any of them to her death?"

"Pete's working on it."

"It still isn't enough."

"We got the case two days ago, Rosie."

"You know that I'm not the most patient person in the world. The prelim is a week away."

The unyielding voice of reality.

Her tone softened. "Do you think there's any real chance that you might be able to get the charges dropped at the prelim?"

"Ask me the same question in a couple of days. Kids okay?"

"Yes. Grace and Chuck are busy working on a new film. Tommy is studying for finals. He said that he would come over for a visit next week."

"Your mom?"

"Feisty as always."

All accounted for.

She finished her wine. "Are you starting early again tomorrow?"

"Not that early."

"Are you planning to stay here tonight?"

"I need to pick up a few things at the apartment."

"I'll make it worth your while."

How can I possibly say no? "I'll stay."

Her eyes darted toward the bedroom. "Good."

My phone vibrated four hours later. I answered right away.

"You up, Mick?" Pete asked.

"I am now." I glanced at my watch. Five-ten AM. "Do you ever sleep?"

"Not much. How soon can you get downtown?"

I glanced across the bed at Rosie, who was covered by a sheet and sleeping soundly. "Give me forty-five minutes."

"Meet me at Victoria Pastry in North Beach. Tyler Benson comes in almost every morning."

16
"IT'S THE NEXT BIG THING"

"You sure he's coming?" I asked.

Pete looked out the window of the café at the corner of Columbus and Filbert in the heart of North Beach. "My sources tell me that Tyler Benson comes here every day at this time."

His sources are usually right.

At seven o'clock on Wednesday morning, I closed my eyes and enjoyed the sweet aroma of St. Honore cake, homemade cannoli, hand-baked amaretto pignoli cookies, and espresso. We were sitting at one of a half-dozen tables at Victoria Pastry, the century-old bakery where my grandparents bought birthday cakes when they were a little flush. For its first hundred years, it was located at Stockton and Vallejo, across the street from Little City Meats, which is still going strong. About a dozen years ago, it moved to its current location near Washington Square Park, down the street from the magnificent Saints Peter and Paul Catholic Church.

Pete's eyes darted up the street. "Right on time, Mick. Follow my lead."

I would never think of doing otherwise. I took a bite of my apple Danish and waited.

An athletic young man with buzz-cut blonde hair and sporting a navy Patagonia fleece bearing the logo of a failed crypto company entered the café, his phone pressed to his ear. He informed whomever he was talking to that he would consider his proposal.

I started to stand, but Pete stopped me. "Not yet," he whispered. "Wait until he orders."

Got it.

Benson went up to the counter and ordered a pastry and a cappuccino. He grabbed his breakfast and looked around.

Pete smiled and gestured at the empty chair at our table. "We'll be leaving in a few minutes. Feel free to join us."

"Thanks." Benson took a seat, sipped his coffee, and resumed looking at his phone.

Pete pretended to take a drink of coffee from his empty cup. "You're Tyler Benson, aren't you?"

"Uh, yes."

"I've read a lot about you. You've had an amazing run of investments."

"Uh, thank you."

"It's an honor to meet you. This is my brother, Mike."

I love watching Pete work.

I played along. "Nice to meet you. You've been involved in some very exciting projects."

Benson's phone was now on the table. "I have."

"Congratulations."

Pete held up a finger—the signal for me to let him do the talking.

"You live around here?" he asked Benson, already knowing the answer.

The tech entrepreneur pointed at Coit Tower. "Telegraph Hill."

"I'm a bit surprised that you aren't living in one of those new towers down by the ballpark and Chase Center."

Benson smiled. "I have a condo down there, too."

I wasn't surprised. According to Pete, Benson also had an estate in Atherton, a condo in Maui, a McMansion next door to Charles Schwab near the seventh fairway at Pebble Beach, and a six-thousand square foot pied-a-terre on Central Park West.

Benson added, "I like North Beach. I'm a fourth-generation native of San Francisco. My great-grandfather ran a dry-goods store a few blocks from here and played baseball on the North Beach playground."

He also made a boatload of money when he sold his business to the affluent Magnin family and moved into a mansion around the corner from Dianne Feinstein in Presidio Terrace.

Pete feigned admiration. "Mike and I are only second-generation."

Benson gave us a well-practiced phony smile. "It isn't a contest."

With guys like you, everything is a contest.

Pete kept his voice conversational. "How did you get started in the investment business?"

He inherited a lot of money and got really lucky.

Benson seemed willing to overshare with a couple of strangers. "I started in college at Harvard."

Everybody who attends Harvard always finds a way to mention it.

He added, "I was in the same dorm as Mark Zuckerberg."

I'm impressed.

"Then I got my MBA at Stanford."

Stanford alums always manage to work that into the conversation, too.

Benson feigned modesty. "I worked at Andreessen Horowitz for a few years."

Where you took advantage of your family's connections and wealth.

He added, "About five years ago, I decided that I wanted a little more flexibility than Andreessen could offer, so I went out on my own." He nodded as if to reassure himself that he had made the right call. "It's worked out nicely."

Pete nodded repeatedly and pretended to be impressed as Benson listed a dozen investments he had made which returned billions. He neglected to mention any losers.

"You still big on crypto?" Pete asked.

"Never was," Benson insisted. "I've pivoted to AI. It's the next big thing. It's going to disrupt the world."

We'll see.

We chatted for a few more minutes as Benson nursed his coffee, ate his pastry, and expounded upon his investing acumen. He struck me as a pretty smart guy with excellent credentials, even better connections, and, most important, family money. In fairness, if I had found myself in similar circumstances, I probably would have done the same thing.

"You got any kids?" Pete asked.

"Not yet," Benson said. "Maybe someday."

"I have a daughter who is finishing her sophomore year at UC Santa Barbara. Mike's daughter graduated from USC and is working at Pixar. His son is at Cal."

"Fine schools," Benson said dismissively. He might have added, "But not Harvard or Stanford."

"You married?"

"Divorced."

"Sorry." Pete gave him a reassuring nod. "Mike and I have both been divorced. It was hard at the time, but it worked out for the best. I've been married for a long time. Mike has a long-term relationship. Hopefully, things will work out for you."

"Thanks." Benson finished his coffee and reached for his phone. "Thanks for sharing your table. Nice meeting you."

"Nice meeting you, too. Actually, there was something else that I wanted to ask you about." Pete kept his voice even. "Mike is with the Public Defender's Office. He's representing César Ochoa. I'm an investigator and helping with the case. Your name appeared on a list of people who were at For Gentlemen Only on Friday night."

Benson tensed, but he didn't say anything.

"You probably heard that the body of a dancer named Chloe Carson was found in the alley behind the club on Saturday morning. We're trying to find out what happened."

"I don't know anything about it."

"You were there on Friday night?"

"Yes."

"You go there often?"

His voice filled with irritation. "Occasionally."

"I'm not passing judgment, Tyler. I've probably spent more time at clubs than you have. Did the police ask you for a statement?"

"Yes. I told them that I didn't know Chloe Carson, I don't know your client, and I don't know anything about what happened on Friday night."

"Did you ever talk to César?"

"He's the doorman, right?"

"Right."

"I may have said hello when I entered the club."

"Did you know Chloe Carson?"

"No."

That conflicts with the information provided by Jerry Henderson.

"Did you see her on Friday night?"

"If she was onstage, I saw her."

"Did you talk to her?"

"No."

This also conflicts with Henderson's account.

"Did she interact with César?"

"Briefly. It looked like they were arguing about something."

"Do you know what they were arguing about?"

"No."

"Did she get into it with anybody else that night?" Pete asked.

"She got angry at the sound guy after the sound went out during her performance."

"Jerry Henderson?"

"I don't know his name."

"Anybody else?"

"She got into an argument with a lawyer."

"How do you know it was a lawyer?"

"Because he was on the opposite side of a deal that I was working on a few years ago. His name is John Foreman."

17
"WE HAVE AN UNDERSTANDING"

"Nice to see you again, John," I lied.

The managing partner of the megafirm of Story, Short, and Thompson extended a hand, flashed a practiced smile, and lied back to me. "Nice to see you, Mike. It's been a long time."

At one-forty-five on Wednesday afternoon, I was standing in his corner office on the fortieth floor of Four Embarcadero Center. While most big law firms have opted for smaller spaces even for senior partners, John Foreman's thirty-by-forty-foot space retained the splendor of a bygone era. Then again, it was probably fitting for the chairman of the third-largest law firm in the world, where revenues hit five billion dollars last year.

I admired his panoramic view extending from the Marin Headlands to the Golden Gate Bridge to Mount St. Helena to the Berkeley Hills and finally the Bay Bridge. "Nice view."

"Thank you."

Foreman was a couple of years older than I was, with chiseled features, a Roman nose, a head of coiffed silver hair, and the supreme self-confidence of a man with a twenty-five-million-dollar book of business. Notwithstanding the fact that big law firms had transitioned to business casual years ago, he still wore a top-of-the-line Armani suit, a custom Egyptian cotton dress shirt, and a three-hundred-dollar Salvatore Ferragamo necktie. My source at the firm (Nady's husband) told me that Foreman takes home a cool twenty million a year.

I took a seat in the soft leather chair across from his immaculate desk that was handcrafted from fine oak. A matching conference table, credenza, and bookcase finished the ensemble. His walls displayed a half-dozen Picasso lithographs that cost more than his undergrad and law school tuitions at Harvard.

He sat down in his ergonomic chair and glanced at a state-of-the-art laptop—the only nod to Twenty-first Century technology in the opulent space. He was one of the most successful mergers and acquisitions attorneys in the world, but his office showed no signs of day-to-day legal work. A rainmaker of his stature had an army of junior partners and associates for such drudgery.

He was still displaying the phony smile. "I don't think we've chatted since you left the firm."

"Probably not," I replied.

Foreman and I were partners for a short time at Simpson and Gates, a megafirm at the top of the Bank of America Building where I worked after Rosie and I split up. White-shoe firms like S and G don't like attorneys who represent criminals because they don't have a lot of money and they scare away the corporate clients. I was unceremoniously fired after five years when the power partners—including Foreman—decided that I wasn't pulling my weight. Foreman moved over here after Simpson and Gates broke up.

He feigned sincerity. "You and Rosie have done very well."

I can play this game, too. "Thank you. So have you." I pointed at a photo of a supermodel-beautiful young woman posing in front of the eighteenth hole at Pebble Beach. "I remember when your daughter was in grammar school. She's very pretty."

"Actually, that's my wife."

Oops. "Sorry."

"Diane and I split up shortly after you left the firm. It was difficult, but we're on good terms. I was married to another woman named Marla for five years. That didn't work out, either. Amy and I have been together for three years."

"Congratulations."

"Thank you."

Marla was his paralegal at Simpson and Gates. I don't know where he met Amy.

"Thank you for seeing me on short notice," I said.

"Professional courtesy. Besides, we go back a long way. And I've always believed that it's good policy to cooperate with the PD's Office."

This is probably the first time you've ever spoken to anybody from the PD's Office.

"How can I help you?" he asked, trying to sound genuine.

"I'm representing César Ochoa, the doorman at For Gentlemen Only. You may have read that he's accused of killing a dancer named Chloe Carson on Saturday morning."

"I heard about it. Very sad."

Here goes. "This is a bit awkward. The police reports included a list of people who were at the club on Friday night and Saturday morning." I cleared my throat. "Your name was on it."

The phony smile finally disappeared. "I was there."

"You go there often?"

"From time to time. I live in the neighborhood."

I glanced at the photo of his wife, but I didn't say anything.

He spoke up again. "We have an understanding."

Open marriage? Polyamory? Swinging? Old-fashioned infidelity?

His tone remained conversational. "Amy understands that I'm going to watch young women dance on occasion, and I understand that she's going to meet men when she and her girlfriends go to Italy in the summer. We're adults. We're completely honest about it."

"I'm not judging." *Yes, I am.*

"I recall that you were once a priest. I suspect that you're probably a little more judgmental than I am."

This wasn't covered at the seminary. "I'm not a priest anymore."

The fact that he and his wife agreed that it's okay to cheat didn't surprise me. I was, however, a bit taken aback that he was so nonchalant about it. Then again, when I was at Simpson and Gates, it seemed as if I was the only partner who *wasn't* sleeping with an associate, secretary, or another partner. Even during the dark days when Rosie and I were getting divorced, neither of us ever cheated, and we wouldn't consider the possibility nowadays. Pete says that I'm old-fashioned. I guess I like it that way.

"Do you know César?" I asked.

"I didn't know him well, but I said hello to him when I entered the club."

"Did you see him have any interactions with Chloe Carson on Friday night?"

"No."

"Did you know her?"

"I know that she was an excellent dancer."

My eyes found their way to the photo of his wife, who bore a resemblance to Chloe. "Did you talk to her on Friday night?"

"Briefly. I told her that I enjoyed her performance." He eyed me. "If you're wondering whether I ever requested additional services, the answer is no."

I was, and your answer conflicts with what we heard from Benson. "Tyler Benson was also at the club on Friday night. He told us that you got into an argument with Chloe."

"Not true."

"He was lying?"

"Let's give him the benefit of the doubt and say that he was mistaken."

"What time did you leave?"

"Around one." He said that he went straight home. "I live on Green Street about a ten-minute walk from For Gentlemen Only."

"Your wife can corroborate your whereabouts?"

"She's in Italy."

There was a knock on the door, and his secretary entered the office. She was another attractive young woman.

"Your two o'clock is here, Mr. Foreman," she said.

"Thank you. We were just finishing."

She excused herself and left the office.

I sensed that this interruption was planned. "You talked to the police?"

"I did. I told them that I didn't kill Chloe Carson, and I don't know who did."

"Do you think that César is capable of murder?"

"He's always been nice to me."

Not exactly the answer to my question. I handed him the printout of the customers who were at For Gentlemen Only on Friday night. "Recognize anybody?"

He scanned the list. "F.X. Quinn is an organizer for the theatrical union. He lives in North Beach and is planning to run for supervisor."

"Did you see him have any interactions with Chloe Carson?"

"Briefly. They were arguing in the back of the club as I was leaving. I don't know what it was about."

"Do you know where I can find him?"

He gave me a knowing look. "He's a political guy, Mike. He won't be hard to find."

18

"I WAS WORKING"

Francis Xavier Quinn took a draw of his Stella Artois, wiped his lips with a paper napkin, and set his mug down on the table. "Good to see you, Pete. It's been a few years."

My brother nodded. "Good to see you, too, F.X."

At three-thirty PM, Quinn, Pete, and I were sitting at a wobbly table with mismatched chairs next to the bar at Gino and Carlo's, which the Rossi family has operated on Green Street in North Beach since 1942. The dive is housed in a ramshackle two-story building two blocks east of Columbus Avenue. Flanked by Caffe Sport and Golden Boy Pizza, Gino and Carlo's smelled of beer, shrimp scampi, and pizza. It's always been popular among cops, firefighters, longshoremen, and blue-collar workers because it opens at six AM. In addition to hosting countless celebrations and memorials, it was once the informal office of the legendary one-eyed muckraking journalist, Warren Hinckle, who held court at a table in the back with capable assistance from his ever-present basset hound, Bentley.

Pete took a sip of coffee. "Thanks for meeting us on short notice."

"Always happy to help an old friend."

That's a bit of a stretch. Ten years ago, Quinn hired Pete to keep an eye on his now-ex-wife. It took Pete a couple of days to confirm Quinn's suspicions that his wife was cheating. Pete's efforts led to a favorable divorce settlement, and Quinn had referred other clients to him.

Pete grinned. "Still fighting the good fight for the union?"

Quinn returned his smile. "Solidarity forever."

The native of North Beach was a few years younger than I was. He was a big man: six-two and close to three hundred pounds. He had a wide face, thinning gray hair, and jowls that wiggled as he talked. His father was a carpenter at the American Conservatory Theater on Geary. He was also a hard-drinking rabble-rouser who convinced the employees at A.C.T. and other theaters to join the International Alliance of Theatrical Stage Employees, Moving Picture Technicians, Artists and Allied Crafts, which represents almost 175,000 workers in theater, movie and TV production, and concerts. Although he never worked in the theater, F.X. followed in his father's footsteps and became an organizer for IATSE.

Pete kept his tone conversational. "You really going to run for supervisor?"

"Maybe. It's going to be a crowded field. I think I have a decent chance of getting into the runoff. After that, anything can happen." The inveterate glad-hander pulled at the collar of his worn gray sport jacket. "How can I help you?"

"Mike is representing César Ochoa. I trust that you heard that he's been accused of killing a dancer named Chloe Carson in the alley behind For Gentlemen Only?"

"I did. Helluva thing."

"Helluva thing," Pete repeated. "We got a list of people who were at the club on Friday night. Your name was on it."

Quinn's perpetual smile disappeared. "You think I had something to do with it?"

Maybe.

"We're just looking for information," Pete said. "You were there, right?"

"I was working."

"Working?"

"I've been trying to convince the dancers and the staff to unionize."

"How was it going?"

"Slowly."

"Did you know Chloe Carson?"

"I'd talked to her a couple of times." He quickly added, "Strictly union business."

Of course.

"Did you talk to her on Friday night?" Pete asked.

"Briefly. After she finished her performance, I asked her if we could set up a meeting outside of work to strategize. She promised to text me."

"How was her demeanor on Friday night?"

"She was pleasant enough, but she seemed a little nervous. She told me that she didn't want her boss to see her talking to me."

"Dave Callaghan?"

"Right. As you might surmise, he doesn't want his employees to unionize."

"They have a right to do it if they want to."

"It doesn't mean that management is going to be happy about it."

"Did you talk to Callaghan about it on Friday night?"

"No."

"Have you ever talked to him?"

"Briefly. He's a hard-ass."

"That will make union negotiations interesting."

Quinn smirked. "That's the fun part."

"Did you talk to César?"

"I said hello to him when I entered the club. He's always been nice to me."

"Do you think he's the kind of guy who might have killed somebody?"

"He didn't strike me as a violent guy, but you never know."

"Do you know if anybody was mad at Chloe Carson?"

"I don't know."

"Did you talk to anybody else at the club?"

"A dancer named Sheema Smith. She's been there a long time. I figured that if I could convince her to work with me, the others might follow. She listened to my pitch, but she didn't make any commitments. I also talked to the sound guy, Jerry Henderson, but he's only there when the regular guy is out, so he wasn't interested." He took a sip of beer. "I think there was something going on between Henderson and Carson. She snapped at him after the show."

"Any idea why?"

"Afraid not."

Pete kept his voice even. "Did you see anybody else get into it with Ms. Carson?"

He arched an eyebrow. "You ever heard of a lawyer named John Foreman?"

Pete nodded. "I recognize the name."

"He tried his best line on Chloe, but she wasn't interested. You might also talk to Tyler Benson. He was hitting on Chloe, too. I think she turned him down."

"We'll talk to them. Anybody else?"

He grinned. "Have you talked to 'The Franchise'?"

Pete and I exchanged a glance. Jason "The Franchise" Strong was the Giants' All-Star leftfielder. After a torrid start to the season, he had been sidelined with a shoulder injury.

"I didn't see his name on the list of people at the club," I said.

"He probably paid cash. He didn't want the Giants or, more important, his wife, to see a credit-card charge from For Gentlemen Only."

"He's married with a couple of young kids."

"It isn't the first time I've seen him at the club." His grin broadened. "My sources tell me that he has somebody in every city in the National League."

I was disappointed, but not entirely surprised. "Do the Giants know about this?" I asked.

"I'm sure they do."

"Did he talk to Chloe?"

"Yes. He got in the middle of the argument between Chloe and Henderson. Henderson grabbed Chloe's arm, and Strong pushed him away from her. She pushed Henderson, too. It lasted just a second or two. She told Strong to leave her alone."

"Are you willing to testify if we need you?"

"If I have to. My dad always told me that you have to tell the truth in court."

19
"WHAT WAS HE THINKING?"

An hour later, I stopped at the cubicle outside my office and greeted my former client and long-time receptionist, paralegal, and process server, Terrence "The Terminator" Love. "Welcome back. Good trip?"

"Excellent." The six-six, three-hundred-pound former professional boxer and former not-so-professional shoplifter smiled broadly, exposing his signature gold front tooth. "My new granddaughter is a beauty."

"Good to hear, T."

"Dazzle filled me in on what's been happening. Any progress on César's case?"

"Working on it. You ever been to For Gentlemen Only?"

"My strip club days are over. Besides, it's too upscale for me. I used to visit some earthier places South of Market." He wiped the sweat from his shaved dome. "Rolanda said that Jason Strong was there on the night that Chloe Carson was killed."

"So it seems. Pete's trying to track him down."

"He won't be hard to find. In the meantime, the Giants had an afternoon game. They beat the Cubs 4-3."

"That's the best news that I've had today."

"You think he was involved in Chloe Carson's death?"

"I don't know. I guess we'll have to ask him."

His brown eyes danced. "Can you turn him in to the cops after the season ends? He was having a great year until he got hurt."

I smiled. "I'll see what I can do. Anybody looking for me?"

"Rosie and Rolanda are in the conference room. They want to see you right away."

Rosie looked up from her laptop when I entered the conference room. "Jason 'The Franchise' Strong was at For Gentlemen Only on Friday night?"

"So it seems."

"The guy with the supermodel wife, the two beautiful kids, a three-hundred-million-dollar contract, and a family charity that promotes women's rights and family values?"

"Uh-huh."

"What was he thinking?"

"Evidently, he wasn't."

Rosie pushed out an exasperated sigh. "Do you have any idea how many problems in the world would be solved if you men would just learn how to keep your pants on?"

Rolanda burst out laughing. "It may also have an adverse impact on his sponsorship deal with Nike if word gets out."

"It'll get out," I said. "It always does. It also makes him a potential suspect in Chloe Carson's murder."

"Are you going to talk to him?"

"Absolutely. Pete is looking for him. Ordinarily, I would go through our sources with the Giants, but the team might not make him available in the circumstances."

"You think they know?"

"I wouldn't be surprised. Pro sports teams monitor their assets to protect the value of their brand. In some cases, they hire private investigators and resolve issues quietly."

"That makes them complicit. If they knew about it, they should have said something to his wife."

Agreed. "Maybe they did."

Rosie spoke up again. "Have the Giants ever hired Pete to watch one of their players?"

"Yes. He wasn't allowed to tell me who it was."

"That's no fun."

"I told him the same thing."

She closed her laptop. "I'm heading home. Don't stay too late." She headed out the door.

I turned to Rolanda. "Did you go over and see César today?"

"Yes. He isn't doing very well." She said that César wasn't eating or sleeping. "He couldn't stop pacing. He's going to wear himself out before the prelim next week. He's going to be a train wreck by the time we go to trial."

"Did you ask him about Tyler Benson, John Foreman, and F.X. Quinn?"

"Yes. He saw all of them at the club, but he didn't see them get into it with Chloe."

"And Jason Strong?"

"César said that Strong got into a shoving match with Henderson. It looked like Strong was trying to protect Chloe."

"I'll go see him tomorrow. Did anything else come in from the DA?"

"More police reports. Additional crime scene photos. Nothing exculpatory, but nothing incriminating, either. I'm putting together motions to file before the Friday deadline. The usual stuff: no cameras in the courtroom, a gag order on all parties, limits on crime scene photos, requests for fingerprint reports and DNA analysis."

"Any hints on the DA's case?"

"My guess is that it will be short. The guy who found the body. The first officer at the scene. The Assistant Medical Examiner. Fingerprint and DNA experts. Inspector Wong will tie their case together. I bet it won't take more than a couple of hours."

"Bottom line?"

"Unless we find some compelling evidence that somebody else did it, or we have a 'Perry Mason Moment' in court, it's going to be difficult to get the charges dropped at the prelim."

Rolanda had inherited Rosie's propensity for exhibiting clear-eyed realism.

"Please send me the drafts of the motions," I said. "I'll be here for a few more hours."

"I'm also going to keep going through the video and police reports."

"Don't stay too late. You have kids at home."

The corner of her mouth turned up. "It's kind of fun to be back in the middle of the action. I missed the adrenaline rush of trial preparation when I was out on maternity leave."

Just like Rosie. "If you want an adrenaline rush, wait until your kids are teenagers."

"I just want to get them out of diapers."

At eight-ten that same night, I was reviewing the drafts of Rolanda's motions when my phone vibrated, and Pete's name appeared on the display.

"You still at the office?" he asked.

"Yes."

"Meet me at Momo's right away."

It was the popular watering hole and grill across the street from the ballpark.

"Fifteen minutes," I said. "Why?"

"I found 'The Franchise.'"

20

"THE FRANCHISE"

Pete held up a hand. "Over here, Mick."

I joined him at a table on the patio of Momo's. The Giants game had ended four hours earlier, so the crowd was thin. I took the seat across from him and under a heat lamp. The light towers of the ballpark across the street were engulfed in fog. The aroma of burgers and nachos wafted across the patio.

"Where is he?" I asked.

Pete pointed across at the ballpark. "Getting treatment on his shoulder. He should be coming back soon."

"How did you find him?"

He pointed at the upscale condo complex at the corner of Second and King, kitty-corner to the ballpark. "He lives there during the season. I know the woman at the security desk."

"Her boss will be unhappy if he finds out that she provides information about the residents to private investigators."

"He won't. I know the security people in every upscale building in town."

I'm not surprised. "What do we do now?"

"You order dinner, and we wait for Strong."

I ordered a cheeseburger and an iced tea and ate in silence. Pete nursed his coffee as his eyes shifted from his phone to the ballpark and back. The patio emptied as the wind picked up. Fifteen minutes passed. Then a half hour. We ordered more coffee. I paid our bill.

And we waited.

At nine-fifteen, Pete jammed his phone into his pocket. "Here we go."

I followed him to the sidewalk in front of the restaurant. I recognized Jason "The Franchise" Strong, who was wearing a Giants hoodie and carrying a Nike duffle bag. We waited as he crossed King Street, eyes down, phone pressed to his ear.

Pete smiled as Strong approached us. "You're my daughter's favorite player. I hope your shoulder is better and you're back in the lineup soon."

Strong looked up. "Thank you. A few more days."

Pete reached inside his pocket, pulled out a baseball and a pen, and offered it to Strong. "I'm sorry to bother you, but would you mind signing this to Margaret?"

"Uh, sure."

"Thank you so much. She'll be thrilled."

"You're welcome." Strong grabbed the ball and pen and scribbled a signature.

"Mind if we take a quick photo?" Pete asked.

"Okay."

"By the way, my name is Pete, and this is my brother, Mike. We've been Giants fans since we were kids."

"Nice to meet you."

I pulled out my phone and took a picture of Pete and Strong with the ballpark in the background.

Strong picked up his duffle bag. "I need to get home."

Pete didn't move. "I saw the commercial that you did with your wife and kids to promote your charity. She seems like a super mom and a really nice person."

"Thank you. She is."

"It must be hard on her and the kids when you travel so much."

"She and the girls live in Arizona. They come up a once a month during the season."

"That's great." Pete's expression turned serious. "Mike is an attorney at the Public Defender's Office. I'm an investigator. Mike is representing a guy named César Ochoa. He's the doorman at a club called For Gentlemen Only."

The Franchise froze. "I have to get home."

Pete kept talking. "César has been charged with killing a dancer who worked at For Gentlemen Only. A couple of witnesses saw you at the club on Friday night. We'd like to ask you a few questions."

Strong's movie-star features hardened. "I don't know anything about it. If you want to talk about legal stuff, you'll need to contact my lawyer."

"Actually," Pete said, "we were going to contact the Giants, but we wanted to give you a chance to talk to us first."

"I don't know anything about it, and I have nothing to say to you."

"We aren't accusing you of anything, Jason. We're just trying to get information." Pete looked my way.

"We can do this the easy way or the hard way," I said. "We can go for a walk, ask you a few questions, and have a private conversation. Or we can send a request to your lawyer and the Giants and inform the media that you were at For Gentlemen Only on Friday night. Your call."

"I don't know what happened to that dancer," he insisted.

"Then you have nothing to hide," I said.

He thought about it for a moment. "You have to promise that you won't tell anybody."

I answered him honestly. "I can't do that. On the other hand, if you tell us the truth, I promise that I will do my best to avoid any personal embarrassment for you."

"Let's go for a walk."

"I don't know what happened to the young woman," Strong said.

"You were at For Gentlemen Only on Friday night?" I asked.

He nodded.

"Did you know Chloe Carson?"

"I watched her dance."

It was ten PM. Pete, Strong, and I were standing in the otherwise empty plaza between the back of the center-field scoreboard and the Bay. Dozens of yachts were lined up in South Beach Harbor. The boarding ramps to the Alameda, Larkspur, and Vallejo ferries were empty. The wind whipped through the mature palm trees.

"Did you talk to her on Friday?" I asked.

"Briefly. I told her that I enjoyed her performance."

"You'd seen her before?"

A hesitation. "Once or twice."

Which means that you're a repeat customer at the club. "What time did you arrive?"

"Around midnight." He said that he went alone.

"How long were you there?"

"Until last dance." He left a few minutes before one.

"You left through the front door?"

"No. I left through the back door."

"Did you see anybody in the alley?"

"No."

"Where did you park?"

"A couple blocks away on Sansome."

I sensed that he wasn't being entirely forthcoming.

Pete spoke up again. "Did you see our client interact with Ms. Carson on Friday night?"

"Yes." He waited a beat. "They got into an argument. I don't know what it was about."

"How long did it last?"

"Just a few seconds."

"Did Ms. Carson get into it with anybody else?"

"The sound guy."

"Jerry Henderson?"

"I don't know his name."

"Big guy with a bushy beard?"

"Yes."

"Do you know what they were arguing about?"

"I'm not sure, but at one point he grabbed her by the arm. I pulled his arm away from her and told him to lay off."

"How did she react?"

"She was really pissed off. She told him never to touch her again."

"Did she interact with anybody else?"

"I don't know. I didn't see anything."

21
"AREN'T YOU GETTING A LITTLE OLD FOR THIS?"

The gregarious bartender tossed his dish towel over his shoulder, gave me a wide smile, and spoke to me in a phony Irish brogue. "What'll it be, lad?"

"Have I ever ordered anything other than a Guinness, Joey?"

"Nope." His grin broadened. "Coming right up, Mike."

At ten-thirty on Wednesday night, the aroma of fish and chips and Guinness wafted through the inviting Irish pub at Twenty-third and Irving, around the corner from the house where I grew up. I looked at the framed black-and-white photo of my uncle, Big John Dunleavy, who had opened Dunleavy's Bar and Grill sixty-five years ago after my dad helped him build the long mahogany bar. Except for the flat screen TVs and the Wi-Fi password on the blackboard, the wood-paneled watering hole looked the same as it did when I drank my first beer at fourteen and tended bar on weekends when I was in college. Twenty years ago, Big John handed over the day-to-day operations to his grandson, my cousin Joey, but he kept coming to his beloved saloon to make his fish and chips and visit with his regulars. He died of a heart attack two years ago as he was counting the day's receipts and sipping a twenty-five-year-old single-malt Irish whiskey.

Joey filled Pete's cup with Folgers. Big John steadfastly refused to serve fancier coffee. Then he turned to the third person sitting at our table. "How about you, Roosevelt?"

The most decorated homicide inspector in SFPD history pointed at his empty mug and spoke in a raspy baritone. "Thanks."

Joey filled his mug. "You okay?"

"Doing fine for an eighty-seven-year-old." My father's first partner took off his glasses and wiped them with a napkin. He spoke in the familiar voice that I heard on Sunday nights when Roosevelt and his family used to come over for dinner. He reported that he was healthy, but an old knee injury required him to walk with a cane. His wife, Janet, had passed away a couple of years earlier. His granddaughter had just given birth to his third great-grandchild.

Joey's tone was respectful. "Your fish and chips are ready. I'll pack them up and you can take them home." He headed to the kitchen.

Roosevelt turned to us. "You boys okay?"

Pete and I nodded in unison. "Fine, Roosevelt," I said.

"I heard you picked up César's case."

"We did."

"Did he do it?"

"He says he didn't."

"You going to be able to get him off?"

"We'll see."

His lips turned down. "His situation is sad. He was a good cop, but he was his own worst enemy. I didn't think he was malicious, but he had a temper." His voice remained even. "Melinda Wong is a good inspector. Catherine O'Neal is a fine prosecutor. You're going to have your hands full."

"I know."

His eyes twinkled. "This is going to be an interesting battle. I'll be watching."

Joey returned with Roosevelt's order of fish and chips. The old warhorse thanked him, excused himself, and headed for the back door.

Joey dropped the phony brogue. "Roosevelt looks good. I have more fish and chips in the back. You interested?"

"I'm in," I said.

Pete nodded. "So am I."

"How's business?" I asked.

"Not bad," Joey said. "We're almost back to pre-Covid numbers."

When Covid hit, Joey transitioned to takeout only. He reopened for indoor dining in early 2021, but many of his customers stayed away or sat on the makeshift patio in the back.

I took another look at the photo of Big John. The consummate barkeep was also a savvy businessman. Dunleavy's had put his children and grandchildren through college, paid off his house around the corner, and got him a nice condo in Palm Springs.

"He would have been pleased that you stayed open during the pandemic," I said.

"Dunleavy's never closes," Joey said.

"How's Margarita?"

His eyes danced. "We're thinking of moving in together."

"That's great."

He had just turned forty. At six-four and two-forty, he had continued our family tradition of playing football at St. Ignatius. The former offensive lineman was still imposing, although he was getting a little soft in the middle. His bright red hair had turned gray, and his jowls had expanded along with his girth. He got a business degree from State and went to work for Big John. He almost got married to his high school sweetheart, but it didn't work out. About a year ago, Rosie's mother introduced him to the granddaughter of one of her neighbors. Margarita Mares worked for a tech start-up and was smart, ambitious, and independent. Rosie and I were hoping that Joey and Margarita would make their relationship a permanent one.

We exchanged gossip for a few minutes. He invited me to the annual Memorial Day fish-and-chips marathon. I invited him to join us for brunch on Sunday after church. It seemed as if we'd been having the same conversation for forty years.

His voice finally turned serious. "I hear you're representing César. Are you going to do it yourself, or are you going to hand it off to somebody else?"

"I'm going to take the lead for now," I said. "Rolanda is back in the office, and she's going to help. Pete is lending a hand on the investigation."

"I always liked César. He's a hard-ass, but you always knew where you stood with him." He turned to Pete, "After everything that happened, you're helping him?"

"We go back a long way."

"Not in a good way."

"He stood up for me. Now I'm going to stand up for him."

Joey knew better than to argue. "Did he do it?"

"That's what we're trying to find out."

"Do you think he did?"

"If you had asked me twenty years ago, I would have said no. Nowadays, I don't know."

Joey turned back to me. "Why don't you let Rolanda handle it?"

"We're trying to manage her workload. She has two kids in diapers at home."

The corner of his mouth turned up. "Aren't you getting a little old for this?"

"I'm not that much older than you are, Joey. And by the way, shut up."

He chuckled. "Have you talked to Jason Strong yet?"

Pete and I exchanged a glance. "As a matter of fact, we just did."

"I heard that he was at For Gentlemen Only on Friday night. I take it that he didn't confess to killing Chloe Carson."

"No, he didn't. How did you know?"

"Everybody knows." Joey pointed at the TV, which was tuned to SportsCenter. "It was on the news. Somebody took a video of Strong at the club. He was talking to Chloe Carson. A big guy with a beard interrupted them and grabbed her arm, and Strong shoved him out of the way. The guy who took the video posted it on X, or whatever they call Twitter now. It probably has ten million views."

Pete and I pulled out our phones and searched Twitter. He found it first. The video was barely five seconds long. It showed Strong talking to Carson. Henderson came over and grabbed Carson's arm. Strong pulled Henderson's arm away. Carson said something to Henderson. Strong walked away.

We watched it a half-dozen times. We couldn't hear what was said. It was already the top story on the *Chronicle*, ESPN, and countless other news outlets. Strong had issued a tweet admitting that he was at the club and apologizing to his wife and children. He asked for privacy and understanding while he worked out a "personal matter" with his family. His agent put out a damage-control statement that Strong was not involved in Chloe Carson's death and was cooperating with police. The Giants issued their own statement saying that the team was investigating the incident. Major League Baseball said that it was aware of the situation.

Pete grinned. "A lot of lawyers and PR people are going to be up all night. Strong can't blame us for it going public."

"I feel for his wife and kids."

"So do I. He isn't going to be doing commercials for Nike much longer."

"He brought it upon himself."

"Yes, he did. When he woke up this morning, he was a hero to millions and one of the highest-paid players in the big leagues. Now he's just another jerk who sneaked off to a strip club while his wife was out of town."

Joey grinned. "He's still highly paid," he observed.

Pete returned his smile. "Yes, he is. He is also now a suspect in a murder case."

22

"THINGS WILL LOOK BETTER IN THE MORNING"

"Where are you?" Rosie asked.

"I just passed the south tower of the bridge," I said.

At eleven-forty-five that same night, I was talking to Rosie via the hands-free as I drove my Prius north on the Golden Gate Bridge through what tourists would correctly call rain, and natives would describe as mist. Traffic was light. I couldn't see anything to my left except the blurry headlights of cars driving in the southbound lanes. I could make out the Alcatraz Beacon in the middle of the Bay. The Berkeley Hills wouldn't reappear until tomorrow.

"Are you at home?" I asked.

"I was at a meeting at City Hall that ran late, so I decided to stay at the apartment in the City. You're up late."

"It's been a long day. Pete and I went for a beer at Dunleavy's."

"Are Joey and Margarita still an item?"

"Yes. They're talking about moving in together."

"I'll let Mama know. She will be very pleased."

I drove up the hill and into the Robin Williams tunnel separating the Marin Headlands from Sausalito. The fog broke as I exited the tunnel and headed downhill.

Rosie's voice turned serious. "I saw the video of Jason Strong at For Gentlemen Only. Rolanda said that you talked to him."

"We did. He didn't confess to killing Chloe Carson."

"You believed him?"

"Let's just say that I remain appropriately skeptical."

She chuckled. "When you took this case, I'll bet that you didn't expect that the Giants' left fielder would be a suspect."

"At the very least, we know that he was there, and he had a conversation with Chloe Carson and Jerry Henderson."

"You're going to need some solid evidence to suggest that he killed Chloe."

"That's why we have Pete."

"Why do men always pander to their magical parts?" She quickly added, "Present company excepted."

"Thank you. It seems to be in the male DNA."

"Do you have anything substantial enough to get the charges dropped at the prelim next week?"

I answered her honestly. "I'm not wildly optimistic."

"You have some potential alternate suspects."

"Trying to blame Jason Strong, Jerry Henderson, Tyler Benson, John Foreman, F.X. Quinn, or even Dave Callaghan might help us get to reasonable doubt at trial, but it won't be enough to get the charges dropped at the prelim."

Her tone softened. "You sound tired."

"We'll get through it. We always do."

"Are you going to stay at the house tonight?"

"I'm heading to the apartment. I have to pick up a few things, and I need to check on Wilma."

"Give her a hug for me."

Wilma is the snow-white cat who lives in my apartment. She used to live next door. When my neighbors had twin boys, Wilma started coming over to my place for peace and quiet. It turned out that the twins were allergic to cats, so my neighbors asked me to adopt Wilma since she was already spending most of her time with me. I was happy to do so, and Wilma was delighted to have her own space and a human who changed her box and kept her water bowl and kibble dish full. I checked in on her at least once a day. She's one of the sweetest creatures on Planet Earth. As far as I can tell, she spends about twenty hours a day sleeping on the sofa and pondering the things that cats ponder.

"Have you been to the gym?" Rosie asked.

"It's been about a week."

"Dr. Partida wants you to stay active. At the very least, you should get out and walk the steps in the morning. It's good for you, and it will make Zvi happy."

"I can't keep up with him."

"Neither can I."

Our friend, neighbor, and hero, Zvi Danenberg, is a relentlessly upbeat ninety-eight-year-old retired science teacher who stays in exemplary shape by climbing the one hundred and thirty-nine steps connecting Magnolia Avenue in downtown Larkspur with the houses on the adjacent hill. He used to do it every day, but he slowed down to twice a week after he turned ninety-five, and his doctors advised him to preserve what was left of his overworked knees. I join him from time to time. The classical music afficionado still goes to the symphony regularly, and he maintains a magnificent collection of classical records that he accumulated over eight decades.

"Give my best to Zvi," she said. "And get some rest, Mike. Things will look better in the morning."

My phone vibrated at six AM. I answered on the second ring.

Pete's voice was raspy. "You up, Mick?"

"I am now."

My eyes struggled to adjust to the darkness in the bedroom of my cozy apartment behind the Larkspur Fire Station. The mismatched furniture included a mattress perched on a wooden frame held up by cinder blocks, a second-hand nightstand, and a dresser from IKEA. Wilma was sleeping next to me—she wouldn't be up for at least another hour.

Pete cleared his throat. "Meet me at Café Trieste at eight AM. We're having coffee with somebody who knows everybody in North Beach."

23
"INDEED I AM"

"Are they still coming?" I asked.

Pete pulled up the collar of his bomber jacket to fend off the morning fog as he stood in line underneath the cheerful green awning in front of Café Trieste, which has been serving espresso and pastries on the corner of Grant and Vallejo since 1956. "Any minute now."

I looked up Grant Avenue, the narrow street that bisects Chinatown and North Beach. Nowadays, the Italian restaurants in the two- and three-story post-Earthquake buildings are interspersed with sushi bars, burger joints, Nepalese cafes, burrito shops, dive bars, and, more recently, marijuana dispensaries. The air is always filled with the glorious aroma of tomato sauce, garlic, olive oil, parmesan cheese, espresso, and cannoli.

Pete pointed at the top-of-the-line black Cadillac Escalade with tinted windows pulling into the red zone in front of Café Trieste. "They're here, Mick."

The chauffeur opened the door to the back seat. A diminutive man wearing a three-piece Brioni suit, a blindingly white shirt, and a Turnbull and Asser silk necktie emerged, tugged at the fresh rose on his lapel, and smiled at the dozen people standing in line.

"Good morning," he chirped in a singsong voice.

Everyone in line returned his smile, and several sang out, "Good morning, Nick."

His rubbery face transformed into a broader grin as he turned to Pete. "Great to see you, Pete. How the hell are you?"

"Great, Nick." He pointed at me. "You remember Mike?"

"Indeed I do. Good to see you, too."

I shook his hand. "Same here, Nick."

Nick "The Dick" Hanson was still spry at ninety-five. He had founded the Hanson Investigative Agency seventy-five years ago in an office above the Condor Club around the corner at Broadway and Columbus. He was the chairman emeritus of the biggest private eye operation on the West Coast.

A young woman also emerged from the Escalade, asked Nick's long-time driver to come back in an hour, and headed toward us. Her face bore a resemblance to Nick's, but she towered over him by at a foot, and her jet-black hair had a magenta streak.

Nick handled the introductions. "You remember my great-granddaughter, Nicki?"

"Of course," I said, shaking her hand. "Nice to see you again."

"Same here." She smiled as she exchanged greetings with Pete.

Nicki was the head of the agency's cybersecurity group. The thirty-year-old had a computer science degree from UC San Diego and a master's in data analytics from UCLA. She was one of dozens of Nick's children, grandchildren, and great-grandchildren who worked at the agency.

Nick pointed at the door to Café Trieste. "Shall we?"

I couldn't resist. "Indeed we shall. After you."

The people in the queue parted like the Red Sea as Nick led us inside and past the display case filled with Italian pastries, cannoli, cookies, brownies, bagels, and other treats. The aroma of espresso, cappuccino, latte, and mocha filled the intimate room, which had a half-dozen small tables along the window and a few larger ones in the back. The walls were lined with photos of generations of North Beach notables. Opera music played on the sound system, and four dedicated employees made perfect drinks at the classic espresso machine. A hand-lettered sign reminded patrons that Café Trieste is still a cash-only operation.

We followed Nick to a table where a hand-lettered sign said, "Reserved." He took a seat with his back to the wall so that he could see his domain, and his admirers could see him. He was the son of Russian immigrants who became small-time vaudeville stars. They got tired of the travel and moved to San Francisco, where Nick's uncle was a longshoreman. Nick's father opened a magic shop next door to the Tosca Café. Nick played baseball with Joe DiMaggio on the North Beach playground. During the Great Depression, he helped his father make ends meet by sweeping up at the Valente, Marini, Perata Funeral Home on Green Street, handing out towels at the Italian Athletic Club, and bilking tourists at three-card monte.

I took my seat and admired the photo of a younger Nick sitting at this very table with Francis Coppola, who wrote portions of the screenplays for *The Godfather* movies here.

"Have you talked to Francis lately?" I asked him.

"Indeed I have. We were up at the winery a couple of weeks ago. He's doing okay."

"Was he working on the Godfather when that picture was taken?"

Nick turned and admired himself. "I think it was *Godfather II*. It took a little time, but I persuaded him that Fredo had to die at the end."

I find that hard to believe.

Without being asked, one of the servers arrived with a cappuccino and three pastries for Nick, and a latte and a bagel for Nicki. I ordered a cappuccino. Pete requested black coffee. I offered to pay, but Nick informed me that he had a running tab that dated back to the fifties.

Nick lived a few blocks away in an Earthquake-era mansion near the top of Telegraph Hill. A savvy businessman and astute investor, he accumulated a portfolio of apartment buildings rumored to be worth a cool fifty million. In his spare time, he wrote mystery novels that were embellishments of his cases. Danny DeVito played Nick in a long-running Netflix series.

A visit with Nick requires time, patience, and an empty stomach. By the time my cappuccino arrived, Nick had finished his second pastry and was expounding upon the growth strategy for this agency (still going strong), his real estate portfolio (he was trying to acquire the building housing Café Trieste), and his plans for the summer (a gathering in Calistoga followed by a family reunion at his compound at Poipu Beach).

In response to my question about the TV series, Nick took a big bite of his third pastry. "We paid Danny a boatload of money to do one more season. Then the Hollywood writers went on strike, and everything went on hold. Fortunately, everybody's working again, so they should start shooting soon."

We shot the breeze for another twenty minutes. Nick was never in a hurry, and Nicki was content to sip coffee and let him talk. Nick was a natural storyteller, and he was always the hero in his stories. A few people stopped at our table to say hello and ask for selfies. Most private eyes are loath to have their pictures taken, but Nick had a million followers on Instagram.

He finally turned to business. "I heard you picked up César's case."

Pete answered him. "We did. Mike is handling César's prelim next week. I'm helping out with the investigation."

"Even after everything that happened?"

"César and I go back a long way, Nick."

"Suit yourself. Did he do it?"

"He said that he didn't."

"You believe him?"

"That's what we're trying to find out. You're as tuned in as anybody here in North Beach. Have you heard anything?"

"Afraid not."

"Have you ever been to For Gentlemen Only?"

"It's been a few years."

Nicki interjected. "We didn't let Grandpa eat at indoor locations during Covid. And with the TV show, it's almost impossible for Grandpa to do surveillance without being noticed."

Nick grinned triumphantly. "The price of fame."

Pete spoke to Nicki. "Any chance you had somebody working at For Gentlemen Only on Friday night?"

"Afraid not."

"Do you know any of the employees?"

Nicki exchanged a glance with her great-grandfather, who spoke up again. "We've paid Dave Callaghan to provide information on a few cases. Most of it has been reliable."

"Is he a good guy?"

"No, he's a dick."

"The kind of dick who would kill one of his dancers?"

"Doubtful. He's just a garden-variety dick."

"The decedent had a relationship with the sound guy, Jerry Henderson."

"He's a dick, too. He was abusive to a couple of his ex-girlfriends."

"Was he abusive to Chloe Carson?"

"I don't know."

I asked if he knew anybody else who worked at the club.

"Talk to Sheema," he said. "She has an edge, but she's been a reliable source of information. Who else was there?"

"You know Tim Volpe?"

"Everybody knows Tim. Solid cop. Not the hardest-working guy in town, but he tries."

"You think he's the kind of guy who would kill somebody?"

"Also doubtful."

"John Foreman was at the club on Friday night."

Nick responded with a knowing grin. "I'm not surprised. He's been going there for years. It blew up his first two marriages."

"You know him?"

"We're neighbors. He's an excellent lawyer."

"Good guy?"

"He's a prick."

By my count, that's two dicks and a prick in the last three minutes.

Nick was still talking. "His first ex-wife hired us to see if he was cheating. It took us two days to confirm it. His second ex-wife hired us to do the same thing. It took us less than a day. He and his current wife have an arrangement: he gets to watch naked girls dance, and she gets to sleep around. I'm not sure that it's psychologically healthy, but it works for them."

"Is he the kind of guy who might kill somebody if she refused his advances?"

Another grin. "You never know."

"Jason Strong was at For Gentlemen Only, too."

Nick grinned. "I saw the video. Evidently, so has the rest of the world."

Nicki added, "He visits For Gentlemen Only on occasion. He's a good-looking dick who can hit a baseball a mile."

We're up to three dicks now. "Did his wife hire you?"

"The Giants hired us. We're on retainer. We try to be discreet."

"The Giants know that Strong hangs out at strip clubs?"

"So does his wife. That's why she lives in Arizona with the kids."

"The Giants are okay with this?"

"They're trying to contain the damage. He isn't doing anything illegal. His relationship with his wife is between the two of them. And they owe him north of three hundred million dollars."

I wondered how I would have handled the situation if they had come to me for marriage counseling when I was a priest. "Is he the kind of guy who would stab somebody?"

"Also doubtful," Nicki said. "He isn't very bright, but he's probably smart enough to avoid doing something that would jeopardize the rest of his contract."

"Anybody else?" Nick asked.

"F.X. Quinn was there."

"F.X. is everywhere. He's going to run for supervisor. He has no chance."

At least he didn't call him a "dick." "Does he know that?"

"Union organizers are inherently optimistic."

"Is he the type who might have stabbed a dancer in an alley in the middle of the night?"

"I wouldn't think so, but you never know."

"Tyler Benson was there, too."

Nick grinned at his great-granddaughter. "I'm not surprised."

"Neither am I," she said. "One of his investors hired us to watch him when he was selling crypto. He was at a different club every night."

Pete looked at Nick. "You think he's a dick, too?"

"No, he's a punk. There's a difference."

I'm not sure of the precise distinctions between a "dick," a "prick," and a "punk," but I'm not inclined to ask. "The kind who would kill a dancer if she didn't sleep with him?"

"You never know."

Nicki finished her coffee and nodded at her grandfather. "We need to get over to the Italian Athletic Club for another meeting, Grandpa."

"In a sec." He looked at me. "You going to get the charges dropped at the prelim?"

"I'm not wildly optimistic. Is there anybody we should talk to who may have been in the vicinity of For Gentlemen Only on Friday night?"

"Talk to Clive Williams. He's a homeless guy who hangs out near the strip clubs."

Pete grinned. "By my count, Nick identified three dicks, a prick, and a punk."

"Can you explain the difference?" I asked.

"It doesn't matter."

We were still sitting at Nick's table in the back of Café Trieste. Nick and Nicki had departed. The line outside had dissipated. A few regulars lingered over coffee. Some picked at laptops. Most looked at their phones.

"You going back to the office?" he asked.

"I'm going to see César. You?"

"I'm going to find Clive."

24
"YOU NEED TO GET ME OUT OF HERE"

Perspiration covered César's face and his voice was filled with the unmistakable sound of desperation. "You need to get me out of here."

"I'm working on it, César."

"You need to work faster."

"We talked about this. It's going to be almost impossible to get you pretrial release."

He paced in the cramped consultation room in the Glamour Slammer. "Ask again."

"I will." *It isn't going to happen.* "The judge won't reconsider until the prelim."

"I may not last that long."

"I need you to stay strong."

I inhaled the stale air as we stared at each other. César looked a lot worse than the last time I saw him, only a day earlier. His eyes were bloodshot. His skin had a yellow cast.

"You getting any sleep?" I asked.

"No."

"You eating?"

"Not much."

I could only offer a platitude. "You need to take care of yourself, César." I pointed at a bandage on his right hand. "What's that?"

"Nothing."

"Come on, César."

He sat down across the table from me. "A guy shoved me. I shoved him back. He had something in his hand. It wasn't a knife, but it was sharp. It wasn't bad. I'll be fine."

I invoked a nonconfrontational tone. "You know how things work. It's in your best interest to stay away from people and avoid trouble."

"I know." His expression softened. "You find anything that we can use next week?"

I summarized our conversations with Callaghan, Henderson, Volpe, Foreman, Strong, Quinn, and Benson. "It gives us some options."

His expression turned skeptical. "Options are good. Evidence is better."

True. "A couple of people said that Jerry Henderson had a toxic relationship with Chloe Carson. He had a history of being abusive."

"That wouldn't surprise me."

"He's never been convicted of a crime."

He invoked his cop-voice. "Victims of abuse are often reluctant to come forward."

Sad, but true. "Do you know anybody who might be able to corroborate this information?"

He thought about it for a long moment. "Talk to Sheema again."

Rolanda entered my office at five-fifteen PM. "How did it go with César?"

"He's starting to panic."

"Not good. I emailed you updated drafts of our motions."

"I'll give them a look." She started to walk away, but I stopped her. "You okay?"

"Fine."

"Good. We're going to be very busy for the next week or so."

I was reviewing Rolanda's motions at nine o'clock the same night when Rosie strolled into my office and sat down in the chair opposite my desk.

She smiled. "Having a high job satisfaction day?"

"Absolutely."

"Good. It makes me happy when my subordinates are happy."

"How did it go at the fundraiser tonight?"

"Another twenty grand. We're going to bury my opponent before the campaign starts."

"She'll never know what hit her."

"That's the idea. Are you going home soon?"

"Maybe in an hour or so. Our motions for César's case are due in the morning. I want to go over them once more."

"You want me to give them a look?"

"That's okay. Rolanda is excellent."

"I'll see you at home." She headed out the door.

My phone vibrated. I opened a text from Pete. It read, "I found Clive."

25
CLIVE

The aroma of cheeseburgers and fries filled the narrow diner on Broadway, between Columbus and Stockton, where Chinatown converged with Nob Hill and North Beach. Opened in 1966 by Mike ElShawa, and now run by his son, Emad, Sam's Burgers has a counter, a dozen ketchup-red stools, and three Formica tables bolted to the wall. It caters to cops, firefighters, maintenance workers, and the drinking crowd from the nearby bars seeking sustenance after midnight. Mike's picture hangs on the wall, a Styrofoam cup in his hand, a cigarette in his mouth. It's next to a photo of the late Anthony Bourdain, who proclaimed that the double cheeseburger was one of the top three burgers in the world. In a framed note on the wall, Bourdain observed "That is a good motherf—kin' burger." Mike expressed his gratitude by naming the twenty-dollar double-cheeseburger special after Bourdain.

I stopped at the last table against the wall where Pete was sitting with an African American man of indeterminate middle age with a leathery face, a gray beard, and jet-black eyes surrounded by deeply embedded crow's feet.

Pete handled the introductions. "This is Clive Williams."

I reached across the table and shook his calloused hand. "Mike Daley. Nice to meet you."

"Same here."

Pete pushed a double cheeseburger and fries toward me. "We got you a Bourdain."

"Thanks." I looked over at Clive, whose grease-soaked paper plate was now empty. "You want another burger?"

"Sure. Thanks."

I pushed my burger over to Clive, who unwrapped it and took a bite. I figured that my cardiologist would be pleased by my decision.

Pete spoke up again. "Clive lives in the neighborhood."

"Whereabouts?" I asked.

Clive ate a handful of fries. "Here and there."

"It's tough out there."

"Not as bad as the Tenderloin or South of Market."

True. "We have people at our office who can help you find a place to live."

"Been there. I'd rather live on the street than in an SRO in the Tenderloin."

It's a close call. Some of the single room occupancy hotels, or "SROs," aren't bad. Others are vermin-infested nightmares filled with addicts, drug dealers, sex workers, and the mentally ill.

I wanted to keep Clive talking. "You from around here?"

"East Oakland."

"McClymonds?"

"Oakland Tech." He said that he enlisted in the Army after high school but was discharged after injuring his leg during basic training. He returned to Oakland and did construction work until the Great Recession. He picked up part-time security work, but his leg injury made it difficult to stay on his feet. He became addicted to painkillers and started drinking, which led to his eviction from his apartment and life on the street.

"Do you spend much time near For Gentlemen Only on Broadway?" I asked.

"Sometimes. They stay open late. People are pretty friendly. Sometimes they drop me a few dollars or give me some leftovers."

"Do you know César Ochoa?"

"I met him a few times. I never gave him any trouble, so he didn't give me any trouble."

"I trust that Pete explained that I'm representing him?"

"He did."

"Were you anywhere near For Gentlemen Only on Friday night?"

"I walked by around eleven that night. I didn't see what happened to Chloe Carson."

"Did you know her?"

"I saw her leaving the club a few times. She didn't say much. She gave me some leftovers once."

"Did you ever see her talk to César?"

"Once or twice. Nothing out of the ordinary."

"You ever see anybody else give her a hard time?"

He thought about it for a moment. "Dave Callaghan threatened to fire her after she showed up late one night. She didn't take crap from anybody, so she gave it right back to him."

"Did you see them get into it on Friday night?"

"No."

Pete showed him photos of Tim Volpe, John Foreman, Tyler Benson, and F.X. Quinn. Clive recognized them. He had never seen any of them get into it with Carson. "Sergeant Volpe gave me a couple of dollars once. The others ignored me."

"You ever see Jason Strong?" Pete asked.

Clive smiled. "A few times. He's a nice guy. He signed a Giants cap for me."

"Do you know if he had any contact with any of the dancers?"

"All of them. He would chat them up in the alley." His grin broadened. "It was a running joke that he hit better when he was getting a little action."

"Have you ever seen him get into any arguments with any of the girls?"

"He gave Sheema some crap one night, but she gave it right back. He tried to pick up a new girl named Kelly, but she turned him down."

"And Chloe Carson?"

"Not that I saw."

Pete showed him a photo of Jerry Henderson. "Recognize him?"

"He works at the club every once in a while." Clive hesitated. "He asked me to watch his car once. He promised me twenty bucks, but he didn't pay me. He gave me some coke instead." He paused. "I think he was dealing coke and meth in the alley behind the club."

"Was he selling drugs to Chloe Carson?"

"I don't know."

"He used to be her boyfriend."

"I didn't know that." Clive took a drink of Coke. "They got into a big argument a few weeks ago. She told him to leave her alone."

"Did he get physical with her?"

"He grabbed her arm. She told him to keep his hands off of her."

Pete probed for details, but none were forthcoming. "You want anything else to eat?"

Clive shook his head. "I'm good."

"We appreciate your time, Clive." Pete reached inside his pocket, pulled out five twenties, and slid them across the Formica table to Clive. "This is for your time tonight. We may need you to testify next week. We'll pay you for your time and reimburse you for a cab ride."

Clive pocketed the bills. "How much for my time?"

I answered him. "A hundred bucks an hour."

"Two hundred."

"I might be able to make it one-fifty."

"I might be able to help you. When do you need me?"

"Probably Wednesday or Thursday of next week."

Pete handed him a prepaid burner phone. "We'll call you on this phone to let you know."

Clive grinned. "It's a pleasure doing business with you gentlemen."

26

"IS THERE ANY POSSIBILITY THAT WE CAN RESOLVE THIS?"

The Honorable Elizabeth McDaniel motioned Rolanda and me to the open chairs opposite her polished redwood desk. "Come in."

"Thank you, Your Honor," I said. Rolanda and I nodded at O'Neal, who was sitting in the other chair. "Nice to see you, Catherine," I lied.

"Nice to see you, too, Mike."

Right.

Judge McDaniel was an elegant woman of seventy-five with stellar credentials, a razor-sharp mind, and a thoughtful presence. Her paneled chambers were on the third floor of the Hall overlooking the slow lane of the I-80 Freeway.

I admired the framed photos of her grandchildren on her credenza between her laptop, multiple volumes of California Jury Instructions, and several signed first-edition Donna Leon novels. "Grandkids okay?"

"Everybody's fine, Mike." Although she had lived in the Bay Area for almost a half-century, you could still hear a trace of her native Alabama in her voice. "I saw Rosie at Pilates yesterday. She seems to be doing well." She asked about Grace and Tommy.

"Status quo. Grace is still working at Pixar. Tommy is at Cal."

"Good to hear. Is Grace going to make you and Rosie grandparents anytime soon?"

"Maybe in another year or two. Rosie's mother is getting impatient."

"So is Rosie."

To those who had never met Betsy, it was hard to imagine that the Hall of Justice's resident mother hen had been a tenacious prosecutor for a quarter of a century. She brought the same intensity to the bench, albeit in a more nurturing way. Then again, if you made a poorly researched or ill-reasoned argument, she wouldn't hesitate to skewer you.

She turned to Rolanda. "It's nice to have you back at the office. Are your children okay?"

"Fine, thank you, Your Honor."

"Good to hear." She looked at O'Neal. "How is your mother?"

"A little better."

"Good. Please give her my best." The judge glanced at her computer, signaling that the social portion of our meeting was over. "César Ochoa," she said to nobody in particular. "Preliminary hearing on Wednesday." She looked my way. "What's the rush?"

"My client has the right to a prelim within ten days after his arraignment. That's how he would like to proceed."

"That's his legal right. It's not my job to tell you how to conduct your case."

But you might offer a few suggestions.

She turned to O'Neal. "I presume that you'll be ready?"

"Yes, Your Honor."

"How much time will you need?"

"A couple of hours. Just a few witnesses. The evidence is straightforward."

"How about you, Mr. Daley?"

It did not go unnoticed that I was once again "Mr. Daley." "Two or three days. The evidence isn't as straightforward as Ms. O'Neal has suggested."

"Is there any possibility that we can resolve this before Wednesday?"

O'Neal spoke up. "Not unless Mr. Daley's client is willing to change his plea to guilty."

Here we go. "Your Honor, Ms. O'Neal is being unreasonable and jumping to conclusions."

O'Neal fired back. "We found a bloody knife with your client's fingerprints."

"You didn't find any blood on his hands, clothes, or car."

"You aren't seriously going to make that argument, are you, Mr. Daley?"

"Damn right I am, Ms. O'Neal. Either way, this isn't a first-degree murder case. You and Inspector Wong are rushing to justice."

"No, we're not."

"Yes, you are."

Judge McDaniel let us argue it out for the next five minutes. Over the years, she had learned that it's sometimes productive to give lawyers time to vent. I guess she figured that if we do it in chambers, we're less likely to do it in court.

The judge finally stopped us. "It sounds like we aren't going to settle this today. I have reviewed your motions." She looked my way. "First, your request to exclude the knife is denied. There is no evidence that chain of custody was breached.

"Second, while I understand your desire to see the evidence as soon as possible, you have no right to see it prior to the prelim. While I would encourage Ms. O'Neal to provide any remaining police reports, crime scene photos, the autopsy report, and other relevant evidence, she is under no legal obligation to do so. As a result, your motion is denied."

This isn't going well, but it isn't unexpected. It's the correct interpretation of the law.

"Third," the judge continued, "I encourage you to exchange witness lists before the prelim to ensure an orderly process, but you are under no legal obligation to do so."

Also a correct statement of the law.

"Fourth," she said, "I am going to continue Judge Tsang's gag order on all parties and counsel. I don't want any of you talking to the press or trying this case in social media. If you talk, tweet, or post, it will cost you.

"Finally, I want to make it clear that I will not allow the prelim or later proceedings, if any, to be televised."

"But, Your Honor—," O'Neal said.

"I've ruled, Ms. O'Neal. You know as well as I do that people change their behavior when the cameras are on. And it isn't for the better."

"Yes, Your Honor."

Judge McDaniel leaned back in her leather chair. "I know that you are all good lawyers and you're reasonable. I would encourage you to go back to your respective offices, take a deep breath, and give some serious thought to this case. Then I would suggest that you go out for a cup of coffee and see if you can work something out. Otherwise, we'll see you on Wednesday."

27
"HE'S A FUNDAMENTALLY DECENT MAN"

Dazzle was sitting at her cubicle when I walked toward my office at one-ten PM. "How did it go with Judge McDaniel?" she asked.

"About what I expected. No big wins or losses. She was a little perplexed that we want to move forward to the prelim so quickly."

"I might have asked the same question."

"César insisted." I smiled. "Have you ever thought about going to law school? You would be a terrific lawyer."

"Not a chance." She grinned. "I spent eight years as a paralegal at a big law firm."

"I thought it was Terrence's turn to work today."

"He caught a cold from his granddaughter. You know how it goes. The baby will be fine in a day or two. Terrence will be sick for a couple of weeks."

Probably true. I pointed at Rosie's office. "Anything I need to know from the boss?"

"No."

"You heard from Pete?"

"Nothing." Her expression turned serious as she pointed at the closed door to Rolanda's office. "César's ex-wife just showed up without an appointment. She's in with Rolanda."

Selena Ochoa stood up, forced a smile, and greeted me with a firm handshake and a tense voice. "It's been a long time, Mike. I'm sorry that I didn't make an appointment."

"No worries. Thanks for coming in." I looked at Rolanda, who was sitting at her desk. "How much have I missed?"

"We were just getting started."

I sat down in the chair next to Selena's. "How have you been?" I asked her.

She clutched her water bottle. "Not bad."

"Are your son and grandson both okay?"

"Fine."

I gave her a moment to get her bearings. The native of the Mission and alum of Sacred Heart Cathedral High School was fifty-five. She met César when he was a rookie cop, and she was working in SFPD Dispatch. They were married for a dozen years. Things blew up after César and Pete were fired. César and Selena have remained on strained speaking terms. César has minimal contact with his son and grandson.

"You still working?" I asked her.

"Yes. I'm going to retire in a couple of years when my City pension is fully vested. You?"

"I promised Rosie that I would stick around until she finishes her next term."

Like most City employees, I knew exactly when it would be most advantageous to take my generous pension and retirement benefits.

Selena arched an eyebrow. "You sound confident that she'll win re-election."

"I am. Why did you come to see us?"

"I wanted to thank you and Rolanda for representing César. You could have assigned his case to one of the younger attorneys. I appreciate the fact that you didn't."

"You're welcome." *Don't react. Let her talk.*

"I wanted to thank Pete, too," she said. "It's especially nice of him since. . ."

"What happened," I said.

"Yes."

"They were partners, Selena."

"They got fired, Mike. You know the history."

"Personal loyalty trumps unfortunate circumstances. I will pass it along. Pete's moral compass has always been pointed in the right direction. The same is true for César."

She measured her words. "César was a good cop. He's always had a temper, but I still believe that he's a fundamentally decent man. I sometimes wonder if I could have done something to make things easier for him."

"Don't be too hard on yourself. It was a long time ago." I tried again. "Why did you really come to see us?"

"I was wondering if there is anything that I can do to help."

"It would be great if you could come to the prelim and provide a little moral support. It would mean a lot to César, even if you stay for just a short time."

"I don't know, Mike."

"You don't have to decide right now. Is there any chance that you might also be able to persuade your son to come to the prelim? Maybe for just a few minutes?"

She scowled. "Doubtful."

"Understood. Will you ask him?"

"I will." She swallowed hard. "César has a lot of issues, but he isn't a murderer."

Pete was sitting on my windowsill an hour later. "It was nice of Selena to stop by."

"She was very appreciative of your efforts on behalf of César," I said. "Anything new?"

"I've interviewed all the employees and most of the customers who were at For Gentlemen Only on Friday night. I talked to people who live and work nearby. I haven't found any evidence absolving César."

"The prelim doesn't start until Wednesday. We've been working on this case for less than a week. You'll find something."

He looked at Rolanda. "What do you think?"

It no longer bothers me that Pete trusts Rolanda's and Rosie's instincts more than mine.

She responded with a reassuring smile. "You'll find something, Pete. You always do."

He took the compliment in stride. "We may need to try to foist the blame onto somebody other than César. Who do you like?"

"We follow the evidence where it takes us."

"Sometimes, you need to give the evidence a little shove."

The corner of Rolanda's mouth turned up. "Who do *you* like?"

"Ideally, you look for somebody who is unsympathetic. Our options include Dave Callaghan, Jerry Henderson, John Foreman, Tyler Benson, F.X. Quinn, Jason Strong, and maybe even Tim Volpe. On the Pete Daley 'Asshole Scale,' Volpe is a two, Quinn is a five, Strong is a seven, Callaghan and Benson are both eights, and Foreman is a ten."

"You left out Henderson."

"He's an eleven." His eyes shifted my way. "Let's go pay him another visit, Mick. Maybe we can rattle his cage."

28
"I CAN'T TALK"

Pete knocked on the metal gate covering the door to the basement apartment three steps beneath a dry cleaner's on Green Street, around the corner from Café Trieste. "Jerry?"

No answer.

He waited a few seconds and tried again.

Still no answer.

The aroma of tomato sauce and mozzarella from Golden Boy Pizza floated up Green Street at three-thirty on Friday afternoon. The sun was out, and pedestrian traffic was light.

"Maybe he isn't home," I said.

Pete pointed at his operative sitting in his car across the street. "Tony said that Henderson hasn't left his apartment since this morning." He pounded on the door again.

It opened halfway. An exhausted-looking Henderson wore a Giants hoodie. His eyes were red. His complexion was pale.

His raspy voice was barely a whisper. "What are you doing here?"

"We need to talk," Pete said.

"I can't talk."

"Just a few minutes."

"I literally can't talk. I lost my voice."

"Can we come in?"

"Not unless you want to catch Covid. I tested positive yesterday."

Oh hell.

Pete waited a beat. "Do you need anything?"

"I'll be fine. They gave me Paxlovid."

"Mike needs you to testify at César's preliminary hearing that starts on Wednesday."

"I don't know if I'm going to be healthy enough by then."

I stepped forward. "We need your help, Jerry." *And I may want to throw you under the bus.* "If you're still testing positive, I can try to persuade the judge to let you testify remotely."

"I'm not sure."

"I'll send you a subpoena if I have to. I'd rather not."

"Send me whatever you want. Now get the hell out of here." He closed the door.

Pete looked my way and deadpanned, "I thought that went pretty well."

"Me, too. You think he's really sick?"

"He didn't look like he was faking to me." Pete pointed at his operative. "Tony will keep an eye on him and let us know if anything changes."

"I'll have Rolanda draft a subpoena."

"Let me know when it's ready. You may need to ask for a continuance if he's still sick next week."

"For now, we'll proceed on the assumption that he'll be available. Where to now?"

"Let's go over to For Gentlemen Only and talk to Dave Callaghan again."

Callaghan feigned irritation when Pete and I walked into For Gentlemen Only at four o'clock that same afternoon. "I don't have time," he snapped.

"We can wait," I said.

"We open in a few minutes. A couple of my people are sick with Covid. I'm trying to arrange for coverage."

Pete's voice was even. "No worries, Dave." He pointed at a table in the otherwise empty bar. "Mike and I are going to have a drink. Come see us when you have a minute."

Pete and I took our seats at a table against the wall. Pete looked at his phone. I watched the pre-opening choreography. Servers set tables. Bartenders prepared lemons and limes. Through the door to the kitchen, I saw cooks chopping lettuce, peeling potatoes, and cutting vegetables. A technician adjusted the lights and tested the sound. Two dancers headed toward the dressing room, gym bags over their shoulders. It reminded me of my days working as a bartender at Dunleavy's, although Big John's bar operated on a smaller scale, and there were no dancers.

I glanced at Pete, who was staring at his phone. "What now?"

"We order drinks. Then we wait for Callaghan to apologize for snapping at us."

He turned back to his phone, and I looked at the TV, which was tuned to ESPN. A server came over. Pete ordered coffee. I asked for a club soda. A few customers trickled inside.

Ten minutes later, the houselights went down, music started playing, the bartenders manned their stations, and the servers started working the room.

Callaghan joined us and spoke in a subdued voice. "Sorry for snapping at you."

"We caught you at a busy time," I said.

Pete took a sip of coffee. "You get everything covered?"

"For now."

"We heard that Jerry Henderson got Covid."

"He did. Hopefully, he'll be okay."

Pete looked around the empty room. "How's business?"

"Not great. They say that all publicity is good. That isn't necessarily the case when one of your dancers is killed behind your club. I take it that you're here to talk about César?"

I answered him. "Yes."

"I don't know anything more than I told you last time."

"We heard that Jerry and Chloe were seeing each other, but she broke up with him."

"Who told you that?"

"A couple of people. Did you know about it?"

"Uh, no."

"We were told that the breakup was acrimonious."

"I wouldn't know."

"We also heard that Jerry and Chloe were arguing on Friday night. Did you know what they were fighting about?"

"No."

I probed for a few more minutes, but Callaghan wasn't forthcoming. "César's preliminary hearing starts on Wednesday. We need you to testify."

"If I have to." He said that the DA had also contacted him. "Catherine O'Neal wants me to confirm that Chloe worked here and the time that she left on Friday night."

Makes sense. "We may need you to identify some other people who were here on Friday."

"Fine."

"Have you seen Jason Strong since Friday?" Pete asked.

"No, but I saw the video. His wife, agent, lawyer, and the Giants probably have him on a short leash."

"No doubt. Tim Volpe?"

"Haven't seen him, either." In response to Pete's inquiries, he said that he hadn't seen Foreman or Benson. "F.X. Quinn stopped by for a few minutes last night."

"Does it bug you that he's trying to get your employees to join a union?"

A shrug. "He's within his legal rights. He's also a paying customer."

"Do you think he'll be successful?"

"I hope not. There will be unintended consequences."

In other words, people will lose their jobs.

Callaghan looked at his phone. "I need to deal with some stuff in the back of the house." He headed to the kitchen.

"Now what?" I asked Pete.

"We follow Dazzle's advice." He pointed at Sheema Smith, who was chatting with one of the bartenders. "If you want to know what's going on at a club, you talk to the dancers."

29
"FROM TIME TO TIME"

"Got a sec?" I asked.

Sheema Smith's eyes darted from the bartender to me to Pete and then back to me. "I need to get ready for work."

Pete stepped in front of me. "Just a few minutes, Sheema. We know that you're busy."

She gave us a practiced smile, slung her gym bag over her shoulder, and led us to the nearest table. "Five minutes."

Pete and I took seats across from her.

Her tone was even. "I don't know anything more than I told you last time."

Pete eyed her. "We talked to Jason Strong. Did you see the video?"

"Everybody's seen it. I hope his soon-to-be-ex-wife gets a lot of money from him."

Seems like a good bet.

"How often did he come in?" Pete asked.

"Once or twice a month. He wasn't a regular." She said that he usually came in alone.

"Did you ever talk to him?"

"It's my job to talk to customers. Decent tipper."

"Did he ever ask you for any personal attention?"

"I'm not his type."

"What is his type?"

"Young and pretty." She flashed a knowing smile. "Like Chloe."

"He hit on her?"

"Yes. He always paid extra for a lap dance. She said that he was a jerk."

"Not exactly the wonderful family man that he portrays in those Toyota commercials?"

"Uh, no."

"Did he ever get physical with her?"

"I don't know."

I was about to ask her about John Foreman when I heard a commotion behind us. I turned and saw Callaghan arguing with Kelly Ryan.

"You were supposed to be here an hour ago," he snapped.

"I'm here now," Ryan said. She started to walk away, but Callaghan grabbed her arm. Her voice filled with anger. "Don't touch me."

"Don't be late."

She stormed into the dressing room.

I looked over at Sheema. "That didn't look good."

"Dave's been on her case. She would make her life easier if she showed up on time."

I left it there. "Have you seen John Foreman?"

"Not since Friday."

"We've been told that he and Chloe argued on Friday night."

"I didn't see it."

"Did you ever see them argue?"

"Once or twice." A knowing smile. "He's a rich old guy who is used to getting what he wants."

"Was he getting it from Chloe?"

"For a while. She cut him off."

I asked her about Tyler Benson.

"He's a rich *young* guy who is used to getting what he wants."

"And if he didn't?"

"His second ex-wife asked for a restraining order."

Good to know. "F.X. Quinn said that he talked to you on Friday."

"Briefly. He's trying to get us to unionize."

"Union organizing can have some rough edges."

"You think he stabbed Chloe because she was reluctant to sign a union card?"

"I don't know. We talked to Jerry Henderson. He has Covid."

"I guess I'd better take a test before I go on tonight."

"A couple of people have told us that he has anger management issues."

"He does."

"And that he directed that anger toward Chloe on more than one occasion."

"It wouldn't surprise me."

"César's preliminary hearing starts on Wednesday. We may need you to testify that César and Chloe knew each other. We'll pay you for your time and reimburse you for an Uber."

"I'll do it if I have to." She picked up her bag. "Your five minutes are up." She headed to the dressing room.

I started to put on my jacket when Pete held up a hand.

"Wait a sec, Mick." He beckoned to Kelly Ryan, who had emerged from backstage. "Ms. Ryan? Can we talk to you for a minute?"

"I need to get ready for work. Besides, I've already told you everything that I know."

"Did you see the video with Chloe and Jason Strong?"

"Everybody's seen it."

"Did Chloe ever talk about him?"

"She said that he wouldn't leave her alone. Anything else?"

I spoke up. "César's preliminary hearing starts on Wednesday. We may need you to testify about her relationships with Jerry Henderson and Jason Strong. We'll compensate you for your time."

"And if I say no?"

"I'll have to send you a subpoena."

"Wonderful." She sighed. "Let me know when you need me. I'll be there."

"Thank you."

She headed back to the dressing room without another word.

Pete looked my way. "I'm going to try to talk to Benson again. Are you heading back to the office?"

"I'm going to see if I can talk to Foreman again."

30
"I HAVE NOTHING ELSE TO SAY"

John Foreman glared at me as he exited the lobby of Four Embarcadero Center. "Now you're accosting people at the office?"

Actually, I waited for you downstairs. "I left messages by email, text, and voicemail. You didn't return any of them."

"I'm busy."

I kept my voice even. "I wanted to let you know that we may need you to testify at César's prelim next week."

"You could have emailed me."

"I did. As a matter of professional courtesy, I also wanted to tell you in person."

"You're wasting your time." He added, with gratuitous snark, "I will testify if you serve me with a valid subpoena, and I determine that I am legally compelled to appear. I will also expect you to compensate me at my hourly rate of nineteen hundred and fifty dollars an hour."

Ouch. "You know that a subpoena is a court order that requires you to testify. We are under no obligation to compensate you for your time."

"What on earth do you need me to testify about?"

"That you saw Jerry Henderson, Tyler Benson, Jason Strong, and F.X. Quinn at For Gentlemen Only on Friday night."

"There were dozens of people at the club on Friday night. You can find somebody else to confirm that information."

Yes, I could. "It will be more convincing coming from somebody of your stature."

He rolled his eyes. "I don't know who killed Chloe Carson."

"I don't expect you to testify that you do."

"I will fulfill my legal obligations."

"Thank you." *Good to hear—especially since you're a lawyer.* "Did you see Jason Strong?"

"Only on the video that's gone viral." He invoked his best "big-firm-lawyer" voice. "If you make the slightest suggestion that I was involved in Ms. Carson's death, I will sue you and your office for defamation. I have hundreds of extraordinarily aggressive associates at my disposal who would love to impress me by notching a victory against the PD's Office. It will not enhance the reputation of your office or your ex-wife's re-election prospects if someone of my reputation in the legal community files a lawsuit. My grunts will bury you in paperwork and make your life miserable for the next five years."

I'm terrified. "Thank you for bringing that information to my attention, John."

Pete chuckled. "Foreman really threatened to sue you?"

I pressed my phone to my ear. "Yes."

My brother who almost never laughs let out a hearty guffaw. "You sound intimidated, Mick."

"I'm shaking."

I was standing in the plaza between Four Embarcadero Center and the Ferry Building. The fog had rolled in, and the wind was whipping through the hideous Vaillancourt Fountain, a monstrosity built of concrete cubes in the sixties to generate white noise to drown out the sound of the traffic on the old double-decked Embarcadero Freeway that once separated the plaza from the Ferry Building. The freeway was damaged during the 1989 Earthquake, and it was subsequently torn down. The fountain was still standing, but there have been discussions about removing it as well. One can hope.

Pete was still laughing. "Foreman understands that you're judgment-proof, right?"

"It's just bluster. He'll show up in court in a Brioni suit and answer all of my questions in a polished voice. The judge will probably believe everything he says."

"You going to accuse him of murder?"

"Possibly. It would make me very happy if you could find some hard evidence implicating him. Or Henderson. Or Benson. Or anybody other than César."

"Working on it. Speaking of which, how soon can you meet me outside the Bay Club?"

It was the upscale gym at the foot of Telegraph Hill. "Ten minutes. Why?"

"Tyler Benson is inside playing squash. We should be able to catch him as he's leaving."

31

"I'VE TOLD YOU EVERYTHING THAT I KNOW"

"What's the count so far?" I asked.

Pete looked up from his phone. "Two squash players, six basketball players, four aerobics, five Pilates, and eight people whose athletic preferences I can't identify."

I grinned. "How can you tell the basketball players from the people doing Pilates?"

"The basketball players walk with a limp. They always seem to wreck a hamstring or tear an Achilles. That's why I quit playing hoops when I turned fifty."

Pete was sitting in the driver's seat of his Crown Vic, which he had parked illegally on Greenwich between Sansome and Battery. I was on the passenger side. The upscale San Francisco Bay Club sits in the flatlands between Telegraph Hill and the Bay, about halfway between downtown and Fisherman's Wharf. A century ago, it was an industrial area where the businesses provided services to the port. Nowadays, it's a mix of refurbished older buildings and modern offices. The Bay Club is housed in a two-story building across the street from Levi's Plaza, a complex of red-brick buildings that's the headquarters of the denim manufacturer founded in San Francisco a hundred and seventy years ago.

Pete pulled down his Giants cap. "A lot of attractive women work out at the Bay Club."

"I'm going to tell Donna."

"She lets me look, Mick. I let her look, too. Neither of us gets to touch." He grinned. "You don't take a peek every once in a while?"

"Rosie would kill me."

"She's still got you after all these years."

Yes, she does.

He glanced at his phone. "Get ready to roll. Benson is leaving the club."

"How do you know?"

"I give a nice Christmas present to the young man who works at the front desk."

I should have known.

Benson emerged from the club, pulled up his windbreaker, and slung a squash racquet over his shoulder. Pete got out of the car and approached him. I tagged along.

Benson saw us coming and started walking in the opposite direction.

Pete spoke to him in a respectful voice. "Tyler, can we talk to you for a minute?"

The tech entrepreneur stopped. "I need to be somewhere."

"We'd be happy to give you a ride."

"That won't be necessary."

"Just a few minutes?"

"I've told you everything that I know."

Pete glanced my way.

"Tyler," I said, "we wanted to tell you that we're going to need you to testify at my client's preliminary hearing that will be starting on Wednesday next week."

"You could have called."

"I like talking to people in person."

"I'm going to be out of town."

"We would appreciate it if you'd stay."

"I can't change my plans."

"I'd rather not send you a subpoena, but I will do so if I have to."

"Let me talk to my lawyer. What on earth do you want me to talk about?"

"We need you to identify some people who were at For Gentlemen Only on Friday."

"That's it?"

Not necessarily. "That's it."

His tone softened. "I think I can work it into my schedule."

"Thank you." *Easier than I thought.*

Pete spoke up again. "Have you been back to the club since Friday?"

Benson shook his head. "No."

"We talked to John Foreman."

Benson's eyes perked up. "Do you think he had something to do with Chloe's death?"

"Maybe." Pete eyed him. "We've been told by a couple of witnesses that Foreman had words with Chloe."

"I don't know anything about it."

"Have you ever seen them together outside the club?"

He paused to consider his answer. "I saw them having dinner at Fior d'Italia once."

"Have you seen the Jason Strong video?"

A smirk. "Everybody on Planet Earth has seen it."

"Did you ever see Strong with Chloe Carson?"

"Afraid not."

"We've been told by several sources that Jerry Henderson and Chloe went out for a while and had a bad breakup. One person said that Henderson may have been abusive to her."

"I don't know anything about it."

"Was he selling drugs to her?"

Benson shrugged. "No idea. I really need to go."

We watched as Benson walked west toward the Filbert Steps leading up to Coit Tower.

When he was out of hearing distance, Pete spoke up again. "You think there's any chance he's involved in Chloe's death?"

"I don't know. At the very least, maybe we can get him to point a finger at Foreman or Quinn or even Strong in court."

"They'll point their fingers back at him."

"That could work to our advantage, too. "

He glanced at his watch. "We need to get over to the Italian Athletic Club for dinner."

The Italian Athletic Club was a century-old private club on Washington Square. It wasn't as upscale or exclusive as the

Olympic Club, the University Club, the Bohemian Club, or the Pacific Union Club, but anybody who was anybody in North Beach was a member.

"We don't have time," I said.

"We'll make time. It's Stag Dinner night."

Once a month, the members of the IAC gather for a raucous feast of antipasto, salads, prime rib, chicken marsala, and tripe accompanied by copious amounts of red wine. The food is more hearty than gourmet, the company is excellent, and the bawdy jokes last into the wee hours.

"It always sells out," I said. "We don't have tickets."

"Nick Hanson left us a couple of passes. Everybody who is anybody in North Beach shows up." He arched an eyebrow. "I'll bet you a hundred bucks that F.X. Quinn will be there."

32
"I HOPE I CAN COUNT ON YOUR VOTE"

Pete and I pushed through the crowded bar of the historic San Francisco Italian Athletic Club, which was housed in an off-white building with red trim across the street from Washington Square. The Stars and Stripes and the Italian flag had flown on parallel poles on the roof since 1917. In addition to the clubby wood-paneled bar, the ground floor had a banquet room with carved ceilings and ornamental chandeliers. The gym upstairs had a miniature basketball court. If you wanted to do Pilates or CrossFit, you needed to go to the Bay Club.

I inhaled the aroma of prime rib, spaghetti, and perspiration as I inched past older club members who were tossing back Manhattans, gesturing with unlit cigars, and playing liar's dice. The younger generation sipped Chardonnay and stared at their phones. North Beach had changed a lot since 1917, but the IAC hadn't.

Pete pointed at the diminutive man sipping Chianti and holding court at the bar. Nick "The Dick" was regaling an audience of admirers with one of his semi-truthful stories about his high school teammate, Joe DiMaggio.

As we approached him, Nick greeted us with an enthusiastic, "How the hell are you?"

"Couldn't be better, Nick," I said. "Thanks for the tickets."

"My pleasure. Have you figured out who killed Chloe Carson?"

"Working on it. Have you seen F.X. Quinn?"

He pointed at the banquet hall. "Inside."

Pete and I made our way into the ballroom and scanned the dozen long tables filled with well-dressed male revelers who were consuming red meat and red wine. The roar was deafening as glasses clinked and people exchanged gossip, coarse stories, and off-color jokes. The Mayor was busy glad-handing at the table near the door. Judges, restaurateurs, tech entrepreneurs, and fishermen mingled. The head of the Teamsters Union chatted amiably with the owner of San Francisco's biggest trash collection company. The Chairman of the Port Commission offered a toast to the Executive Director of the Telegraph Hill Neighborhood Center, a century-old nonprofit. The head of the San Francisco AIDS Foundation chatted with the chairman of San Francisco's Republican Party. Just another night in North Beach.

Pete and I made our way to the table where F.X. Quinn was talking to the general manager of Ghirardelli Square. Pete and I sat down in two open chairs nearby. We nibbled at lukewarm pasta while Quinn schmoozed. Sensing that there was nothing more to be gained from the people in his immediate vicinity, he turned to us.

"Good to see you again," he lied.

"Same here," I said. "Are you a member?"

"Of course."

"You aren't Italian."

"Doesn't matter. You pay the initiation fee, buy a couple of rounds for the Board, and they let you in."

"Do you run the Statuto?"

"Not anymore."

The IAC's annual 8K race was first run through North Beach in 1919. It commemorates the Italian Constitution (the Statuto Albertino), and it raises funds for charity. It's more of a bacchanalia than an athletic event. The postrace brunch features all-you-can-drink mimosas.

"Did you come to the Triple-I on St. Patrick's Day?" I asked.

"I haven't missed one in years."

The San Francisco Irish-Israeli-Italian Society, affectionately known as the "Triple-I," was hatched in the fifties by George Reilly, a member of the Board of Supervisors who twice ran for mayor (and lost), and Nate Cohn, a theatrical trial lawyer whose clients included Frank Sinatra, Melvin Belli, Duke Ellington, and the Birdman of Alcatraz. The "Society" has no dues, no website, and almost no organization. Its members don't need to be Irish, Jewish, or Italian. Its sole purpose is organizing boisterous luncheons at the IAC on St. Patrick's Day, Israeli Independence Day, and Columbus Day, where politicians, cops, lawyers, labor leaders, business execs, and other hangers-on rub elbows for old-fashioned civic bonhomie. I used to accompany my dad and Big John to the festivities every year.

"When are you planning to file your paperwork to run for supervisor?" I asked.

"In the next couple of weeks. I hope I can count on your vote."

"I'm registered in Marin, so I can't vote for you." *That's true.* "I would be happy to spread the word." *A small white lie, but well short of a whopper.*

"Much appreciated."

I leaned over and shouted into his ear. "César's preliminary hearing starts Wednesday."

He feigned interest. "You figured out what happened yet?"

"Working on it. Did you see the Jason Strong video?"

"Everybody in this room has seen it. Do you think he was involved in Chloe Carson's death?"

"I don't know." *It would help César's defense if he was.*

Quinn's eyes darted over my shoulder in search of more people to glad-hand, so I turned to business. "We need you to testify that you saw John Foreman, Tyler Benson, Jason Strong, and Jerry Henderson at the club on Friday night."

His lips turned down. "I will if I have to."

"Henderson and Chloe Carson went out for a while and had a nasty breakup. Did you ever see them together?"

"Only when she was dancing, and he was working the soundboard."

"They got into an argument on Friday night."

"I didn't see anything."

"He has a history of domestic abuse."

"I don't know anything about it."

"We have reason to believe that he was selling drugs."

"I don't know anything about that, either."

"Is there anybody else that we should talk to?"

"Not that I can think of." He waved at the owner of Mario's Bohemian Cigar Store on the opposite side of Washington Square. "I need to talk to some people."

Always working the room. "We'll be in touch," I said.

He was already on his way across the room.

I looked at Pete. "You want to stick around for dinner?"

"No time, Mick. I need to get back to work."

I was sitting in my office at ten o'clock that same night when my phone vibrated. The name of one of the big downtown law firms appeared on the display. I was tempted to let it roll over into voicemail, but I decided to answer.

"Michael Daley speaking."

"Mr. Daley, my name is Stephen Bean." He spoke with the affected tone of a Boston Brahmin. He informed me that he was a partner at the law firm whose name appeared on the display. "I represent Jason Strong."

I'm not surprised that Strong has lawyered up. "Good to hear from you, Mr. Bean."

"Steve."

"Mike. How can I help you?"

"I am reaching out because I understand that you spoke with my client."

"I did." *Let him talk.*

"I would ask you not to contact him again unless I am present."

"Of course."

"Mr. Strong also forwarded a subpoena that he received from your office asking him to appear at a preliminary hearing for your client, César Ochoa."

"That's correct."

"The Giants are out of town, so my client will not be available next week."

"Your client told us that he would be rehabbing his shoulder here at home for at least another week. If he cannot appear in person, I can ask the judge if he can do so remotely."

"I'm afraid that's not possible, either."

"Mr. Bean—,"

"Steve."

"Steve," I said, "your client was very professional and cooperative when I spoke to him. I would hope that he would continue to comport himself in a similar manner as we go forward."

"He will."

"Good to hear. I expect him to honor his legal obligations under the subpoena and appear in court next week."

"My client had nothing to do with Chloe Carson's death."

"Then he has nothing to hide, and nothing to lose by cooperating. I have the legal right to call him as a witness. Everybody knows that he was at For Gentlemen Only on Friday night, and we believe that he has information concerning Ms. Carson's relationship with a man named Jerry Henderson, who argued with Ms. Carson that night."

"He has no such information."

"Perhaps I am mistaken. Either way, I need him to testify."

"It's a waste of his time—and yours."

"If that's the case, I offer my apologies in advance. If he doesn't show up pursuant to a valid subpoena, I will leave ask the judge to impose appropriate remedies."

He spoke with lawyerly precision. "I will look at the subpoena. If it's legally binding, my client will fulfill his legal obligations."

Good to hear. "Thank you, Steve."

33

"YOU'RE SITTING IN EDUARDO'S SEAT"

Sylvia Fernandez took a bite of scrambled eggs and washed it down with a sip of coffee from a white mug. "I saw the video of Jason Strong at For Gentlemen Only on the night that Chloe Carson was killed. I read in the *Chronicle* that he said that he wasn't involved in her death. Will you call him as a witness in César Ochoa's case?"

"Maybe." I placed my half-eaten cheeseburger on the plate in front of me. "Other than the fact that he was there, we don't have any evidence connecting him to Ms. Carson's death."

"He seems like a nice young man with a beautiful family."

"Sometimes nice young men like to go to strip clubs."

Rosie's mother was born eighty-seven years earlier in Monterrey, Mexico. Sylvia was an older, stockier, and equally intense version of Rosie. At twenty-four, she and her late husband, Eduardo, a carpenter, made their way to San Francisco's Mission District along with Rosie's older brother, Tony, who was a baby. Sylvia and Eduardo worked grueling hours and saved for a down payment on the little house that cost twenty-four thousand dollars. Today, Sylvia could sell it to a tech entrepreneur for almost two million, but she has no intention of ever doing so.

Sylvia was still razor-sharp and remarkably spry for someone with two artificial knees and an artificial hip. She lived around the corner from the apartments on Garfield Square where my parents had grown up, and not far from where my mom, dad, two brothers, baby sister, and I lived until we moved to a house in the Sunset.

Sylvia finished her eggs. "Rosita told me that Ms. Carson had a nasty breakup with the sound guy at the club. Is he a suspect?"

"Yes."

"Do you have any hard evidence against him?"

"No."

"Does that mean that you aren't going to be able to get the charges dropped at the preliminary hearing?"

I pointed at Rolanda, who was sitting across the table from me. "Your granddaughter is a very resourceful attorney."

Sylvia's eyes filled with pride. "Yes, she is."

Rolanda responded with Fernandez family realism. "We'll see how it goes, Grandma."

Sylvia, Rolanda, Rosie, and I were sitting in a booth in the back of the St. Francis Fountain which has been serving breakfast, burgers, and milkshakes at the corner of Twenty-fourth and York since 1918. The classic ice cream parlor looked much the same as it did when my mom and dad used to take us there after church when I was a kid. It was two blocks from St. Peter's Catholic Church where we had just attended Sunday Mass. My parents were baptized and married at St. Peter's. So were Rosie and I. So was our daughter, Grace. The humble wooden church was built in 1885 and survived two fires and changing demographics as the neighborhood transitioned from working-class Irish, German, and Italian families to Latino families to the more recent influx of tech entrepreneurs. It carries on the traditions of the legendary Father Peter Yorke, who served from the late 1800s until his death in 1925. Father Yorke was an old-school priest who ran his own newspaper, defended union workers, helped settle strikes, sent money to the rebels in Ireland, and served as a regent of the University of California. St. Peter's still embodied the hard-working community that it served with distinction for more than a century.

Sylvia adjusted the collar of one of her several navy "going-to-church" dresses, then she spoke to Rolanda. "Is your father going to watch the kids this afternoon?"

"Yes, Grandma. Zach and I need to go to the office for a few hours."

Rolanda's father, Tony, ran a produce market down the street. He and Rolanda's husband, Zach, had taken Maria and Antonio to a nearby playground after they became fidgety at lunch. Maria was named after Rolanda's late mother. Antonio was named after Tony. Rolanda's dad reveled in his role as "Papa Tony."

"You and Zach work too hard," Sylvia said.

Rolanda looked at Rosie. "I have a very demanding boss."

Rosie grinned. "You can take the afternoon off."

Rolanda returned her smile. "Papa Tony likes having the kids to himself for a few hours." She arched an eyebrow. "And Zach and I appreciate a few hours of peace and quiet."

Sylvia touched Rolanda's hand. "I want you and Zach to take advantage of every minute with the babies. Time goes by very quickly. Soon you'll be an old woman like I am."

"You'll always be young to me, Grandma."

"My heart agrees with you, honey. My knees aren't so sure."

In response to Sylvia's questions, Rolanda reported that Maria was enjoying her preschool, and Antonio occasionally slept through the night. She and Zach were planning to take the kids to Disneyland over the summer.

"God help you," Sylvia deadpanned.

Rolanda smiled. "You want to join us, Grandma?"

"I'd love to, honey, but I'm a little old for Star Wars rides."

"Are you playing tonight?"

"Of course, dear. It's Sunday."

Sylvia and a rotating cast of her friends had been playing mah-jongg on Sunday nights since Rosie was a kid. When Covid hit, they started playing online. They recently resumed in-person games. Sylvia was the second-youngest of the group. Jan Harris was the baby at eighty-six. Mercedes Crosskill was in her late eighties. Marge Gilbert and Flo Hoffenberg were in their early nineties. Char Saper and Yolanda Cesena were ninety-five. A few years ago, at the suggestion of Ann-Helen Leff, a nonagenarian hippie, great-grandmother, and lifelong rabble-rouser, they switched the refreshments from sherry to marijuana. Sylvia received a regular delivery of edibles from a young woman who ran a designer dispensary on Valencia Street and took orders after Mass at St. Peter's.

Rolanda reached into her backpack, pulled out a magenta box about the size of a deck of cards, and handed it to Sylvia. "This is for your game tonight, Grandma."

Sylvia's eyes lit up. "Weed?"

"Edibles. Zach and I tried them last night to take the edge off. They're very smooth."

"I'll give them a try, honey."

Rosie and I exchanged a glance. Even though the gift was perfectly legal, we had never anticipated that the young woman for whom we had babysat and who was the front-runner to succeed Rosie as PD would be giving her grandmother—Rosie's mother—a tin filled with cannabis. Times change.

Rolanda and Sylvia chatted for a few more minutes. Then Rolanda excused herself to catch up with her husband, her father, and her kids.

Sylvia looked across the table at Rosie and smiled. "She's a good kid."

"She's almost forty, Mama."

"She'll always be a baby to me. How are your babies?"

"Everybody's fine. Grace is finishing post-production on a short film. Tommy is in the middle of finals. They promised to come over and see you next Sunday." She winked. "They were hoping that you might bring them here for burgers and shakes."

"It can be arranged." Sylvia looked my way. "You're sitting in Eduardo's seat."

"I know."

When the Fernandez clan dined at the St. Francis, they always sat in this booth, and Rosie's father always sat in the seat that I was now occupying so that he could see the faces on the kids as they walked by the candy counter. I never met

Eduardo. I think he would have enjoyed meeting my mom and dad."

Sylvia got a faraway look in her eyes. "It's been a long time." She pointed at my chocolate shake, which was served the traditional way—in a tall glass with the extra in a metal container next to it. "Do you think the shakes are as good as they used to be?"

"Absolutely."

They were made from scratch with ice cream from Mitchell's, about a mile south of here at Twenty-ninth and San Jose. In the Daley family, there was a difference of opinion as to the best shakes in San Francisco. My older brother, Tommy, and I were partial to the St. Francis. Pete and our baby sister, Mary, preferred Bill's Place at Twenty-third and Clement. My mom and dad liked the long-gone Zim's at Nineteenth and Taraval.

Sylvia looked over at Rosie. "How's the campaign?"

"We're going to win, Mama."

"I know, dear. Jerry Edwards in the *Chronicle* said that your not-so-worthy opponent might drop out of the race."

"If she's smart."

"Is she?"

Rosie grinned. "We'll see."

Sylvia looked my way. "The *Chronicle* also said that César Ochoa is guilty. Any chance you can get the charges dropped at the prelim?"

"I'm not sure." *If Sylvia had been born twenty years later, she would have been the managing partner of one of the big law firms downtown.* "Pete is looking for evidence."

My ex-mother-in-law eyed me. "You don't have anything, do you?"

I never tried to BS Sylvia. "It's always tough to get the charges dropped at a prelim."

"What do you think?" she asked Rosie.

I learned long ago that Sylvia valued Rosie's opinions more than mine.

Rosie glanced my way. "It's always tough to get the charges dropped at a prelim, Mama."

I appreciate the show of support.

Rosie added, "If anybody can do it, Rolanda and Mike can."

Sylvia smiled. "You want to come over to the house for a little while, Rosita?"

"Of course, Mama."

She turned to me. "Care to join us, Michael?"

"I'm going to see César," I said. "Then I need to spend some time in the office."

"Don't work my beautiful granddaughter too hard."

34

"IT ISN'T ENOUGH"

Rolanda looked up from her laptop. "How is César?"

"Not great," I said. "I spent an hour with him this afternoon. He still hasn't been eating."

Pete, Rolanda, and I were meeting in Rolanda's office at eight-forty on Sunday night. The PD's Office was quiet, although a few of our colleagues had come in to prepare for trials starting the following morning. The air conditioner wasn't working, so the warm air was heavy. My polo shirt was sticking to my back.

I looked at Pete, who was leaning against the wall. "You know him better than I do. How do you think he'll handle the prelim?"

"First, he'll act tough. Second, he'll get frustrated. Third, he'll just want it to be over."

"He may already be at Act Three."

"Anything more on Henderson?"

"My guy is still watching him. He hasn't left his apartment since we saw him on Friday. A few people have stopped by for short periods. Henderson hasn't let anybody inside. My guess is that he's selling coke and maybe fentanyl out of his apartment, but I don't know for sure. I told Tim Volpe about it. He said that his people would monitor the situation."

I asked if there was any connection between Henderson's customers and Carson's death.

"Not as far as I can tell. I talked to Callaghan again. He claimed that he didn't know that Henderson was dealing. I think he knows more than he let on. I tracked down the guys in Henderson's band, too. Let's just say that they weren't shocked to hear that Henderson may be dealing. Bottom line: I haven't found a direct line between Henderson's potential drug dealing and Chloe Carson's death."

Which takes us back to square one. I turned to Rolanda. "Anything more from the DA?"

"Nothing."

So much for Catherine O'Neal's heartfelt promise to provide any exculpatory evidence as soon as possible. "I presume this means that she didn't send over a preliminary witness list?"

"Afraid not. She's under no legal obligation to do so. Do you still want to put on a full defense?"

"For now. We'll re-evaluate at the end of the prosecution's case. If it looks like we have no chance of prevailing at the prelim, we may decide to keep our powder dry until trial." I pulled up a draft of our witness list. "Our blood spatter expert will suggest that they should have found Carson's blood somewhere on César's hands, clothes, or car. Our fingerprint guy will challenge the prints on the knife. Our DNA person will challenge their DNA analysis."

Pete chuckled. "You're stretching, Mick."

"You go to court with what you have, Pete."

"You going to try to deflect blame to somebody else?"

"Possibly. Jerry Henderson is the most obvious alternate suspect."

"He has Covid. He may not be able to testify."

"Then he won't be able to defend himself. We can also call Callaghan, Foreman, Quinn, Benson, and Strong."

"You don't have any hard evidence connecting them to Chloe Carson's death."

"You'll find something."

"You're more confident than I am."

"You're too modest."

His tone turned serious. "You aren't going to get the charges dropped by trying to foist blame onto other people who were at For Gentlemen Only unless we find some hard evidence."

"It can't hurt to give the judge some options. At the very least, it will give the media and the potential jurors some alternate possibilities to think about if we go to trial."

He grinned. "You're already trying to work the refs?"

"It's our job to play every angle to get one juror to reasonable doubt."

"It isn't enough." His eyes darted over to Rolanda. "You're okay with this strategy?"

"It's the best that we can do, and I learned from the best."

Pete looked my way and feigned exasperation. "You and Rosie are a bad influence."

"I like to think that we're a good influence." I turned back to Rolanda. "I think you should take the lead in court. I think our defense will be more effective coming from you."

"Happy to do it."

"For now, you should go home, play with your kids, and get some rest. Grandma Sylvia thinks you're working too hard."

"I still have a few things to finish."

"Never disobey your grandmother." I looked over at Pete. "You going home?"

"I'm going back to North Beach."

"What are you looking for?"

"I'm not sure."

35

"TRY HARDER"

At ten-fifteen on Tuesday morning, Judge McDaniel sat behind her desk in her chambers, pushed her glasses to the top of her head, and rested her chin in her palm. "César Ochoa."

O'Neal, Rolanda, and I nodded.

The judge squinted at her computer. "You're ready to start the prelim tomorrow?"

We nodded again.

The judge's eyes shifted my way. "Are you sure that you want to move forward so quickly, Mr. Daley?"

No. "Yes, Your Honor. My client wishes to exercise his right to a speedy prelim."

"Fine." Her eyes moved to O'Neal. "You're good to go?"

"Yes, Your Honor."

"Any last-minute issues?"

"None," I said.

O'Neal nodded. "Nothing from us, Your Honor."

"You've provided all relevant information as required by law to Mr. Daley?"

"Of course, Your Honor."

"We were hoping for more," I said. "Ms. O'Neal sent over a couple of police reports, a copy of the preliminary autopsy report, a fingerprint report, and a DNA report."

O'Neal feigned irritation. "That's all that you're entitled to, Mike."

"You can do better, Catherine." *Well, maybe not.*

"We will provide you with everything that you're entitled to before trial."

"If you can provide enough evidence to convince Judge McDaniel to move forward from the prelim."

"We will."

Probably true.

Betsy McDaniel's eyes moved back and forth as O'Neal and I took turns sniping at each other. Finally, she spoke in a voice sounding as if she was lecturing a couple of teenagers. "Mr. Daley, if you have issues with the evidence that Ms. O'Neal has provided, you can file a motion seeking additional information. However, I will not be predisposed to rule in your favor."

Got it. "Understood, Your Honor."

She turned to O'Neal. "Any chance that you and Mr. Daley might be able to get together to try to resolve this matter before we expend the court's time and resources on this case?"

"Mr. Daley isn't listening to reason."

"I have always found Mr. Daley to be very reasonable."

Nice to hear.

"Perhaps you and Mr. Daley can sit down and see if you could work something out."

O'Neal's voice was flat. "Yes, Your Honor."

The judge looked my way. "You'll confer with Ms. O'Neal?"

"She isn't listening to reason, Your Honor." I realized that I sounded whiny as I said it.

"You'll try?"

"We've tried."

"Try harder."

"Yes, Your Honor."

When I returned to the office an hour later, Dazzle was hunched over her laptop, and Terrence "The Terminator" was in his usual spot in the cubicle next to hers.

I stopped in front of Dazzle. "I thought it was Terrence's day."

"It is." She looked up from her computer. "Rolanda asked for help organizing your exhibits while she talked to a couple of your witnesses."

"Thanks for coming in, Dazz."

"No problem, Mike. I'll be here all day."

I turned to Terrence. "Anything I need to know?"

"Rolanda needs to see you right away."

"Thanks, T." I headed into Rolanda's office. "Terrence said that you wanted to talk?"

"I just got an email from O'Neal. She wants to see us at four o'clock this afternoon."

36

"NO WAY"

Catherine O'Neal sat behind her desk, eyes focused on mine. "Thank you for coming in."

"You're welcome," I said.

Rolanda nodded.

The DA's Office was buzzing at four o'clock on Tuesday afternoon. We were eighteen hours from the start of the prelim. O'Neal's door was closed. The air conditioner hummed.

She tried to freeze me with an icy glare. "You ready to go tomorrow?"

"Yes."

"I won't object if you want to ask for a continuance."

"No."

"You sure?"

"Yes." *Why are we here?*

Rolanda spoke up. "You wanted to talk to us?"

"Yes." O'Neal's stern expression didn't change. "Judge McDaniel asked us to talk again about a potential resolution." She looked my way. "She assured me that you would be reasonable."

Always. "Of course." *Let her talk.*

"I had a long talk with Vanessa after I got back from court. I was able to persuade her to authorize me to offer your client a deal for second-degree murder."

Rolanda and I didn't react. *Let's hear the rest of it.*

O'Neal added, "No enhancements. Credit for time served."

That's a week and a half. "Recommended sentence?" I asked.

"High end of the scale."

The scale is fifteen to life. "How high?"

"Fourteen." She waited a beat. "It's a good deal."

No, it isn't. "No deal."

She responded with a melodramatic sigh. "It took all of my persuasive powers to get Vanessa to agree to go down to second-degree."

No, it didn't. "No deal."

"I can't do any better."

"Yes, you can."

"No, I can't."

You're making a token offer so that you can tell Judge McDaniel that you offered something.

She tried again. "We can resolve this right now, Mike. Your client was there. He got into an argument with Chloe Carson."

"A lot of people were there. Several of them had history and harsh words with Ms. Carson."

"Your client's fingerprints were on the knife."

"He used it earlier that night."

"Come on, Mike."

"You come on, Catherine."

She decided to try Rolanda. "I'm offering you a gift. Ninety-nine times out of a hundred, we wouldn't be talking about a deal until we got closer to trial."

Rolanda glared at her. "That's because your evidence is so flimsy."

"His fingerprints were on the knife," she repeated.

"There wasn't any blood on his hands, clothes, car, or apartment."

"He washed his hands, got rid of his clothes, and cleaned his car and apartment."

"You would have found traces of blood somewhere if he had stabbed Chloe Carson."

Sensing that she wasn't making any headway with Rolanda, O'Neal decided to plead her case to me once more. "He's an ex-cop, Mike. He knew how to get rid of evidence. At the very least, you won't be able to get the charges dropped at the prelim."

Probably true. "No deal."

"You're going to regret this decision."

Maybe. "I don't think so."

"What would you suggest?"

She seemed more willing to horse-trade than I had anticipated. "I might be able to sell him on voluntary manslaughter with a reasonable sentence."

"How reasonable?"

The minimum sentence for vol man is three years, the maximum eleven. "Three."

"No."

"Four."

"No."

"Five."

"No way. I'll never be able to sell it to Vanessa."

"Then I think we're done."

"You have a legal obligation to take my offer to your client."

"We will, but we won't recommend it."

"Then we'll see you in court tomorrow."

César's response was succinct. "No deal."

"I don't think they'll offer us something better," I said.

"No way."

Rolanda gave him one more chance. "You sure?"

"I didn't kill Chloe Carson. I'm not going to cut a deal saying that I did."

The anger in César's voice was genuine, his resolve absolute. Rosie always says that the hardest cases are the ones where you think your client may be innocent.

I looked across the dented metal table in the consultation room in the Glamour Slammer. "The prelim starts at ten AM. Rolanda and I will bring you a suit and a tie. We need you to be alert and ready."

"I will."

"Judge McDaniel is a stickler for decorum. Since there is no jury at a prelim, we will be playing to an audience of one: the judge. I need you to be respectful. Under no circumstances should you show any emotion or say anything unless I tell you to do so."

"Got it. What's the plan?"

"We will challenge everything the prosecution says. We will do a hard cross-exam of all of O'Neal's witnesses."

"Are you going to put on any witnesses?"

"Yes. We will call a blood spatter expert to testify that they should have found blood on your hands, clothes, car, and apartment. We will call a fingerprint expert to testify that there are questions about the prints that they found on the knife. We'll call a DNA expert to question their finding that Chloe's DNA was on the knife. We'll hammer Inspector Wong. And we'll put Jerry Henderson on the stand and accuse him of murder."

"Will it be enough to get the charges dropped?"

Doubtful. "It's going to be a heavy lift, César."

A look of resignation crossed his face. "Do I get to testify?"

"Not at the prelim."

His tone became more emphatic. "I want to testify."

"No, you don't."

Conventional wisdom says that you don't put your client on the stand unless you're desperate.

"It's too risky," I said, "especially at a prelim."

"What about at trial?"

"We'll make that decision if we have to. In the meantime, I want you to keep eating and try to get a good night's sleep."

Rolanda leaned forward. "Is there anything that we can do to make this a little easier for you?"

He considered his answer for a moment. "Please call Selena and tell her that I love her."

37

"I'LL BE THERE"

Rolanda was sitting in the chair opposite my desk at ten o'clock that same night. "Pete talked to Jerry Henderson," she said. "He tested negative for Covid, but he's feeling like crap. I'm not sure that he'll be able to testify tomorrow."

"Then we'll need to stretch things out to see if he's feeling better on Thursday. Do you want to go through your narrative once more?"

"I think I've got it nailed."

"Good." I added Rosie's customary advice. "Keep it short."

She grinned. "I will."

We had spent the evening working on our exhibits and questions for the witnesses that we presumed O'Neal would call. O'Neal's presentation would probably be short, so we needed to be ready to start our defense tomorrow.

"Who do you think will be on their final witness list?" I asked.

She glanced at her laptop. "The guy who found the body. The first officer at the scene. An evidence tech or two. The Medical Examiner. A fingerprint expert will verify that César's prints were on the knife. A DNA expert will confirm that Chloe's blood was on the knife. Then Inspector Wong will wrap up their case."

"And our list?"

"Our blood spatter expert will testify that the police should have found blood on César's hands, clothes, and car. Our fingerprint expert will say that there were smudged prints. Our DNA expert will say that there was blood on the knife that didn't match Chloe or César."

Rolanda continued to read from her witness list. "Dave Callaghan will confirm that Jerry Henderson had words with Chloe on the night that she died. Sheema Smith will do the same. Then we'll call Foreman, Quinn, and Benson and try to shake them. We've also included Jason Strong on our witness list, but I don't know that we'll want to call him." She looked up. "Do you really think the Giants' leftfielder killed Chloe Carson?"

I grinned. "You'll just have to ask him about it."

She remained skeptical. "You want me to get up there and accuse everybody of killing Chloe Carson?"

"Yes."

"Do you have a favorite?"

"Henderson. He had the closest relationship to Carson, and we have evidence that he was abusive."

"What if he can't make it to court because of Covid?"

"We'll ask for a delay if we need to. We'll hope he's available on Thursday. In the meantime, we'll try to get one of the other witnesses to make the case that Henderson killed Chloe. I figure that there are several other people who would be happy to point a finger at him if they think it will exonerate themselves."

"What's our narrative?" she asked.

I expected the question. When I was a new Deputy Public Defender, the first thing that Rosie taught me was that trial work is theater, and lawyers are storytellers. The best trial lawyers identify a compelling and easy-to-understand narrative that the judge or jury can follow. Everything you do in court is in support of that narrative. It was the first piece of advice that Rosie and I passed along to Rolanda when she joined the PD's Office.

"Rush to judgment," I said. "The DA and Inspector Wong are ignoring other potential suspects who had motive, means, and opportunity. Henderson is our best alternative."

"It won't be enough to get the charges dropped at the prelim unless Pete comes up with some hard evidence that Henderson or somebody else did it."

"Probably true, but I still think we should challenge their case and put on a full defense."

"Have you heard anything more from Pete?" she asked.

"Not yet. Never underestimate my brother."

Terrence "The Terminator" knocked on the open door. "Selena Ochoa is here to see you."

"Ask her to come in."

Terrence motioned at Selena, who was standing in the hallway. She walked into my office, expression grim, eyes determined.

"Sorry for coming in so late," she said.

"No worries."

She pointed at a garment bag that she had draped on Terrence's cubicle outside the door. "I brought a suit, tie, and dress shirt for César. I also brought along socks and a pair of shoes."

"Thank you. That's very helpful."

Her lips formed a tight line across her face. "How is César holding up?"

"As well as can be expected in the circumstances."

"Is he eating?"

"Some."

"Sleeping?"

"Not much."

She pushed out a heavy sigh. "Is there any chance that you'll be able to get the charges dropped at the prelim?"

Rolanda answered her. "The odds aren't great, but we're planning to put on a full defense."

"Understood. Thank you."

We sat in silence for a long moment. Finally, I spoke up again. "Is there anything else you'd like to talk about, Selena?"

Her eyes narrowed. "You said that it would be helpful if I showed up in court tomorrow to provide support for César. I wanted to let you know that I'll be there."

"Thank you, Selena. That's great. And your son?"

"He won't."

38

"IT ISN'T LOOKING GOOD"

Rosie handed me a glass of Cab Franc as I sat down on the sofa in her living room at eleven-fifteen that same night. "It sounded like you needed a glass of wine," she said.

"Thanks. I'm fine. Kids okay?"

"Fine. So is my mother."

"Good."

Her post-Earthquake bungalow seemed bigger now that Grace was married, and Tommy was in college. The evening fog had rolled in, and a cool breeze was coming in through the open window. I still expected to see the lights on in Grace and Tommy's bedrooms.

"You didn't sound like your usual jovial self on the phone," she said.

"Just busy." *My head feels like somebody hit me with a two-by-four.* "How did the fundraiser go?"

"Not bad. We raised twenty thousand."

"Your opponent isn't going to catch up."

"Probably not. We are engaging in psychological warfare to get her to believe that it's hopeless, and that she should drop out of the race."

"If I were in her shoes, I would."

"You're smarter than she is."

I'd like to think so. "Is it possible that you're taking her candidacy a little too seriously?"

"I don't like to lose, Mike."

Neither do I.

Her expression turned serious. "Are you good to go in the morning?"

"Yes. Rolanda and I decided that she should take the lead."

A nod. "She's very good. She'll play well to Betsy."

"That's the idea."

"Do you have enough to get the charges dropped?"

"It isn't looking good. Our statistics may take a hit."

"We'll persevere."

She listened attentively as I summarized our strategy. "We'll challenge the prosecution's witnesses. We'll put on our own blood spatter, fingerprint, and DNA experts. If that doesn't seem to be working, we'll call some of the people who were at For Gentlemen Only on the night that Chloe Carson was killed. We'll try to foist the blame onto somebody else. Jerry Henderson is probably our best candidate, but he's recovering from Covid, so he may not be able to testify."

"It would be better if Rolanda could go after him on the stand."

"Agreed. On the other hand, he won't be able to defend himself."

"Seems like a stretch, Mike."

It is.

She eyed me. "Any real evidence?"

"It's thin."

"And your narrative?"

"Rush to judgment. Shaky evidence. Somebody else did it."

"You sure that you want to show the prosecution so much of your case?"

She was making an excellent point. It's often better to let the prosecution show its evidence and strategy and not show all of our cards until trial.

"We'll see how it goes," I said.

"Maybe Pete will come up with something. How is César holding up?"

"Not great. He runs hot and cold. At times, I think he's ready to fight. Other times, I think he just wants it to be over. Selena said that she would come to the prelim to provide a little support."

"That's good."

"Their son won't."

"That's not so good. How's Rolanda?"

"Fine."

"Mama thinks she's working too hard."

"She's very protective." I winked. "She thinks you're working too hard, too."

"Mama isn't crazy about the fact that I decided to run for another term. I explained to her that I was trying to clear a path for Rolanda."

"She worries about you, too."

"That she does." She reached over and clasped my hand. "Are you feeling okay?"

"Fine."

"Your heart working properly?"

"Perfect."

"This prelim is going to be stressful."

"We've been through worse."

"I'm going to need you to run the office as the campaign heats up."

"Piece of cake. Your opponent is going to drop out of the race. And Terrence and Dazzle run the office anyway."

She finished her wine and flashed the million-watt smile that still got my heart pounding. "We should go to bed. You need your rest."

"I need to look at a couple of things on my computer."

"It can wait until morning." She squeezed my hand. "I'll make it worth your while."

I returned her smile. "It can wait until morning."

39
"A PRELIM IS DIFFERENT FROM A TRIAL"

At nine-thirty on a balmy Wednesday morning, Rolanda and I kept our heads down as we lugged our laptops, trial bags, and exhibits past a handful of reporters who were waiting for us on the front steps of the Hall.

"Mr. Daley? Is your client going to cut a deal?"

"Ms. Fernandez? Is there anything that you would like to say to Chloe Carson's mother?"

"Mr. Daley? Is it true that your client's fingerprints were found on the knife?"

Rolanda and I stopped and turned around. I looked into the nearest camera and recited the platitudes that every defense attorney says on the steps of every courthouse before the start of every legal proceeding. "Ms. Fernandez and I are pleased to have the opportunity to defend our client in court. We are confident that he will be exonerated."

The reporters drifted over to Vanessa Turner, who had emerged from a black SUV. Our media-savvy DA gave them a moment to position their cameras before she offered the usual DA catechisms in an appropriately somber tone. "Chloe Carson's death is a great tragedy. The evidence is overwhelming. Our office prosecutes criminals to the fullest extent of the law. We are confident that César Ochoa will be convicted of first-degree murder."

As Turner played to the cameras, Rolanda and I slipped inside the Hall.

"All rise," the bailiff intoned.

At the stroke of ten AM, an uneasy César stood between Rolanda and me at the defense table in Judge McDaniel's courtroom. Freshly shaved and sweating through the navy suit that Selena brought over last night, he looked as if he was ready for hand-to-hand combat.

I whispered, "Stay calm and look the judge in the eye."

A standing fan moved the heavy air from one side of the courtroom to the other as Judge McDaniel emerged from her chambers and glided to her chair. She switched on her computer, glanced at her docket, and raised a hand. "Please be seated."

She wouldn't touch her gavel.

César, Rolanda, and I took our seats. Catherine O'Neal sat at the prosecution table wearing a subdued black pantsuit, eyes locked onto the judge. A young ADA sat beside her along with Melinda Wong. As the lead homicide inspector, she was the only witness allowed in court before her testimony.

The gallery was full. In a display of institutional support, Turner was sitting behind O'Neal. She would probably stick around until the lunch break and issue another round of sound bites to the media. Chloe Carson's mother sat next to her in dignified silence.

Rosie sat in the front row with two Deputy Public Defenders. I appreciated the show of solidarity. Selena was in the same row, eyes forward, demeanor stoic. The crime beat reporter from the *Chronicle* sat in the third row next to Mike Herlihy, my Berkeley classmate who has been a reporter at Channel Two for three decades. The courthouse regulars occupied the remaining seats. In a sign that the Covid era was finally drawing to a close, nobody was wearing a mask.

Judge McDaniel nodded at Turner. "It's always a pleasure to welcome our distinguished District Attorney."

"Thank you, Your Honor."

"Likewise, it's nice to see our Public Defender."

Rosie nodded.

Judge McDaniel looked at the bailiff. "We are on the record. Please call our case."

"The People versus César Ochoa. Preliminary hearing. First-degree murder."

"Counsel will state their names for the record."

"Catherine O'Neal and Richard Kramer for the People."

"Michael Daley and Rolanda Fernandez for the defense."

Judge McDaniel spoke quickly and without notes. "I would like to remind everyone that a prelim is different from a trial. There is no jury, so I will make all rulings from the bench. The burden of proof is also different. At trial, the prosecution must prove every element of its case beyond a reasonable doubt. The purpose of a prelim is to determine whether there is a reasonable basis to conclude that there is sufficient evidence that the defendant has committed the crime for which he is charged. Under California law, if there is any ambiguity on evidentiary matters, I am required to give the benefit of the doubt to the prosecution. At trial, such determinations will be made by a jury."

The judge's eyes shifted from O'Neal to me. "Any last minute issues?"

"None," we said in unison.

"Ms. O'Neal, do you wish to offer a brief opening statement?"

"Yes, Your Honor."

She wasn't obligated to do so, but I had never seen a prosecutor decline the invitation. Moreover, most judges don't give prosecutors and defense attorneys the opportunity to present an opening statement at a prelim.

"Please proceed."

O'Neal stood at the lectern and pointed at an enlarged high school graduation photo of Chloe Carson on the flat screen TV. "Chloe was a bright, beautiful, and talented young woman who was only twenty-two years old when she was brutally killed by the defendant."

César tensed. I could have objected on the grounds that César was innocent until proven guilty, but Betsy McDaniel didn't need the reminder. Moreover, it's considered bad form to interrupt during an opening.

O'Neal showed a montage of photos of Chloe from preschool through young adulthood. "She was a beloved daughter and a cherished friend. Her death is an unspeakable tragedy."

Yes, it is. I whispered to César, "She's going to point at you. Look her right in the eye."

O'Neal pointed at César—the way every prosecutor is taught. "The defendant, César Ochoa, is sitting at the defense table."

César stared right back at her.

She lowered her arm. "We will introduce incontrovertible evidence that the defendant stabbed Chloe to death in the early morning of Saturday, May sixth, in the alley behind the club where she worked. She bled to death. These facts are indisputable."

We will dispute them anyway. O'Neal was following the conventional playbook. She would refer to Chloe by name to humanize her. Conversely, she would refer to César only as "the defendant." It may seem trivial, but trial work is theater, and every nuance counts.

O'Neal's voice was somber. "Chloe's mother is here today, and she is overwhelmed with grief. Chloe's family, friends, and co-workers are devastated. We cannot bring her back, but we must bring the person responsible for this brutal and senseless crime to justice."

O'Neal glared at César for a moment, then she addressed the judge. "Chloe was a talented dancer, performer, and artist. She aspired to become a ballerina, but she did not have the resources to pay for professional training. She worked as a dancer at a club here in the City, where she was widely admired and genuinely loved. On Friday, May fifth, she was doing what she loved: dancing. After last dance, she argued with the defendant. She left via the back door into the alley where the defendant was waiting for her. He stabbed her with a steak knife that the police found in the adjacent Dumpster. Chloe's blood was on the knife. So were the defendant's fingerprints. That is more than enough evidence to move this case forward to trial."

César leaned over and whispered, "Can you stop this?"

No. "It will be our turn in a few minutes."

O'Neal described the discovery of the body and the knife, the securing of the scene, and the Medical Examiner's determination of cause of death. Judge McDaniel listened attentively and unemotionally.

O'Neal shot a disdainful glance my way, then she faced the judge. "The defense is going to argue that the defendant didn't stab Chloe. Or that it was an accident. Or that somebody else did it. That's their job. As Your Honor noted, we are not required to prove our case beyond a reasonable doubt at this time. That will come at trial. However, I will provide more than enough evidence for you to move this case forward."

O'Neal returned to the prosecution table and sat down.

Judge McDaniel looked my way. "Opening statement, Mr. Daley?"

"Ms. Fernandez will handle our opening." We could have deferred until after O'Neal had completed her case, but we wanted to make a few points right away.

Rolanda walked to the lectern and placed a single note card in front of her. "César Ochoa has been wrongly accused of a horrible crime that he did not commit. The prosecution is rushing to judgment. It is our job to correct this error and see that justice is served.

"César Ochoa is a San Francisco native, a lifelong member of St. Peter's Parish, and a former police officer. He is a good man who has gone through some difficult times. For the last two years, he has worked as a doorman at For Gentlemen Only, an adult entertainment venue. He is a father and a grandfather. He is honest. He is kind. He is resilient. And he isn't a murderer."

Judge McDaniel was listening.

"César was working at For Gentlemen Only on Friday, May fifth. As always, he arrived on time and performed his duties professionally. As was his custom, he had dinner at the club shortly before closing time. He had a hamburger, fries, and a soft drink. He cut the burger with a knife that he left on the table. It is the only knife that he touched that night. Somebody picked it up and used it to stab Chloe Carson."

O'Neal stood up. "This is pure speculation, Your Honor."

Yes, it is.

"Noted," the judge said.

Rolanda picked up the note card. "Chloe's death is a tragedy. It was a horrible and bloody crime. However, the police found no traces of her blood on my client's hands, clothing, car, or apartment. It is a gaping hole in their case. There were many other people at the club that night, several of whom had strained relationships with Chloe. Her former boyfriend, Jerry Henderson, was working the soundboard. We will present testimony that he had been physically and emotionally abusive. He and Chloe exchanged harsh words that night. Yet the prosecution refuses to consider the possibility that Mr. Henderson was involved in her death."

"Move to strike," O'Neal said. "There is no evidence supporting these unsubstantiated assertions."

"We will provide such evidence," Rolanda said.

"The objection is overruled—for now."

Rolanda lowered her voice. "Your Honor, we will demonstrate that the prosecution is rushing to judgment without sufficient evidence to move this case forward to trial."

She headed back to the defense table.

The judge's eyes shifted to O'Neal. "Please call your first witness."

"The People call Mr. Stewart Baird."

It was a logical starting point. Baird found Chloe's body.

40

"I WAS WALKING MY DOG"

O'Neal stood at the lectern. "Please state your name and occupation for the record."

"Stewart Baird. Retired. I was a partner at a major law firm for forty years."

"What type of law did you practice?"

"Commercial litigation."

In his navy sport jacket, powder-blue shirt, and striped necktie, the gray-haired and soft-spoken Baird evoked understated authority. I had met him at several Bar Association functions, and he was always gracious. He had a reputation as conscientious and scrupulously honest. Notwithstanding his low-key demeanor, like most big-firm litigators, he had the capacity to go full-on barracuda when the circumstances called for it.

O'Neal's tone was conversational. "Could you please tell us where you were at approximately seven AM on Saturday, May sixth, of this year?"

"I was walking my dog, Archie."

O'Neal responded with a fake smile. "What kind of dog is he?"

"A golden retriever." Baird sat up a little taller. "He's the sweetest dog in the world."

This was, of course, completely irrelevant to César's case, but there was nothing to be gained by objecting. Archie probably was a wonderful dog.

O'Neal asked for permission to approach Baird, which Judge McDaniel granted. She stopped a few feet from the box and pointed at the flat screen, which showed a Google Maps photo of the blocks surrounding For Gentlemen Only. "Where did you and Archie start your walk?"

"From my house on Vallejo Street. We continued east to Montgomery, then we headed south toward Broadway."

"You and Archie stopped before you got to Broadway, didn't you?"

"Objection," Rolanda said. "Please remind Ms. O'Neal that she isn't allowed to lead the witness." She wanted to disrupt O'Neal's rhythm.

"I'll rephrase," O'Neal said. "Could you show us where you stopped?"

Baird pointed at the screen. "At the entrance to the alley behind For Gentlemen Only."

"Why did you stop?"

"Archie saw a dead body in the alley and became agitated."

"Move to strike," Rolanda said. "With respect, Mr. Baird is not qualified to render a medical conclusion as to whether the individual in the alley was deceased."

"Sustained."

O'Neal asked if the person in the alley was moving.

"No."

"Did you check for a pulse?"

"Yes. As far as I could tell, there was none."

"Did it appear to you that the person was dead?"

"Yes."

O'Neal had put the first points on the board. In a murder case, you need a decedent. She pointed at the TV again. "Could you please show us where you found the body?"

"At the yellow X in the alley next to the Dumpster."

O'Neal was conducting a by-the-book direct exam. She was asking Baird precise questions, and he was responding with short answers.

"Did you call 9-1-1?" she asked.

"Yes." Baird said that the police and EMTs arrived within ten minutes. "I gave my statement to the police and took Archie home."

"No further questions."

The judge looked our way. "Cross-exam?"

Rolanda answered her. "Just a few questions. May we approach the witness?"

"You may."

Rolanda stood, buttoned her charcoal jacket, and headed to the front of the box. "Mr. Baird, you didn't know the decedent, correct?"

O'Neal stood up as if she was thinking about objecting but reconsidered. It was a legitimate question, and on cross, you're allowed to lead the witness.

"No," Baird said.

"Was she already in the alley when you and Archie walked by?"

"Yes."

"You don't know how or when she got there, do you?"

"No."

"Was anybody else around?"

"No."

"You don't know how she died, do you?"

"There was a lot of blood. It looked like she might have been stabbed."

"But you didn't see her being stabbed, did you?"

"No."

"You have no personal knowledge of how or when she died, do you?"

"No."

"And you are not aware of any connection between my client and the decedent, are you?"

"No."

"No further questions."

O'Neal passed on redirect.

"Please call your next witness," the judge said.

"The People call Officer Jeff Roth."

Jeff Roth sat in the box, uniform pressed, star polished, bearing erect. He wouldn't touch the cup of water that he had poured for himself. Strong witnesses never drink water because it makes them look nervous.

He spoke deliberately as O'Neal led him through a crisp summary of his CV. "I have been a sworn officer since 1988." He confirmed that he had started his career at Mission Station and then worked at Taraval, Northern, and Park Stations. "I moved to Central Station in North Beach about ten years ago."

"Were you on duty on the morning of Saturday, May sixth, of this year?"

"I was." Roth said that he had worked the overnight shift. "My partner and I were preparing to log out when we got a call from 9-1-1 dispatch at seven AM. Mr. Stewart Baird had discovered an unconscious woman in the alley behind For Gentlemen Only. The victim was unresponsive. I answered the call and requested police backup and a medical unit. At seven-oh-five AM, I checked out a police unit and drove to the scene. I arrived at seven-oh-nine."

"You met Mr. Baird in the alley?"

"Yes. He directed me to Ms. Carson's body."

"Move to strike," Rolanda said. "Officer Roth is not qualified to determine whether Ms. Carson was deceased at the time."

Judge McDaniel looked at Roth. "Could you please clarify your answer?"

"Yes, Your Honor. Mr. Baird led me to a woman later identified as the victim, Chloe Carson. She was unconscious and, as far as I could tell, she wasn't breathing. Her clothes were covered in blood. I attempted to administer CPR, but I was unsuccessful. The EMTs arrived two minutes later. Unfortunately, Ms. Carson never regained consciousness. She was pronounced dead at the scene by the EMTs who were in real-time contact with an emergency room physician at San Francisco General."

It was solid testimony from a veteran cop.

O'Neal walked Roth through concise descriptions of how he secured the scene and organized a search for witnesses. "Did

Mr. Baird have any information as to how Ms. Carson died?" she asked.

"No."

"Did you search the area?"

"Yes."

O'Neal walked over to the cart and picked up a clear evidence bag containing the steak knife. She introduced it into evidence and handed it to Roth. "Can you identify this item?"

"Yes. I found this knife in the Dumpster next to Ms. Carson's body. It appeared that there was blood on it. I was wearing rubber gloves at the time so that I did not disturb any fingerprints or other evidence."

"Do you know where this knife came from?"

"I have no personal knowledge, but I was told that it matched the knives used at For Gentlemen Only."

"It was later determined that the defendant's fingerprints were on this knife, wasn't it?"

Rolanda spoke from her seat. "Objection. Calls for a conclusion beyond Officer Roth's knowledge and expertise."

"Sustained."

"It was also determined that the victim's DNA was on this knife, right?"

"Objection. Also outside Officer Roth's expertise."

"Sustained."

It would be a short-lived victory. O'Neal would undoubtedly call a fingerprint expert to confirm that César's prints were on the knife. Then she would call a DNA expert to confirm that it was Carson's blood.

O'Neal had what she needed from Roth. "No further questions."

"Cross-exam, Ms. Fernandez?"

"Yes, Your Honor." She walked over to the evidence cart, picked up the knife, and handed it to Roth. "Did you handle this knife?"

"Yes. I was wearing gloves at the time to avoid contaminating the evidence. I placed it in the evidence bag and logged it in accordance with standard SFPD procedure."

"Did you see my client stab Ms. Carson?"

"No."

"Or put this knife into the Dumpster?"

"No."

"So, you don't know what happened to Ms. Carson, do you?"

"I have no personal knowledge."

"Did you find any witnesses who saw my client stab Ms. Carson?"

"No."

"Did you consider the possibility that somebody other than my client may have done so?"

"We consider everybody as a potential suspect until we are able to rule them out."

"Bottom line, you have no direct knowledge of how Ms. Carson died, do you?"

"No, Ms. Fernandez."

"No further questions."

O'Neal spent the next twenty minutes laying the foundation. The lead EMT confirmed that Carson had no pulse when he arrived. Efforts to resuscitate her were unsuccessful. She was pronounced dead at the scene at seven-forty AM. A crime scene technician testified that there were no working surveillance cameras in the immediate vicinity.

Rolanda objected to O'Neal's questions from time to time, but there were few items that she could legitimately dispute. On cross, Rolanda got each witness to confirm that they had no personal knowledge as to how Carson had been killed. More important, they admitted that they had no knowledge of any involvement on César's part. It wasn't going to get the charges dropped, but it inched us a little closer to creating some doubt in the judge's mind.

Having checked off the necessary boxes regarding the discovery of the body and the securing of the scene, O'Neal turned to the next item on her list. "The People call Dr. Ilene Leung of the San Francisco Medical Examiner's Office."

41

"MASSIVE BLOOD LOSS"

Dr. Leung sat in the box, white medical coat pressed. "I have been an Assistant Medical Examiner for five years."

O'Neal was at the lectern. "Where did you train?"

"Undergrad and master's degrees from UC Davis. Medical School at UCSF, where I studied under Dr. Joy Siu."

There was no reason to let her recite her qualifications into the record. "Your Honor," Rolanda said, "we will stipulate that Dr. Leung is a recognized authority in her field."

"Thank you, Ms. Fernandez."

O'Neal introduced the autopsy report into evidence and presented it to Leung as if it was the Ten Commandments. "You performed the autopsy of Chloe Carson on Saturday, May sixth?"

"I did."

"This is the report that you produced?"

"It is."

"You were able to determine the cause of death?"

"I was." Leung pretended to leaf through her report. "The is a homicide case. Massive blood loss caused by a catastrophic stab wound to the neck which pierced the left carotid artery." She explained in medical and then layman's terms that the carotid arteries supply oxygenated blood to the brain, neck, and face.

"Any chance of survival?"

"Minimal. Ms. Carson probably bled out within moments of being stabbed."

"Defensive wounds?"

"None."

O'Neal presented the knife to Leung. "You've seen this knife?"

"Yes. Officer Jeff Roth found it in the Dumpster next to the decedent's body. The blade was covered with blood that was later matched to Ms. Carson's."

"Were you able to come to any conclusions?"

"While it is impossible to match a stab wound to a particular knife the way that we can match a spent round to a particular firearm, this wound was consistent with the serrated blade on this knife. As a result, I believe that this knife was used to stab Ms. Carson."

O'Neal had what she needed. "No further questions."

"Cross-exam, Ms. Fernandez?"

"Yes, Your Honor." She approached the box. "Good morning, Dr. Leung."

"Good morning, Ms. Fernandez."

"Did you find my client's blood on the knife that Ms. O'Neal just showed you?"

"No."

"You testified earlier that Ms. Carson died of a massive blood loss resulting from a stab wound inflicted at close quarters, right?"

"Yes."

"Which means that it is likely that some of Ms. Carson's blood would have found its way to her assailant, right?"

"Objection," O'Neal said. "Ms. Fernandez asked a question on a matter that was not addressed during direct."

"Your Honor," Rolanda said, "we have stipulated to Dr. Leung's expertise on forensic pathology. She testified that Ms. Carson died of a stab wound inflicted at close quarters. She should therefore be able to opine as to the nature and scope of Ms. Carson's wound."

"Overruled."

"In my opinion," Leung said, "it is likely that some of Ms. Carson's blood would have found its way onto the defendant's hands and/or clothing."

"Are you also aware that the police found no traces of Ms. Carson's blood on César's hands or clothing?"

O'Neal could have objected that Rolanda's question was beyond the scope of the matters addressed during direct, but she was confident that Leung could handle it.

Leung's voice didn't waver. "So I was told."

"Wouldn't you have expected to find her blood on his hands or clothing?"

"Possibly. However, the defendant could have washed his hands and laundered or disposed of his clothing."

"Given the current state of technology, isn't it likely that the police would have found traces of blood?"

"Objection. Calls for an opinion on matters outside of Dr. Leung's expertise."

"Sustained."

Our blood spatter expert will deal with this issue during our defense.

Rolanda was now standing directly in front of Leung. "You have no physical evidence connecting my client to the stabbing of Ms. Carson, do you?"

"His fingerprints were on the knife."

"Are you aware that my client has acknowledged that he ate dinner at the club that night and that he used a steak knife of the same type?"

"I'll take your word for it."

"Which means that he could have gotten his fingerprints on it earlier that evening, right?"

"Objection. Speculation."

"Sustained."

"No further questions, Your Honor."

O'Neal passed on redirect.

"Please call your next witness."

"The People call Lieutenant Kathleen Jacobsen."

It was another logical move. Jacobsen was SFPD's most accomplished fingerprint expert.

42
"AN ALMOST PERFECT MATCH"

O'Neal's next witness spoke with authority. "My name is Lieutenant Kathleen Jacobsen. I have been an evidence technician for the San Francisco Police Department for thirty-six years."

Rolanda quickly stipulated to her expertise. Jacobsen was the dean of SFPD's evidence experts. Her badge was displayed in the breast pocket of the jacket of her gray pantsuit. Her makeup was subtle, her salt-and-pepper hair worn in a low-maintenance layered cut. The daughter of an IBM engineer had grown up in Atherton and spent her summers at the pool at the Burlingame Country Club. She played water polo and studied criminal justice at USC, where she graduated summa cum laude. She earned a master's in forensic science from Cal. She had a stellar reputation on forensic evidentiary matters, with specialties in fingerprints and blood spatter. Her wife, Jill, was a retired firefighter.

O'Neal's voice was deferential. "On Saturday, May sixth, were you called to a crime scene behind For Gentlemen Only on Broadway?"

"Yes." She said that she arrived at seven-fifty-seven AM. "The decedent was identified as Chloe Carson. Jeff Roth was the first officer at the scene. Inspector Wong had taken charge."

O'Neal pointed at a photo of the scene on the TV. "Could you please describe what you saw?"

Conventional wisdom says that you should ask precise questions to elicit short answers. With an experienced witness like Jacobsen, it's often better to ask open-ended questions to let the witness tell the story in her own words.

Jacobsen walked over to the TV and gestured with a pen. "Mr. Stewart Baird discovered the decedent's body here." She noted that the EMTs had moved the body slightly during their efforts to administer first aid. "Officer Roth found a bloody steak knife in this Dumpster."

O'Neal handed the knife to Jacobsen. "This knife?"

"Yes."

César leaned over and whispered, "Can you do anything?"

Not really. "It'll be our turn soon."

O'Neal pointed at the knife. "Did you find any fingerprints on this knife?"

"Yes."

O'Neal led her through a rehearsed series of questions in which Jacobsen compared the prints on the knife to those taken when César was booked. Finally, O'Neal lobbed the inevitable softball. "What did you conclude?"

"The defendant's fingerprints were on the knife. It's an almost perfect match."

"No further questions."

"Cross-exam, Ms. Fernandez?"

"Yes, Your Honor." Rolanda moved to the front of the box. "Did you find any prints on the knife other than my client's?"

"There was a partial that we could not identify and a smudged print that was too distorted to match."

"Somebody else must have handled this knife, right?"

"It's possible."

"And it's possible that the partial and the smudged prints were made by different people, which means that two people other than my client might have handled this knife?"

"It's possible."

"It's also possible that the person or persons whose prints you could not identify stabbed Ms. Carson, isn't it?"

"Objection. Calls for speculation."

"Overruled."

Jacobsen didn't fluster. "It's possible, Ms. Fernandez."

Sit down, Rolanda.
"No further questions."

The wiry man with a pasty complexion, widow's peak, rimless spectacles, and dour demeanor hunched forward in the box. "My name is George Romero. I have been a supervising lab technician in the Forensic Services Division of SFPD's Criminalistics Laboratory for eighteen years. Before that, I was an assistant lab technician for twelve years."

O'Neal was standing in front of him. "What is your area of expertise?"

"DNA evidence."

Romero was a dreary but competent little man who had spent his career in a bunker in the basement of the Hall. The native of Bernal Heights had a chemistry degree from State, an inquisitive mind, and a meticulous manner. He wasn't charismatic, but he had a knack for explaining complex scientific concepts in easy-to-understand sound bites. If Lieutenant Jacobsen was the DA's point person on fingerprints, Romero was the go-to guy on DNA.

O'Neal showed him the steak knife. "You're familiar with this knife, Mr. Romero?"

"Yes. It was found at the scene of the murder of a young woman named Chloe Carson."

Come on. "Move to strike the term 'murder,'" I said.

Judge McDaniel rolled her eyes. "So ordered. You know better, Mr. Romero."

O'Neal pressed forward. "Mr. Romero, did you analyze this knife for DNA?"

"Yes."

O'Neal led Romero through a concise explanation of his procedures. His presentation included just enough technical jargon to lend an air of gravitas but was accessible enough to keep the judge's interest. Most important, it was mercifully short.

O'Neal asked Romero if he had obtained a DNA sample from Chloe Carson.

"I did. We had samples of her hair, fingernails, and skin from her autopsy."

"Did you find Ms. Carson's DNA on this knife?"

Romero paused in a ham-handed attempt to build suspense. "I did."

No surprise.

O'Neal nodded triumphantly. "The police also obtained a sample of the defendant's DNA, didn't they?"

"Yes. They found a comb in his apartment with a strand of his hair."

O'Neal feigned surprise. "You can get a DNA sample from a single strand?"

"If you know what you're doing."

"Did you have an opportunity to analyze the DNA?"

"I did."

O'Neal teed it up for him. "Were you able to determine whether the DNA from the hair matched any DNA that you found on the knife?"

"Yes. We were able to obtain a DNA sample from the defendant's fingerprint. I therefore concluded that the defendant handled the knife."

"No further questions."

"Cross-exam, Ms. Fernandez?"

"Yes, Your Honor." Rolanda walked to the front of the box. "Mr. Romero, you found DNA on the knife from people other than Ms. Carson and my client, didn't you?"

"Objection," O'Neal said. "Ms. Fernandez is raising an issue not addressed on direct."

"Your Honor," Rolanda said, "Ms. O'Neal questioned Mr. Romero about DNA tests on this knife. She opened the door. I should be allowed to explore the scope of his investigation."

O'Neal fired back. "Ms. Fernandez can address these issues during the defense case."

True.

The judge opted for expediency. "I'm going to overrule the objection and give you a little leeway, Ms. Fernandez."

Fine.

"Thank you," Rolanda said. She turned back to Romero. "Did you find anybody else's DNA on the knife?"

"Yes."

"How many people?"

"At least one. Maybe two."

Good.

"Were you able to make a positive ID of those other individuals?"

"No."

"Did you run the DNA through the local, state, and federal DNA databases, including the national criminal database commonly known as 'CODIS'?"

"Yes. We found no matches."

"Did you find my client's DNA on Ms. Carson's body, clothing, or other belongings?"

"No."

"Did you find my client's DNA on any other objects in the Dumpster or the alley?"

"No."

"Did you consider the possibility that one of the unidentified people stabbed Ms. Carson?"

"Objection. Calls for speculation."

Yes, it does.

"Sustained."

"Did you find Ms. Carson's DNA on my client's clothing, hands, automobile, or in his apartment?"

"No."

"No further questions, Your Honor."

O'Neal passed on redirect and called her next witness. "The People call Mr. David Callaghan."

43

"THEY WERE ARGUING"

Dave Callaghan looked like one of the bros in San Francisco's South of Market tech gulch in his black sport jacket, gray polo shirt, and no tie. "I am the General Manager of For Gentlemen Only on Broadway."

O'Neal stood in front of the box. "You knew the decedent, Ms. Chloe Carson?"

"I hired her. She worked for me for about six months. She was an excellent dancer. Our customers loved her." Callaghan's voice turned somber. "Our business is like a family where we look out for each other. It was a great loss."

He was laying it on a little thick, but Rolanda and I had no grounds to object.

It was a few minutes before noon. There were now a few open seats in the gallery. The regulars had departed to get in line at the sandwich shops across Bryant. Our esteemed District Attorney left after opening statements. So did Rosie.

O'Neal kept her voice conversational. "Were you at work on Friday, May fifth?"

"Yes."

"Was Ms. Carson working?"

"Yes. She arrived at approximately four-thirty PM. She departed a few minutes after one." He confirmed that he saw her leave through the back door.

"Did you talk to her after her performance?"

"Briefly. I try to spend at least a few minutes with each of our employees every night."

"How was her mood?"

"Objection," Rolanda said, trying to interrupt O'Neal's flow. "Ms. O'Neal is asking the witness to speculate as to Ms. Carson's state of mind."

"I'll rephrase," O'Neal said. "Did you observe her appearance and demeanor?"

"Yes. She appeared distracted and upset."

"Did you ask her why?"

"I did. She said that it was a personal matter."

"Did she mention any names?"

"No."

O'Neal feigned disappointment, then she pointed at César. "You know the defendant?"

"Of course. I hired him, too."

"Was he a good employee?"

"Most of the time."

O'Neal arched an eyebrow. "Most of the time?"

"At times, Mr. Ochoa was a little too forceful during his interactions with customers. On a couple of occasions, he became physical with people who had too much to drink or got a little too friendly with our dancers."

"He became violent?"

"He shoved a couple of people. Nobody pressed charges."

"Did you bring this to the defendant's attention?"

"Yes. I encouraged him to use better judgment. To his credit, he did—most of the time."

"Did the defendant know the victim?"

"Yes. Because of the nature of his position, he knew everybody who worked at the club."

"Did you ever see the victim and the defendant argue or engage in heated discussions?"

"Yes. They argued after Chloe's performance on the night that she was killed."

"Do you know what they were arguing about?"

"I'm afraid not. I couldn't hear them."

"Just to be clear, Mr. Callaghan, the defendant had harsh words with the victim a few minutes prior to the time that both of them exited through the back door of the club?"

"Objection. Ms. O'Neal is mischaracterizing Mr. Callaghan's testimony."

"Sustained."

"No further questions."

"Cross-exam, Ms. Fernandez?"

"Yes, Your Honor." Rolanda strode to the front of the courtroom and stopped an arm's length from Callaghan. "Ms. Carson never complained to you about César, did she?"

"Not that I recall."

"In particular, she never complained that César touched her or threatened to attack her, did she?"

"No."

"And you have no idea what they were talking about after Ms. Carson's performance on the morning of May sixth?"

"I couldn't hear them."

"He didn't touch her, did he?"

"Not that I recall."

"And he didn't threaten her, did he?"

"I don't know what he said to her."

Rolanda inched closer. "You also testified that César left the club at one AM, and Ms. Carson departed a few minutes later, right?"

"Right."

"You didn't follow them outside, did you?"

"No."

"So, you have no knowledge of what happened outside, do you?"

"No."

"Which also means that you have no knowledge of how Ms. Carson died, right?"

Callaghan exhaled. "Right."

Was that so hard?

Rolanda's eyes locked onto Callaghan's. "While Ms. Carson never complained about César, she did complain about at least one other employee at the club, didn't she?"

"Objection. Ms. Fernandez is asking about matters that were not addressed on direct."

Yes, she is.

"Your Honor," Rolanda said, "Ms. O'Neal asked Mr. Callaghan to comment upon individuals who allegedly initiated complaints about my client. I should be able to follow up."

Judge McDaniel considered her answer. "I'm going to sustain the objection, Ms. Fernandez. This is an issue that's more appropriately addressed during the defense case."

Rolanda feigned frustration, but she knew that it was the right call. We would, in fact, deal with it during our defense.

She turned back to Callaghan. "You testified that the employees at the club are like family, right?"

"Yes." Callaghan's expression indicated that he wasn't sure where she was going.

"There were many people at the club who knew Ms. Carson, right?"

"Of course."

"Including some regular customers?"

"Yes."

"Ms. Carson once had a relationship with the sound guy at the club whose name is Jerry Henderson, didn't she? And that relationship ended badly, didn't it? And Mr. Henderson has a history of being violent toward women, doesn't he?"

"Objection. Ms. Fernandez is once again asking about matters that were not brought up during direct exam."

"Your Honor," Rolanda said, "Ms. O'Neal questioned this witness about Ms. Carson's employment and relationships with people at the club. I should be able to follow up."

"I didn't ask about Mr. Henderson," O'Neal said.

"He was an employee of the club," Rolanda noted.

Judge McDaniel listened as Rolanda and O'Neal exchanged legal arguments and a few pointed barbs. "The objection is sustained. It seems to me that these are issues suited for presentation during the defense case. Any further questions for this witness?"

Rolanda feigned disappointment. "No, Your Honor."

"Redirect, Ms. O'Neal?"

"No, Your Honor."
"Please call your next witness."
"The People call Ms. Sheema Smith."

44

"SHE DIDN'T LIKE THE WAY THAT HE LOOKED AT HER"

In a simple white blouse and gray slacks, Sheema Smith looked like a CPA. "Chloe was a fine dancer and a popular employee. I was very sad when she died."

O'Neal spoke to her from the lectern. "Did you see her on the night that she was killed?"

"Yes. We performed at the late show."

"Did you see Chloe interact with the defendant after the show?"

"Yes." Sheema sat up taller. "They had a brief and rather heated conversation."

I understood why O'Neal wanted to corroborate Callaghan's testimony. I was now concerned that Sheema would add some new and damaging details.

"Did you happen to hear their argument?" O'Neal asked.

"I didn't hear much of it, but I distinctly heard Chloe tell him to leave her alone."

"Were those her exact words?"

"I don't recall exactly."

"No further questions."

César leaned over and whispered, "That's not true."

Rolanda was already on her way to the front of the box. "You have no idea what Ms. Carson and Mr. Ochoa were talking about, do you?"

"As I told Ms. O'Neal, I couldn't hear most of the conversation."

"It could have been anything, right? Maybe Ms. Carson didn't hear what Mr. Ochoa said. Or maybe she misinterpreted something, right?"

"It's possible."

"He didn't threaten her, did he?"

"I don't know."

"You don't know," Rolanda repeated. "No further questions, Your Honor."

Kelly Ryan took a long drink of water and spoke in a monotone. "Chloe and I started working at For Gentlemen Only about six months ago."

With her delicate features, minimal makeup, pixie-cut hair, black turtleneck, and designer jeans, Ryan looked like a sophomore in high school. It was hard to imagine that she spent most evenings dancing naked in front of strangers.

O'Neal's voice was calming. "When was the last time you saw her?"

"On the night that she died. We performed in the late show."

O'Neal pointed at César. "Did you see Ms. Carson interact with the defendant on the night that Ms. Carson was killed?"

"No."

Good.

"Did Ms. Carson ever mention to you how she felt about the defendant?"

"Objection," Rolanda said. "Hearsay."

Hearsay occurs when a witness shares something that somebody else said outside of court. Under California Evidence Code Section 1200, it becomes "hearsay evidence" when an attorney attempts to use that statement to confirm a fact. Hearsay is generally inadmissible because it is considered unreliable and the person who purportedly made the statement may not be available for cross-exam. However, there are multiple exceptions to the hearsay rule.

O'Neal's tone was dismissive. "Ms. Fernandez is well aware that Ms. Ryan's testimony is admissible under the exception for spontaneous statements under Evidence Code Section 1240."

"No, it isn't," Rolanda said. "Section 1240 applies only to statements that are not made in response to a question."

"Ms. Ryan did not question Ms. Carson about it. It was spontaneous."

"We have no way of knowing that. And I can't cross-examine Ms. Carson about the circumstances under which she allegedly made such assertions."

Judge McDaniel made the call. "The objection is overruled, and the witness will answer the question."

Crap.

Ryan cleared her throat. "Chloe told me once that she was afraid of him."

What the hell?

"Did she tell you why?" O'Neal asked.

"She didn't like the way that he looked at her."

César was seething. He leaned over and whispered, "This is BS."

"No further questions for this witness," O'Neal said.

"Cross-exam, Ms. Fernandez?"

"One moment, Your Honor." Rolanda leaned over to me and spoke in a whisper. "Should I go after her?"

"We have no choice."

She moved to the front of the box. "Ms. Ryan, when did Ms. Carson allegedly make this statement to you?"

"I don't recall."

"Was it in response to a question?"

"I don't recall."

"She didn't accuse Mr. Ochoa of touching her, did she?"

"No."

"Or threatening her?"

"Not that I recall."

"And you never saw Mr. Ochoa get physical with Ms. Carson or threaten her, did you?"

"No."

"So you have no knowledge as to why Ms. Carson allegedly made the statement?"

"Chloe was my friend. I believed her."

"Is there anybody else who can corroborate your story?"

"I don't know."

Rolanda turned to the judge. "Move to strike Ms. Ryan's hearsay testimony."

"Denied."

"But, Your Honor—,"

"I've ruled, Ms. Fernandez."

"No further questions."

The judge looked at the clock above the door. "We have time for one more witness before the lunch break, Ms. O'Neal."

"The People call Inspector Melinda Wong."

45

"IT'S THE ONLY LOGICAL EXPLANATION"

Inspector Melinda Wong sat in the box, an untouched cup of water at her side. Her charcoal pantsuit matched the color of her short hair. "I am the lead homicide inspector on the Chloe Carson murder case. It is a great tragedy."

We could have objected and insisted that she characterize Carson's death as an "alleged" murder, but it would have irritated the judge.

O'Neal stood at the lectern. "Could you please show us exactly where Officer Roth found the knife that was later determined to be covered in Ms. Carson's blood?"

"Of course." A confident Wong walked over to the flat screen and used a Cross pen to point at an enlarged overhead photo of the alley behind For Gentlemen Only. "In this Dumpster."

"Did your search uncover anyone other than the defendant being in the vicinity at the approximate time of Ms. Carson's untimely death?"

"No."

Wong was here to close the sale with Judge McDaniel. She had been on the stand for only a few minutes, but she and O'Neal were executing a flawless direct exam. Rolanda had objected to several of O'Neal's questions, but the reality was clear: we weren't going to derail O'Neal's case during the prosecution's presentation.

Wong returned to the box and assured us that she had secured the scene and supervised the collection of evidence in accordance with SFPD's best practices. Over multiple objections, she confirmed that there had been no lapses in chain of custody. She said that she had taken statements from everybody in the vicinity and all of the employees and customers at For Gentlemen Only.

"How was the defendant's demeanor when you first talked to him?" O'Neal asked.

"At first, he refused to cooperate. He later reconsidered and admitted that he had been at work at For Gentlemen Only."

"Did the defendant offer any explanation as to how a knife with his fingerprints and Ms. Carson's blood ended up in a Dumpster within a few feet of Ms. Carson's body?"

"No."

"Inspector, could you please summarize your conclusion as to what happened in the alley behind For Gentlemen Only in the early morning of May sixth of this year?"

"Yes, Ms. O'Neal." Wong turned and spoke directly to the judge. "Chloe Carson went to work on Friday, May fifth, as always. She handled her responsibilities professionally, and she entertained her customers. After last dance, she and the defendant got into a heated argument near the back door. The defendant left the building. Ms. Carson departed a few minutes later. In the alley, the defendant stabbed Ms. Carson to death using a steak knife from the club. The first officer at the scene found it in the nearby Dumpster. Our evidence experts determined that Ms. Carson's blood was on the knife. So were the defendant's fingerprints." Wong took a deep breath. "It is very sad."

"No further questions." O'Neal closed her laptop and returned to the prosecution table.

"Cross-exam, Ms. Fernandez?"

"Yes, Your Honor." Rolanda walked over to the evidence cart, picked up the knife, and showed it to Wong. "You found my client's fingerprints on this knife?"

"Correct."

"You understand that my client had a burger for dinner at the club that night?"

"So he said."

"Did you consider the possibility that he used this knife to cut the burger? And that somebody else picked up the knife and used it to stab Chloe Carson?"

"I found no evidence in support of your theory."

"The Medical Examiner concluded that Ms. Carson died of a stab wound which would have caused substantial bleeding, right?"

"Right."

"Yet you didn't find Ms. Carson's blood on my client's hands, clothing, or car, or at his apartment, did you?"

"No."

"How is that possible if he had stabbed her at close quarters?"

"Your client used to be a police officer. He knew how to dispose of evidence."

"Your equipment for testing for the presence of blood is very sophisticated, isn't it?"

"Yes."

"It has the capacity to find even minute traces of blood, right?"

"In most cases. A person familiar with evidence collection procedures would know how to sanitize a crime scene."

"You're saying that my client sanitized his hands, clothing, car, and apartment to such an extent that you couldn't even find a drop of Ms. Carson's blood?"

"It's likely that he disposed of his clothing."

"That doesn't address his hands, car, and apartment."

"As I said, the defendant was once a police officer. He knew how to cover his tracks."

"Ms. Carson had issues with other people who were at the club that night, didn't she?"

"Objection. Ms. Fernandez is asking about matters not addressed during direct."

"Sustained."

Rolanda kept her eyes locked onto Wong's. "In particular, Ms. Carson had broken up with a man named Jerry

Henderson, who was the sound technician at the club, hadn't she?"

"Objection. Same basis."

"Sustained."

"Mr. Henderson had a history of domestic violence, didn't he?"

"Objection."

"Sustained." Judge McDaniel's voice filled with genuine irritation. "You'll need to address these issues when you present your defense, Ms. Fernandez."

"Yes, Your Honor." She turned back to Wong. "Let's be honest, Inspector. You just assumed that my client stabbed Ms. Carson, didn't you?"

"It's the only logical explanation. The evidence is overwhelming."

"You didn't consider any other suspects."

"We found a bloody knife with your client's prints in the Dumpster."

"The fact remains that you don't know what happened, do you?"

"It seems obvious to me."

"Not to me."

"Move to strike."

"Sustained."

Rolanda went after Wong, but the veteran inspector remained resolute. Judge McDaniel was paying attention, but I saw no signs that Rolanda was convincing her. She was also limited in her questioning to subjects raised by O'Neal on direct. She would have to wait until we presented our defense before she could talk about other potential suspects. After ten minutes, she turned to the judge. "No further questions." She made her way back to the defense table.

"Redirect, Ms. O'Neal?"

"No, Your Honor. The prosecution rests."

"Ms. Fernandez, do you wish to make a motion before we recess for lunch?"

"Yes, Your Honor."

Here goes nothing.

"The defense moves that the charges be dismissed as a matter of law because there is insufficient evidence to bind my client over for trial."

"Denied."

No surprise.

Judge McDaniel glanced at her watch. "We will resume at one-thirty PM. Please be ready to start the defense case."

46
"YOU HAVE TO DO SOMETHING"

César paced in the holding cell adjacent to the courtroom during the lunch break. He hadn't touched his sandwich, and his voice was filled with a combination of fear, frustration, and anxiety. "You have to do something."

"The prosecution always has the advantage at first," I said. "It's our turn now."

"You need to do more."

"We will. We need you to remain focused and calm."

"I need you to get the charges dropped."

I could only provide an unsatisfying answer. "We're doing everything that we can."

The air was stale in the windowless room down the hall from Judge McDaniel's courtroom. A burly sheriff's deputy was posted outside the door. Rolanda focused on her laptop as she picked at a Cobb salad. I forced myself to eat half of my tuna sandwich even though I wasn't hungry.

César finally sat down. "O'Neal hammered us. I need you to be better."

I pointed at his sandwich. "Eat something."

"I'm not hungry."

I can't force you to eat. I turned to Rolanda. "Any word from Pete?"

"No."

He'd better find something soon.

The deputy tapped on the door. "Ten minutes, Mr. Daley."

"Thank you."

César pushed his sandwich aside. "What's going to happen this afternoon?"

"Our blood spatter expert will testify that they should have found blood in your car or your house. Our fingerprint expert will confirm that there were prints other than yours on the knife. Our DNA expert will also confirm that there was DNA from other people on the knife. Then we'll put up some of the other people who were at the club on Friday night and try to foist the blame onto them."

"You think somebody is going to confess?"

I hope so. "At the very least, we'll try to get them to point the finger at somebody else."

The deputy returned five minutes later and escorted us back to Judge McDaniel's court.

As we were walking down the hallway, I pulled out my phone and texted Pete. "Need something useful soon."

The reply came immediately. "Looking at some possibilities."

47
"A MASSIVE AMOUNT OF BLOOD"

I stood at the lectern after the lunch break. "Please state your name for the record."

"Dr. Lloyd Russell."

"You're a medical doctor?"

"I have a PhD in criminology. My area of expertise is blood spatter patterns."

Rolanda and I decided that I would handle Lloyd Russell's direct exam because I had known him for decades. Of the hundreds of expert witnesses that I had examined over the years, Lloyd was in my personal Hall of Fame. He knew his stuff. He was great in court. He was a straight shooter of unquestionable integrity. Because of our relationship, he didn't charge me. On top of it all, he was one of the nicest guys I'd ever met.

"Water?" I asked.

"No, thank you, Mr. Daley."

Lloyd was my criminology professor at Cal. At eighty-eight, the relentlessly upbeat academic had a cherubic face, dancing blue eyes, and a trim gray goatee. Though he had moved to emeritus status, he still taught a wildly popular graduate seminar every spring. His credentials were impeccable: BS from Harvard, master's from Stanford, and PhD from Cal. The champion bridge player, scratch golfer, and avid skier always showed up in court in a corduroy jacket with elbow patches, a checkered shirt, and a polka-dot tie to bolster his academic bona fides. Outside of court, he wore Armani.

O'Neal stopped me as soon as I started walking Lloyd through his CV. "Your Honor," she said, "we will stipulate that Dr. Russell is an expert on blood spatter."

Judge McDaniel smiled. "Thank you, Ms. O'Neal." She sat in the same row at the symphony as Lloyd and Joni Russell.

I handed the autopsy report to Lloyd. "You reviewed this document?"

"I did."

"Do you agree with Dr. Leung's conclusion as to cause of death?"

"I have no reason to question her findings. She's an excellent pathologist."

Just the way we rehearsed it. I directed him to the final page. "You noted that Dr. Leung identified the cause of death as a stab wound to the decedent's right carotid artery?"

He flipped to the last page and pretended to study it. "Yes, Mr. Daley."

I returned to the lectern. "Have you ever been asked to analyze a stabbing where the decedent's carotid artery was punctured?"

"Unfortunately, yes. I have studied photos from dozens of cases where the decedent died of a similar wound. The scenes were quite gruesome." He stroked his beard. "The carotid artery is a main vessel from the heart, the muscle that pumps blood. If it stops pumping, you die. If the flow is impeded, you may suffer a heart attack. If a main artery is punctured, the heart frequently keeps pumping for a few moments, which means that blood continues to flow to the site of the wound. A lot of blood leaks through the wound and often flies in a projectile pattern until the heart stops beating and the blood stops flowing."

"Would you have expected to see a lot of blood in the area near the decedent's body?"

"Yes."

"And given the close quarters associated with a stab wound, is it your expert opinion that the person who stabbed Ms.

Carson would have gotten a lot of blood on his hands and clothing?"

"Absolutely."

I pointed at a photo of the crime scene on the flat screen. "You've seen this?"

"Yes, Mr. Daley. It was taken in the back of For Gentlemen Only shortly after Ms. Carson's body was removed." He noted the chalk outline and the yellow markers.

"Could you please show us the blood stains?"

"Of course." He walked over to the TV and removed the wire-rimmed glasses that he always brought to court—even though his eyesight was twenty-twenty—and used them to gesture. "The areas underneath and surrounding Ms. Carson body—especially near the neck—are saturated in blood." He made a slightly larger circle. "There are smaller droplets within a few feet of the body, which suggests that they projected a little farther. This is not uncommon for wounds of this type. As you can see, there was a massive amount of blood."

I gave Lloyd a moment to return to the box. "Dr. Russell, in your expert opinion, how likely is it that a large amount of Ms. Carson's blood would have been found on the hands and clothing of the person who stabbed her?"

"I can't give you an exact percentage, but it's very likely."

"Ballpark? Fifty percent? Seventy-five percent? Ninety percent?"

He went through his entire repertoire of scholarly gestures to give the impression that he was deep in thought, even though he knew the question was coming. He opened and closed his glasses. He played with the elbow patch on his jacket. He stroked his goatee. Finally, he spoke directly to the judge. "Ninety-nine percent," he decided.

"Ninety-nine percent," I repeated. "You would have expected to find the decedent's blood on my client's hands and clothing?"

"Yes."

"And perhaps his car and in his apartment?"

"Correct."

I walked over to the evidence cart and picked up a copy of Inspector Wong's report, which O'Neal had introduced into evidence during Wong's testimony. I brought it over to the box and handed it to Lloyd. "You've reviewed this report?"

"I have."

"Was there any mention of Ms. Carson's blood on my client's hands or clothing? Or in his car or apartment?"

"No."

"Did that surprise you?"

"Yes. In my opinion, it is highly likely that traces of the decedent's blood would have been found on the decedent's person, clothing, car, and/or inside his apartment."

"No further questions."

"Cross-exam, Ms. O'Neal?"

"Yes, Your Honor." She stood at the prosecution table. "Dr. Russell, it's possible that the defendant might have avoided a projectile of blood when he stabbed Ms. Carson, isn't it?"

"Anything is possible, Ms. O'Neal."

"For example, if the defendant had pushed Ms. Carson to the ground and was standing above her while he stabbed her, the blood would not have spattered upward, right?"

"It is possible for blood to spatter upward."

"That would have defied the law of gravity, wouldn't it?"

"Not necessarily."

"And it's also possible that the defendant washed his hands and disposed of his clothing before he got inside his car or entered his apartment, isn't it?"

Lloyd kept his voice even. "Like I said, anything is possible."

"And even the most sensitive equipment can't always find traces of blood if the defendant is diligent, right?"

"That's theoretically true—,"

O'Neal cut him off. "Thank you, Dr. Russell."

"Your Honor," I said, "Dr. Russell had not finished his answer."

The judge nodded. "Anything you'd like to add, Dr. Russell?"

"Yes, Your Honor. Our equipment and technology are state-of-the-art and highly sensitive. As a result, I believe that

Ms. O'Neal's suggestion that no traces of blood would have been found is highly unlikely, if not impossible."

"Any further questions, Ms. O'Neal?"

You should sit down now.

"You're aware that the defendant used to be a police officer?"

"I am."

"He was dismissed from SFPD after he lost his temper and attacked a person in his custody, wasn't he?"

"Objection," I said. "Relevance."

"Sustained."

It was a legitimate objection, and Judge McDaniel was correct to sustain it. She was also undoubtedly aware of the circumstances surrounding César's (and Pete's) dismissal.

"Anything else, Ms. O'Neal?" the judge asked.

"One more item, Your Honor." She turned to Lloyd. "You've known Mr. Daley for a long time, haven't you?"

"More than thirty years. He was my student at Cal."

"You would therefore be inclined to help him, wouldn't you?"

"I would never let my personal relationships color my professional judgment."

Good answer.

"How much is Mr. Daley paying you to appear today?"

I was hoping you would ask.

"Nothing," Lloyd said. "I have reached the point in my career where I don't need the money, and I am more interested in justice."

You should have sat down a couple of minutes ago, Catherine.

"No further questions, Your Honor."

"Redirect, Mr. Daley?"

"No, Your Honor."

"I need to call a brief recess. Please be ready to call your next witness in ten minutes."

"He was good," César said, eyes a little brighter.

"He's a gem," I replied.

We were sitting at the defense table awaiting the judge's return.

"Is it enough?" he asked.

Not even close. "Not yet."

"Who's next?"

"Our fingerprint expert."

48

"FINGERPRINTS"

The slender man with the jet-black hair, trim mustache, and lengthy bags under his eyes spoke deliberately. "My name is Sridar Iyengar. I recently retired after thirty years at the San Mateo County Crime Lab."

I was standing at the lectern. "What is your area of expertise?"

"Fingerprints."

Judge McDaniel's courtroom was half empty at one-fifty on Wednesday afternoon. Many of the regulars had taken the afternoon off or decided to check out the action in other courtrooms.

In response to my question, Sridar explained that he was a native of San Francisco whose parents were born in India and moved to the Bay Area to be closer to his grandfather, a researcher at UCSF. "I earned my bachelor's in criminology from San Francisco State and spent my entire career at the San Mateo County Crime Lab."

O'Neal spoke from her seat. "We will stipulate as to Mr. Iyengar's expertise in fingerprint analysis."

Good decision. Sridar was, in fact, one of California's foremost authorities on fingerprints. He was also my former neighbor, long-time friend, and one of the most meticulous guys I've ever known. His mom and dad operated an Indian restaurant a few doors from Dunleavy's, which became an unlikely hit among the neighborhood's Irish, Italian, and later Chinese families. His scholarly demeanor and engaging manner made him an ideal expert witness. What started as a post-retirement side hustle had turned into a lucrative second career.

I pointed at the flat screen. "Are you familiar with these fingerprints?"

"Yes. The first is a right thumbprint of the defendant, César Ochoa, taken by the police at his booking. The second is a right thumbprint taken from a steak knife found by Officer Jeff Roth in a Dumpster in the alley behind For Gentlemen Only on Saturday, May sixth." Sridar went through a detailed comparison of the characteristics of each print.

"Do they match?" I asked.

"In my opinion, they do."

"Can you tell us when Mr. Ochoa handled the knife?"

"No, Mr. Daley. Fingerprints have an indefinite shelf life. It could have been the same day, the day before, or even weeks or months earlier."

"Did you find any other prints on the knife that matched my client's?"

"No."

I displayed another print on the flat screen. "Was this also in the police report?"

"Yes. It was lifted from the same knife." Sridar confirmed that he had compared the prints to César's. "In my professional judgment, at least one other person handled the knife."

So far, so good. I put a second print on the screen. "Was this also taken from the knife?"

"Yes."

"Were you able to make a determination as to whether it matched my client's prints?"

"Unfortunately, the print was too smudged to make a positive identification."

"Is it therefore possible that a second person other than my client handled this knife?"

"In my opinion, it is."

More progress. "Did you review all of the fingerprints included in the police reports?"

"Yes."

"Did you find any fingerprints on the decedent's person, clothing, or belongings that matched those of my client, César Ochoa?"

"None."

"No further questions."

"Cross-exam, Ms. O'Neal?" the judge asked.

"We have no questions for this witness, Your Honor," she said.

Rolanda was at the lectern a moment later. "What is your occupation?"

Dr. Carla Jimenez spoke with authority. "I am a senior forensic DNA Analyst at the Serological Research Institute in Richmond, California. I have worked at SERI for twenty-four years."

"You're a medical doctor?"

"PhD. I earned my bachelor's degree in chemistry and biological science from San Francisco State, and a master's and then a PhD in forensic science from UC Davis. My area of expertise is forensic serology and forensic DNA."

"You've been called as an expert witness before?"

"I have testified in hundreds of cases in state and federal courts nationwide as well as in federal and military courts."

You're very good at your job.

Carla was our go-to expert on DNA. Rosie's classmate at Mercy High School had graduated second in her class, worked her way through State, and was accepted into UCLA Medical School. She deferred her admission to work in a research lab in the Department of Forensic Science at UC Davis, where her professor offered her a scholarship to earn a master's and then a PhD. She went to work at SERI, the preeminent lab for DNA analysis in Northern California. She was testifying *pro bono* as a favor to Rosie and a promise that we would take her out for dinner at Chez Panisse in Berkeley.

Rolanda moved closer to the box. "You have received many citations for your work over the years, haven't you?"

"I am a Fellow of the American Board of Criminalistics in Forensic Biology with subspecialties in Forensic Biochemistry and Forensic Molecular Biology. I am also a member of the California Association of Criminalists, the Northwest Association of Forensic Scientists, the California Association of Crime Laboratory Directors, and the Association of Forensic Quality Assurance Managers."

O'Neal spoke from her seat. "We will stipulate that Dr. Jimenez is an expert in the fields of forensic serology and forensic DNA."

What took you so long?

Rolanda walked to the evidence cart, picked up an official-looking document, introduced it into evidence, and handed it to Carla. "You're familiar with this report?"

"Yes. It is a DNA analysis of samples obtained from the knife found in the Dumpster behind For Gentlemen Only. It was prepared by Mr. George Romero of the Forensic Services Division of the San Francisco Police Department's Criminalistics Laboratory."

"Do you believe that it was prepared in accordance with highest industry standards?"

"I do. Mr. Romero has an excellent reputation."

"Mr. Romero concluded that Chloe Carson's DNA was on the knife?"

"Yes. He made that determination based upon a sample of her blood."

"We provided you with a DNA sample from our client, César Ochoa, didn't we?"

"Yes."

"Did you find Mr. Ochoa's DNA on the knife?"

"I did. The DNA came from his fingerprint."

"Did the report indicate that there was DNA from anyone other than my client and the decedent on this knife?"

Carla nodded. "Yes, it did. At least one other person handled the knife."

"Were you able to identify that person?"

"No, Ms. Fernandez."

"Dr. Jimenez, did the report contain any DNA samples from my client's hands, clothing, automobile, or apartment?"

"No."

Rolanda arched an eyebrow. "Inspector Wong did not identify traces of the decedent's DNA on my client's hands, clothing, and automobile, or at his apartment?"

"Correct."

"You are aware that the Medical Examiner determined that Ms. Carson died of a stab wound to her neck that would have resulted in blood spattering onto my client's hands and clothing?"

"Yes."

"Would you therefore have expected to see evidence of Ms. Carson's DNA?"

"Yes."

"But the police and the DA provided no such DNA evidence, did they?"

"Objection. Asked and answered."

"Sustained."

"Did it strike you as unusual that the decedent's blood was not found on my client's hands, clothing, car, or apartment?"

"Objection," O'Neal said. "Asked and answered."

"Sustained."

It was as far as Rolanda could go. "No further questions."

"Cross-exam, Ms. O'Neal?"

"No, Your Honor."

"Please call your next witness, Ms. Fernandez."

She looked my way for an instant as if to say, "It's time to start pointing fingers." "The defense calls Mr. David Callaghan."

49

"THEY HAD A CONVERSATION"

Rolanda spoke from the lectern. "I remind you that you're still under oath."

Callaghan's Adam's apple bobbed. "Yes, Ms. Fenandez."

"May we approach the witness, Your Honor?"

"You may."

Rolanda and I had decided that she should handle the direct exams of the individuals who were at For Gentlemen Only on the night that Chloe Carson died. She has a deft touch—until she goes in for the kill. Ideally, somebody would admit that they were involved with Carson's death. More realistically, we were hoping that somebody would point a finger at someone other than César. At the very least, we might obtain some new information. All of the scenarios were long shots, but our only other option was to fold up our tent and take our chances at trial.

Rolanda moved in front of the box and blocked Callaghan's view of the prosecution table. "You testified earlier that on the night that Chloe Carson died, you believe that she had a brief disagreement with my client, didn't you?"

"Yes."

"She also had an argument with at least one other person at the club, didn't she?"

"I don't know."

"You were there, right?"

"Right."

"And you were in charge?"

"Yes."

"So you must have kept your eyes on everything, didn't you?"

"I tried."

"Ms. Carson had a heated argument with your sound guy, Jerry Henderson, didn't she?"

"Chloe was upset that the sound didn't work properly during her performance."

"There was more to it, wasn't there?"

"I don't know what you're talking about."

"I think you do. Ms. Carson dated Mr. Henderson for a few months before her death, didn't she?"

"I just found out about it."

"And she broke up with him, didn't she?"

"I don't know."

"And it was acrimonious. And he was very upset about it, wasn't he?"

"I don't know that, either."

"I think you do."

"Objection. There wasn't a question."

"Withdrawn. You did a background check on Mr. Henderson, didn't you?"

"We do background checks on everybody."

"He has a criminal record, doesn't he?"

"I believe so."

"Including at least one arrest for assault?"

"I don't recall."

"Mr. Henderson also has a history of domestic violence, doesn't he?"

"I heard rumors."

"It's more than rumors, Mr. Callaghan. Mr. Henderson was subject to at least one restraining order relating to one of his ex-girlfriends, wasn't he?"

"Objection. Foundation."

"Overruled."

"I heard rumors," he repeated.

"Chloe Carson was afraid of him, wasn't she?"

"I don't know."

And you don't want your corporate masters to find out that your sound guy was harassing one of your dancers, and you didn't do anything about it.

Rolanda's voice filled with exasperation. "Did you report this information to the police?"

"No."

"Why not?"

"I didn't know about it."

She got right into his face. "What other information did you withhold from the police?"

"Nothing."

"Did you consider the possibility that Mr. Henderson killed Ms. Carson?"

"I had no reason to believe that he did."

"He has a criminal record, including an assault charge. He was very upset about their breakup. He had a history of abuse and violence. He threatened her on the night that she died."

"Objection. Ms. Fernandez is testifying. And she is asking the witness to speculate. And she hasn't provided a shred of evidence for any of these unfounded accusations."

Yes, she is. And no, she hasn't.

"That's because the police ignored any potential evidence," Rolanda snapped.

Judge McDaniel held up a hand. "You've made your point, Ms. Fernandez. The objection is sustained."

Rolanda turned back to Callaghan. "You also got into an argument with Ms. Carson that night, didn't you?"

"I reprimanded her for showing up late."

"It was more than that, wasn't it?"

"No."

"Given your history with Ms. Carson, how can we rule out the possibility that you were involved in her death?"

"Objection. Foundation. Ms. Fernandez and Mr. Daley haven't presented any evidence to back up this claim."

No, we haven't.

"Sustained."

"No further questions."

"Cross-exam, Ms. O'Neal?"
"No, Your Honor."
"Please call your next witness, Ms. Fernandez."
"The defense calls Ms. Sheema Smith."

50
"SHE WAS AFRAID OF HIM"

"Did you know Chloe Carson pretty well?" Rolanda asked.

Sheema's voice was calm. "We were co-workers. We didn't socialize."

"You also know my client?"

"Of course."

"Did he ever give you any trouble?"

"No. He was always professional."

The gallery was almost empty at two-twenty-five on Wednesday. Chloe Carson's mother was fanning herself with the sports section of the *Chronicle*.

Rolanda moved in front of the box. "Did you ever see my client act disrespectfully toward Ms. Carson?"

"No."

"Did you ever see him initiate any physical contact with her?"

"No."

"You also worked with a man named Jerry Henderson, didn't you?"

"Yes. He worked the soundboard from time to time."

"He knew Ms. Carson, didn't he?"

"Yes."

"In fact, they had a relationship for a short time, didn't they?"

"Yes. It didn't work out."

"Could you be a bit more specific?"

Sheema considered her answer. "Chloe ended the relationship, but he kept asking her out."

"Would you describe him as persistent?"

"Chloe thought that he was stalking her."

"Did Ms. Carson ever tell you that Mr. Henderson was physical with her?"

"Objection," O'Neal said. "Hearsay."

Rolanda feigned irritation. "Ms. Smith would have been present for such a conversation and can describe its contents. It is therefore an exception to the hearsay rule."

"Overruled."

Sheema exhaled. "Chloe told me that Jerry hit her in the shoulder once and threatened her a couple of times after they broke up."

"Did she report this to her employer, Mr. Callaghan?"

"She was afraid that she would be fired. She didn't report it to the police, either."

"What did Ms. Carson do?"

"She tried to avoid him."

"Are you aware that Mr. Henderson has a criminal record? And that he was subject to at least one restraining order requested by a former girlfriend who feared for her physical safety?"

"Objection. Calls for information outside the scope of Ms. Smith's knowledge."

"Sustained."

Rolanda lowered her voice. "She was afraid of him, wasn't she?"

"Objection. Speculation."

"Overruled."

Sheema nodded. "Yes."

Rolanda moved back to the lectern. "Mr. Henderson was at the club on the night of Friday, May fifth, wasn't he?"

"Yes."

"He and Ms. Carson got into an argument after she finished performing, didn't they?"

"Yes. The sound went out a couple of times. Chloe was upset about it."

"She swore at him, didn't she?"

"Yes. And he swore at her."

"Do you recall exactly what he said?"

Smith turned to the judge. "Am I allowed to use profanity in court?"

"Perhaps you could paraphrase."

"He called her a word that rhymes with 'runt.'"

Rolanda stood in silence for a moment. "How did Ms. Carson react?"

"She gave Jerry the finger and headed to the dressing room. She left a short time later."

"And Mr. Henderson?"

"He left a few minutes after she did."

"They both left through the back door that leads to the alley?"

"Yes."

"Ms. Smith, based on what you saw and heard, do you believe that it's possible that Mr. Henderson stabbed Chloe Carson in the alley?"

"Objection. Calls for speculation."

"Sustained."

"No further questions, Your Honor."

"Cross-exam?"

"Just one question, Your Honor." O'Neal spoke from her seat. "Ms. Smith, you have no knowledge or evidence that Mr. Henderson attacked Ms. Carson in the alley, do you?"

"No, Ms. O'Neal."

"No further questions."

"Redirect, Ms. Fernandez?"

"No, Your Honor. The defense calls Ms. Kelly Ryan."

"Are you okay?" Rolanda asked.

Kelly Ryan adjusted the collar of her plain white blouse. "I'm sorry that I didn't get here a little earlier. My car was stolen last night."

Rolanda stood a respectful distance from her. "I'm sorry to hear that."

"Thank you." Her delicate features contorted into a pained expression. "It isn't the first time, Ms. Fernandez. That's how we roll nowadays here in San Francisco."

Sad, but a reality of life.

"What is your occupation?" Rolanda asked.

"I am a dancer at For Gentlemen Only. I have worked there for about six months."

"You knew Chloe Carson?"

"Yes. We started working at the club around the same time."

"You knew that she had dated a man named Jerry Henderson?"

"Yes."

"And she broke up with him?"

"Yes."

"Is it fair to say that their breakup was acrimonious?"

"Yes. Chloe was very upset about it. She tried to stay away from him."

"Did she tell you why?"

"She was afraid of him."

Rolanda lowered her voice. "Are you afraid of him, too?"

Ryan waited a long beat. "Maybe a little."

"No further questions."

O'Neal declined cross-exam.

The judge looked at the clock above the door. "I'm going to take a short recess, Ms. Fernandez. Please be prepared to call your next witness when we return."

"Yes, Your Honor." Rolanda returned to the defense table and spoke in a whisper. "Should we call Henderson next?"

I considered our options. "Let's see if we can get somebody to implicate him first. We'll put him on at the end and see if he'll crack."

I picked up my phone and punched in Pete's number.

He answered on the first ring. "What do you need, Mick?"

"Is Henderson well enough to testify tomorrow morning?"

"I think so. He had a couple of visitors today."

"Serve him with the subpoena and make sure that he shows up tomorrow."

"Will do."
"You got anything else?"
"I'll let you know, Mick."

51
"THE KIND YOU CAN'T BUY AT CVS"

Clive Williams gulped a cup of water and pulled up the collar of the gray sport jacket that he had chosen from the donated clothing closet at the PD's Office. "I used to see Chloe after she left work at For Gentlemen Only. She never said much, but she was nice enough to me."

Judge McDaniel's sweltering courtroom was quiet at two-forty-five as we started what was likely to be the final session of the day. A confident O'Neal sat at the prosecution table, her expression alternating between bemused and bored. Judge McDaniel's demeanor never changed, but I could see hints of impatience in her eyes.

Rolanda moved to the front of the box. "Do you live on the street, Mr. Williams?"

"Most of the time. If the weather is bad, I try to find a spot in a shelter."

"How long have you been living on the street?"

"Since I lost my last job about ten years ago."

"Did Ms. Carson ever give you any trouble?"

"No. Sometimes she gave me leftovers."

"You knew some of the others who worked at the club, didn't you?"

"A few."

Rolanda pointed at César. "You knew Mr. Ochoa?"

"Yes."

"Did he ever give you any trouble?"

"No." A shrug. "He told me to stay away from the manager."

"Dave Callaghan?"

"Yes."

"Why?"

"César told me that Callaghan thought that I bothered the customers."

"Did you?"

"No."

"Did you ever see Mr. Callaghan engage with Ms. Carson?"

"Just once." Clive waited a beat. "A few weeks ago, he followed her outside and yelled at her for being late. He told her that if she did it again, he would fire her. She yelled right back at him. He got angry and shoved her hard enough that she lost her balance. She told him that if he ever laid hands on her again, she'd rip his, uh, genitals off."

We get the picture.

Rolanda kept her voice even. "Did you ever observe Ms. Carson having words with anybody else who worked at the club?"

"She got into a big argument with the backup sound guy."

"Jerry Henderson?"

"I don't know his name. He's a big guy with a beard."

"Do you know what it was about?"

"I think she had just broken up with him. He wasn't happy about it."

"Did he threaten her?"

"Yes. He called her a bitch."

"Did it appear to you that she was scared of him?"

"Objection. Calls for speculation."

"Just asking for an observation," Rolanda said.

"Overruled."

"Maybe," Clive said.

We were hoping for a little more.

"Do you know Mr. Henderson?" Rolanda asked.

"I've met him."

"Good guy?"

"Bad guy." Clive was starting to enjoy the attention. "A couple of times, he asked me to watch his car when he parked behind the club. He promised to pay me twenty bucks at the end of the night, but he never did."

"He stiffed you?"

"He gave me food instead of money. Once he gave me drugs."

"What kind?"

"The kind that you can't buy at CVS."

Got it.

"Do you think that Mr. Henderson killed Ms. Carson?"

"Objection," O'Neal said. "Calls for speculation."

"Sustained."

It was the right call.

Rolanda didn't fluster. "Based upon your personal experiences with Mr. Henderson and your knowledge of his relationship with Ms. Carson, do you believe that he was the sort of person who would have killed Ms. Carson?"

"Objection," O'Neal said. "Calls for speculation. And there isn't a shred of evidence for this line of questioning. Ms. Fernandez is simply throwing spaghetti at the wall to see if anything sticks."

Yes, she is.

"Overruled," the judge said. "Please answer the question, Mr. Williams."

Clive sat up taller. "Yes, Ms. Fernandez. I believe that Mr. Henderson was absolutely the kind of person who would have killed Chloe."

"No further questions."

"Cross-exam, Ms. O'Neal?"

"Just one question, Your Honor. Mr. Williams, do you have even a shred of evidence that Mr. Henderson was involved in Ms. Carson's death?"

Clive's triumphant expression disappeared. "No."

"No further questions."

"Please call your next witness, Ms. Fernandez."

"The defense calls Tyler Benson."

Time to throw more spaghetti.

52

"IT WAS A PRIVATE BUSINESS ARRANGEMENT"

A supremely confident Tyler Benson sat in the box, shoulders back, smug grin on his face. "I am a successful technology entrepreneur and investor."

Rolanda feigned admiration. "You've been called a Silicon Valley visionary."

Benson's smile broadened. "Thank you, Ms. Fernandez."

Rolanda and I had gone back and forth as to which one of us should question Benson. We decided that it would play better in front of a smart judge like Betsy McDaniel if Rolanda worked her magic on the perpetually arrogant tech bro.

She stood directly in front of him. "The *Chronicle* says you're worth more than two billion dollars."

"More or less."

"Impressive. Are you married?"

"Divorced."

"More than once?"

O'Neal spoke from her seat. "Objection. Relevance."

"Sustained."

Rolanda inched closer to the box. "You patronize a club called For Gentlemen Only?"

"From time to time."

"You like to watch naked women dance?"

"Sometimes."

Rolanda's tone turned sarcastic. "Would you like to watch me dance, Mr. Benson?"

"Objection."

"Withdrawn. You were at the club on the night of Friday, May fifth?"

"I was."

"You saw Chloe Carson?"

"She was dancing."

"What time did you arrive?"

"Shortly after midnight."

"What time did you leave?"

"Shortly after one AM."

"That would have been around the same time that Ms. Carson left the club, right?"

"I wouldn't know."

"You left through the back door?"

"Yes."

"How did you get home?"

"I walked."

"Did you speak to Ms. Carson while you were at the club that night?"

"I may have said hello."

"You got into an argument with her, didn't you?"

"I did not."

"We have witnesses, Mr. Benson." It was a bluff.

His voice became more emphatic. "I did not."

Rolanda feigned disbelief. "As a regular, you knew some of the other employees?"

"I recognized a few faces."

"Including a man named Jerry Henderson who ran the sound system on occasion?"

"I knew his name was Jerry."

"You knew that Ms. Carson had a relationship with Mr. Henderson, didn't you?"

"I was not aware of that."

"That relationship ended badly, didn't it?"

"I'm not familiar with the circumstances."

"You saw Mr. Henderson and Ms. Carson get into an argument that night, didn't you?"

"I saw them have a conversation. I don't know what it was about."

"Is it fair to say that Ms. Carson appeared upset?"

"Yes. So was Mr. Henderson."

"Are you aware that Mr. Henderson had a history of abusing women?"

"I am not."

"Are you aware that he threatened Ms. Carson?"

"No."

"Did Mr. Henderson strike you as the kind of guy who would have become physically abusive when he was upset?"

"Objection. Speculation."

"Overruled."

"I don't know," Benson said.

Rolanda lowered her voice. "Mr. Benson, you also had a personal relationship with Ms. Carson, didn't you?"

"Briefly."

"You paid her for her services, didn't you?"

"Objection. Relevance."

"It's absolutely relevant," Rolanda snapped.

O'Neal's voice filled with sarcasm. "You're that desperate?"

"It's important information," Rolanda insisted.

Judge McDaniel shook her head. "I'm going to allow the witness to answer."

Benson hesitated. "It was a private business arrangement between consenting adults."

"In other words," Rolanda said, "you paid her for a lap dance."

"She offered. I accepted."

"You paid her for other services outside the club, didn't you?"

"No."

"How many times did you enter into such arrangements?"

O'Neal got to her feet and glared at Rolanda. "Objection. Relevance."

"Sustained." Judge McDaniel was running out of patience. "Move on, Ms. Fernandez."

Rolanda lowered her voice. "Mr. Benson, your arrangement with Ms. Carson ended rather abruptly, didn't it?"

"I decided that I didn't want to procure her services again."

"In fact, *she* made that decision, didn't she?"
"It was my decision."
"You must have been very upset."
"It was unfortunate."
"That's because she rejected you, right?"
"Objection."
"Sustained."
"And on Friday, May fifth, you solicited her again, didn't you? And she rejected you again, didn't she?"
"No."
"So you followed her outside and accosted her, didn't you?"
"No."
"And when she rebuffed your advances again, you stabbed her with a knife that you grabbed from a table by the back door, didn't you?"
"No."

O'Neal was on her feet. "Move to strike, Your Honor. There isn't a shred of evidence in support of Ms. Fernandez's wild and irresponsible accusations."

True.

"Sustained."
"No further questions, Your Honor."
"Please call your next witness, Ms. Fernandez."
"The defense calls Mr. John Foreman."

53

"WE WERE BOTH ADULTS"

Unlike the insufferable Benson, Foreman embodied the role of avuncular grandfather as he took his place on the stand. "I am the managing partner at the international law firm of Story, Short, and Thompson in Embarcadero Center. I have worked there for thirty-eight years."

As Rolanda approached the box, I glanced at the prosecution table where O'Neal couldn't hide a confident half-grin.

Rolanda's voice was businesslike. "Were you at For Gentlemen Only on Friday, May fifth, of this year?"

Foreman pretended to remove an imaginary piece of lint from his ten-thousand-dollar Brioni suit. "Yes."

"Do you go there often?"

"From time to time."

"Is your wife aware that you frequent the club?"

"Yes."

"You knew a dancer at the club named Chloe Carson?"

"I've seen her dance."

"Did you talk to her on May fifth?"

"Briefly. I told her that I enjoyed her performance." Grandpa John disappeared and was replaced by Big-Firm John. "Let's cut to the chase, Ms. Fernandez. I didn't kill Ms. Carson. I don't know who killed Ms. Carson. And I don't have any evidence pertaining to the circumstances surrounding her death."

And that's that.

He started to stand, but Rolanda stopped him with an upraised hand. "Did you notice if she had words with anybody at the club?"

"She seemed annoyed with the sound guy."

"Jerry Henderson?"

"I don't know his name."

"Do you know what they were arguing about?"

"I couldn't hear them."

"Did you know that Ms. Carson and Mr. Henderson had dated, and that they had an acrimonious breakup?"

"I did not."

"Did you know that Mr. Henderson has a criminal record and was subject to at least one restraining order for sexual abuse?"

"No."

"You saw Ms. Carson outside the club on several occasions, didn't you?"

"Objection. Relevance."

"Overruled."

Foreman exhaled. "We were both adults."

"Your relationship ended badly, didn't it?"

"We didn't have a relationship."

"Did your wife know about this relationship?"

"Objection. Relevance."

Rolanda fired back. "The circumstances surrounding Mr. Foreman's relationship with the decedent are relevant."

O'Neal wasn't backing down. "Mr. Foreman just testified that he did not have a relationship with Ms. Carson. Ms. Fernandez is simply trying to muddy the waters without providing a shred of evidence."

Yes, she is.

O'Neal wasn't finished. "Furthermore, her strategy—if you can even call it that—is to accuse everybody at the club that night of killing Chloe Carson."

That, too.

Judge McDaniel's patience was exhausted. "The objection is sustained. Anything more for this witness, Ms. Fernandez?"

"No, Your Honor."

O'Neal declined cross-exam.

"Please call your next witness, Ms. Fernandez."

"The defense calls Mr. Francis X. Quinn."

Quinn sat in the box, arms folded over his ample gut, an off-the-rack suit hanging from his shoulders. "I'm a union organizer."

I was standing a couple of feet in front of him. Rolanda and I decided to let Judge McDaniel hear a fresh voice. Moreover, this was likely to get chippy.

"You're also running for supervisor?"

"Thinking about it."

My eyes locked onto his. "You were at For Gentlemen Only on the night of Friday, May fifth of this year?"

"I was."

"You go there often?"

He gulped down some water. "Occasionally."

"You think that's good for your political ambitions?"

"Strictly business. I was working with some of the dancers to organize a union."

"One of those dancers was a woman named Chloe Carson?"

"Yes."

"You met her at the club?"

"Yes."

"And you saw her outside the club?"

"Once."

"You went out on a date?"

"We talked business."

"You paid her for sex, didn't you?"

"No."

Okay. "You saw her in the early morning of Saturday, May sixth?"

"I watched her dance."

"You talked to her?"

"I said a quick hello. I told her that I wanted to follow up on our discussion about unionizing."

"I understand that she wasn't receptive to the idea."

"She was warming up to it."

"In fact, you had some harsh words with Ms. Carson that night, didn't you? Not only did she refuse to help you with unionization efforts, but she also rejected your advances, didn't she?"

"No."

"We have witnesses, Mr. Quinn." *No, we don't.*

"Objection," O'Neal said. "There wasn't a question there."

"Withdrawn." I got into his face. "You asked her out on a date that night, and she rejected you, didn't she?"

"No."

"Because she didn't like you, right?"

"I don't know why."

"So you *did* ask her out on a date?"

"No."

"You just said you did."

"I misspoke."

"Or you lied."

"I-I was mistaken."

"Which is it? Did you or didn't you ask her out?"

"I didn't." He gulped water. "I mean I asked her out, but she said no."

"So you lied?"

"Objection. Asked and answered."

"Sustained."

I moved a step closer to the box. "You left through the back door right after Ms. Carson, didn't you?"

"I don't know when she left."

"You saw her in the alley, didn't you?"

"No."

"And you got into an argument with her because she rejected you, didn't you?"

"No."

"You lost your temper, and you stabbed her, didn't you?"

"Absolutely not." Quinn was sweating. "Look, Mr. Daley, I admit that I asked Chloe out, but I didn't follow her outside, and I sure as hell didn't kill her."

"A moment ago, you admitted that you lied, and now you're lying again."

"No, I'm not."

O'Neal got to her feet. "I object to this line of questioning. Mr. Daley has presented no evidence that Mr. Quinn had anything to do with Ms. Carson's death."

Technically that's true. "He asked her out on a date, and she rejected him, after which he became irate."

O'Neal fired back. "You have no evidence."

"He just admitted it."

"No, he didn't."

"Yes, he did."

Judge McDaniel held up her hands in the form of the letter "T." "Time out. The objection is sustained. Anything else for this witness, Mr. Daley?"

"Just a couple more questions, Your Honor." *Let's see if he'll point a finger at somebody else.* "Mr. Quinn, did you see Ms. Carson arguing with anybody that night?"

He paused to consider his answer. "She got into it with the sound guy. She also had some sharp words for the manager. She had a blowup with a tech guy named Tyler Benson. And she had a very heated discussion with Jason Strong."

I feigned surprise. "The Giants' leftfielder?"

"Yes." Quinn's eyes were wild. "You must have seen the video on YouTube. He was at the club that night. It wasn't the first time that I saw him."

Maybe some of the spaghetti is sticking to the wall. "No further questions, Your Honor."

"Cross-exam, Ms. O'Neal?"

"No, Your Honor."

"Please call your next witness, Mr. Daley."

"The defense calls Jason Strong."

54

"I PLAY FOR THE GIANTS"

In a double-breasted pinstriped suit and a flashy Zenga necktie, Jason Strong carried himself with the supreme confidence of an All-Star. "I play for the Giants."

I spoke to him from the lectern. "I hope the rehab on your shoulder is going well so that you'll be back in the lineup soon."

"Thank you, Mr. Daley." He flashed a charismatic smile. "We're getting close."

Judge McDaniel's courtroom was full again at three-fifty-five on Wednesday afternoon. Word had spread that the Giants slugger would be taking the stand. Three rows were filled with members of the media. Strong's well-appointed lawyer sat between Strong's agent and the Giants GM. The row behind them was filled with middle-aged men wearing expensive suits—I presumed that they were also lawyers, although I wasn't sure who they were representing.

Strong's lawyer agreed to let his client testify subject to the threat that if I suggested Strong was involved in Chloe Carson's death, he would file a defamation suit by the close of business. It was heavy-handed, and he had little chance of prevailing, but I had no doubt that he would do it just for show. One of the courthouse regulars had tossed Strong a baseball as he was entering court and asked for an autograph. The PR-savvy slugger obliged.

I opted to start in a non-combative tone. "Thank you for testifying today."

"You're welcome. I have nothing to hide."

We'll see. "You were at For Gentlemen Only on the evening of Friday, May fifth?"

Strong glanced at his lawyer, who nodded. "Yes."

"You go there often?"

"On occasion. It helps me relax."

"You like watching the dancers?"

"A lot of people do."

"Does your wife know that you go to For Gentlemen Only on occasion?"

"She does now."

I'll bet. "You knew a dancer named Chloe Carson?"

"I've watched her dance."

"And you also met her outside the club?"

"Once." Another glance at the lawyer. "We had dinner."

"Did that date involve sex?"

"Objection. Relevance."

"Sustained."

"Did you ask her out again in the early morning of Saturday, May sixth?"

"No."

"But you talked to her."

"I said hello."

"You argued with her because she rejected your advances, right?"

"No."

"And you followed her outside to continue that argument, didn't you?"

"No." His casual smirk finally disappeared. "Chloe was a terrific dancer and a nice person. I didn't have anything to do with her death. I don't know who killed her. I don't have any information about who killed her. I came here today because I have nothing to hide and to tell the truth. You now know everything that I do."

He looked over at his lawyer, who gave him a subtle nod as if to say, "Nice work."

Judge McDaniel spoke up. "Anything more for this witness, Mr. Daley?"

"Just a couple more questions, Your Honor." I turned back to Strong. "Did Ms. Carson ever mention a man named Jerry Henderson?"

"Yes. He's the sound guy at the club."

"Did she explain that she and Mr. Henderson had been in a relationship earlier this year?"

"Yes."

"Did she tell you that the relationship ended badly?"

"She did." He cleared his throat. "She also told me that she was uncomfortable being around him."

"You saw Mr. Henderson at the club that night, didn't you?"

"Yes."

"Did he and Ms. Carson talk to each other?"

"Briefly. Chloe was unhappy with the way that Henderson managed the sound during her performance."

"Were angry words exchanged?"

"It looked that way to me."

"In fact, you got into a physical altercation with him, didn't you?"

"I told him to leave Chloe alone."

"You hit him, didn't you?"

"No. He grabbed her arm, so I pulled him away from her. I was trying to protect her."

"That altercation appeared in a video that made its way onto social media, didn't it?"

"Yes."

"No further questions."

"Cross-exam?"

"No, Your Honor."

Judge McDaniel looked at the clock. "I'm going to adjourn for the day. Will you be calling any additional witnesses in the morning, Mr. Daley?"

"Just one, Your Honor. Jerry Henderson."

Rolanda sat in my office an hour later, expression grim. "That didn't go well."

"We'll go after Henderson in the morning."

"Unless we can get him to confess on the stand, it won't be enough."

"We gave the judge a few other plausible options."

"Not enough to get the charges dropped at a prelim."

Just like Rosie: the unyielding voice of reality. "Then we'll deal with it at trial."

"César was unhappy when we left court."

"Comes with the territory. We're good lawyers, but we can't always summon a miracle on short notice."

Her expression softened. "Were you able to summon miracles when you were a priest?"

"No."

"I thought you guys had a private pipeline."

"God is busy."

She chuckled. "Now what?"

"We stick to the plan. We'll call Henderson in the morning and try to foist the blame onto him."

"You think he's going to confess?"

I grinned. "You're a good lawyer, Rolanda."

"And if it turns out that I'm not that good?"

"We'll call Inspector Wong and accuse her of rushing to judgment."

"That strategy might get us to reasonable doubt at trial, but it's going to be a heavy lift at a prelim."

"At the moment, it's all that we have."

"Have you heard from Pete?"

"He served a subpoena on Henderson earlier this afternoon. He will make sure that he shows up in court in the morning."

Terrence "The Terminator" knocked on the open door, expression somber. "Pete's been trying to reach you."

Uh-oh. "My phone ran out of battery."

He handed me his phone. "He couldn't find you, so he called me."

I held the phone to my ear. "Did you serve the subpoena on Henderson?"

"Yes."

"Can you give him a ride to court in time to testify at ten o'clock tomorrow morning?"

He cleared his throat. "No."

"Does he still have Covid?"

"No, Mick. He's dead."

55

"I MISS EDSEL"

Sergeant Tim Volpe took a sip of scalding tea from a white cup. "I miss Edsel."

Pete took a bite of his beef "jook," a rice porridge where the grains melted into a velvety pudding. "So do I."

The aroma of wonton soup and stir-fried noodles wafted through Sam Wo, a Chinatown institution that opened in 1912 on Washington Street. It closed in 2012, when its owner was unable to bring the building up to fire code. In 2015, he reopened on Clay Street. The new place has fresh paint, and the walls are studded with signs and photos from the original, including the one reading, "No Booze, No Jive, No Coffee, No Milk, No Soft Drinks, No Fortune Cookies." Credit cards are now accepted, and the staff actually thanks you for visiting.

"You liked abuse?" I asked.

"It was all an act," Pete said. "Edsel was a teddy bear if you got to know him."

The attraction at Sam Wo was never the food, the décor, the cheap prices, or the late-night hours. We flocked here to enjoy gratuitous abuse from Edsel Ford Fung, whom Herb Caen, the legendary *Chronicle* columnist, anointed as "the rudest waiter in the world." Edsel's real name was Edsel Fung. He added his distinctive middle name to enhance his notoriety. He was further immortalized in Armistead Maupin's *Tales of the City*, the serialized soap opera in the *Chronicle* that became the basis for fifteen novels, two TV series, and a musical. At six-feet tall and an imposing two hundred-plus pounds, Edsel sported a military crew cut, a perennially-stained white apron, and an omnipresent scowl. When it came to insults, he made Seinfeld's Soup Nazi sound like Mother Teresa.

If you climbed the rickety steps to the dining rooms in the old restaurant, Edsel would greet you with a terse "Sit down and shut up." He would cuss out customers, spill soup on their laps, and make them bus their own tables. He steadfastly refused to provide forks to those who weren't adept at using chopsticks. If you looked at the menu for more than a few seconds, he would tell you that "This is a restaurant, not a library." After Edsel unilaterally decided when you were finished eating, he would toss the check on your table and say, "Small check, big tip." Sadly, he passed away in 1984 at the age of fifty-six. There is a bistro in the Giants' ballpark bearing his name where the service is more professional, but not nearly as colorful.

Pete looked at Volpe. "You said you have information about Jerry Henderson."

"You didn't hear this from me."

"Understood."

"Looks like he got some coke laced with fentanyl. Our people think he was testing some new product. He was running a substantial pharmaceutical operation out of his apartment."

"Any chance he was selling to Chloe Carson?"

"I don't know. Our people are trying to crack his cell phone and laptop, but it will take a while. They don't have the passwords."

"Any chance you found any blood in his apartment?"

"Not as far as I know."

I put my credit card on top of the check. "Thanks for the information, Tim."

Pete looked up from his phone. "It was nice of Tim to give us the info about Henderson."

"Yes, it was," I said.

We were standing on the sidewalk in front of Sam Wo's at ten-fifteen on Wednesday night. The street was quiet, except for a few tourists making their way to the ugly Hilton that replaced the old Hall of Justice in the sixties. The summer fog had crept in, and my eyes watered from a cool wind.

Pete's voice turned hopeful. "You can still try to blame Henderson for Carson's death."

True. "We don't have any evidence of a direct connection, Pete."

"You're a good lawyer, Mick. You'll come up with something."

"I was hoping that *you* would come up with something."

We walked across the street to the underground garage beneath Portsmouth Square, the historical center of Chinatown. The elevator wasn't working, so we walked down the stairs that reeked of urine. I opened the heavy door to the second level of the garage and saw my Prius. The driver's-side door was open, and somebody had rifled through my car.

Pete shook his head. "Did they take anything?"

"I never leave anything in my car."

San Francisco has almost a hundred car break-ins every day. The perpetrators are found in fewer than one percent of the cases.

Pete chuckled. "You got lucky, Mick. They didn't even break a window."

"It's always preferable to deal with professional car thieves." I pointed at his beat-up Crown Vic. "Looks like your car is unscathed."

"It's better to drive something downscale in the City. You going home?"

"I need to stop at the office for a few minutes. You?"

"I'm going to see if I can find you some evidence proving that Jerry Henderson was involved in Chloe Carson's death." He gave me a knowing look. "Chloe Carson was stabbed to death."

"So?"

"Maybe I can find some of her blood."

56

"STICK TO THE PLAN"

"Now what?" Rolanda asked.

I was sitting at my desk at eleven-fifteen that same night. "We stick to the plan," I said.

"Our plan was to put Henderson on the stand and blame him for Chloe Carson's death."

"We move on to the next witness: Inspector Wong. We'll try to get her to suggest that Henderson did it."

"It won't be as effective as going after Henderson."

"Unfortunately, that's no longer an option."

Rolanda looked at Rosie, who was sitting in the other chair opposite my desk. "Have you ever had a witness die the night before he was supposed to testify?"

"Yes. I've also had a lot of witnesses who didn't show up."

"How did you deal with it?"

Rosie smiled. "We stuck to the plan. It doesn't change your narrative. You put Wong on the stand and argue that Henderson did it. Then you say that even if he didn't, there is insufficient evidence to charge César. Then you claim that the police didn't consider any other suspects and rushed to judgment. You don't need Henderson to make any of those arguments."

"Wong will be a stronger witness than Henderson."

"It means that the degree of difficulty goes up, but getting the charges dropped at a prelim is always a long shot. You make your points, muddy the waters as much as you can, and set it up to make an even stronger case for reasonable doubt at trial."

"Are you saying that we can't get the charges dropped at the prelim?"

Probably.

"Not necessarily," Rosie said. "I'm just saying that it will be more difficult. You know how it goes, Rolanda. You play your cards as well as you can and see where things fall. In this instance, the worst-case scenario is that you do it all over again in front of a jury in a few months."

"I'm not excited about our odds."

"The odds are never in our favor at a prelim. A lot can happen between now and trial. Who knows? Maybe Pete will find some exculpatory evidence. For now, you should stick to the plan."

57
"THE EVIDENCE IS OVERWHELMING"

It was sunny outside at ten-fifteen on Thursday morning, but nobody inside Judge McDaniel's courtroom was thinking about the weather. The gallery was packed for Inspector Wong's testimony. It's like watching a Warriors game on TV: everybody tunes in for the fourth quarter.

Rolanda stood in front of the box, eyes locked onto Wong's. The battle between one of our best young attorneys and one of SFPD's rising stars was fully engaged.

Rolanda worked without notes. "You interviewed Chloe Carson's family, friends, and associates as well as all of the customers and employees of For Gentlemen Only?"

"I did."

Rolanda pointed at César. "Including my client?"

"Yes."

"Was he cooperative?"

"For the most part."

"Did he attempt to run?"

"No."

"Did that strike you as odd?"

Wong responded with a puzzled expression. "I don't understand."

"How long have you been a homicide inspector?"

"Eight years."

"And how long were you a police officer before you became an inspector?"

"Ten years."

"How many homicides have you investigated over that time?"

"I don't recall."

"Ballpark estimate. A dozen? Two dozen? Fifty?"

"I'd guess about two dozen."

"You've interviewed hundreds of suspects, right?"

"Right."

"Did any of them try to run when you caught them?"

"Some."

"You would probably take that as a sign of their guilt, right?"

"Probably."

"If you had killed Chloe Carson, would you have cooperated with the police?"

"Objection. Speculation."

"Sustained."

"Do you really think César would have talked to you if he had killed Chloe Carson?"

"Objection. More speculation."

"Sustained. That's enough, Ms. Fernandez."

Rolanda hadn't taken her eyes off Wong. "César didn't ask for a lawyer, did he?"

"Not until we placed him under arrest."

"That didn't strike you as odd, either?"

"Not really."

"He was a former police officer. If he was guilty, don't you think he would have asked to speak to an attorney?"

"Objection. Speculation."

"Sustained."

Rolanda exhaled. "Inspector, you heard testimony from Dr. Irene Leung that Ms. Carson died of massive blood loss from a stab wound to her neck. Did you find any blood on my client's hands, clothing, furniture, or car?"

"We found Ms. Carson's blood on a knife in the Dumpster next to her body. Your client's fingerprints were on the knife. The evidence is overwhelming."

Rolanda turned to the judge. "Move to strike as nonresponsive."

"Please answer Ms. Fernandez's question, Inspector."

Wong rolled her eyes. "We did not find blood on the defendant's hands, clothing, furniture, or car."

Rolanda glared at Wong. "My client acknowledged that he had a burger that he cut with a steak knife similar to the knife found in the Dumpster. Did you consider the possibility that somebody else picked up the same knife and used it to stab Ms. Carson?"

"That seemed highly unlikely."

"Please answer the question, Inspector."

"Anything is possible, Ms. Fernandez."

"You rushed to judgment."

"The evidence is overwhelming."

"Especially when you didn't consider any other potential suspects."

"Objection. Argumentative."

"Sustained."

Rolanda lowered her voice. "There were dozens of employees and customers at the club that night, weren't there?"

"Yes."

"Several of whom had acrimonious histories with Ms. Carson, didn't they?"

"We found no evidence suggesting that anyone other than your client was involved in Ms. Carson's death."

"Which conclusion fits squarely within your narrative, doesn't it?"

"Objection. Argumentative."

"Sustained."

Rolanda walked back to the lectern, activated her laptop and the flat screen, and put up a slide reading "Other people at For Gentlemen Only With Relationships to Chloe Carson." It showed photos of Dave Callaghan, John Foreman, Tyler Benson, F.X. Quinn, Jason Strong, and, most prominently, Jerry Henderson.

Rolanda returned to the front of the box. "You interviewed all of these people?"

"Yes." Wong confirmed that they were all present at the club.

Rolanda pointed at Henderson's photo. "Mr. Henderson had a history of domestic violence, didn't he?"

"We are aware of at least one restraining order."

"He was also a drug dealer."

"He was never arrested or charged."

"He provided drugs to Ms. Carson, didn't he?"

"I don't know."

"Mr. Henderson died last night of a drug overdose, didn't he?"

"I don't know the cause of his death."

Rolanda moved right in front of Wong. "You're aware that Mr. Henderson and Ms. Carson were seeing each other for several months earlier this year?"

"Yes."

"And she broke up with him?"

"So we were told."

"And he was very unhappy about it."

"We have no evidence regarding his state of mind."

"Several witnesses reported that Mr. Henderson and Ms. Carson had heated words at the club shortly after she completed her set in the early morning of May sixth, didn't they?"

"Yes."

"Yet you didn't consider the possibility that Mr. Henderson might have killed her?"

"Yes, I did. The problem with your speculative theory, Ms. Fernandez, is that I found no evidence supporting it. We found your client's fingerprints on the knife, not Mr. Henderson's."

Rolanda pounded on Wong for a full ten minutes about the possibility that Henderson might have been involved in Chloe's death, but Wong held her ground. At trial, it might have gotten us a little closer to reasonable doubt. At a prelim, it wasn't likely to move the needle.

Rolanda shifted to the other names on the list. "Dave Callaghan was Ms. Carson's boss. He was angry because she showed up late. They argued that night, didn't they?"

"We have witnesses who said that they did."

"Yet you didn't consider him a suspect in Ms. Carson's death?"

"I found no evidence."

Rolanda pointed at the photo of Benson. "Ms. Carson rejected his advances, didn't she?"

"Mr. Benson denied it."

"It has been reported that his behavior can be volatile, right?"

"I have read media coverage to that effect, but I have no corroborating evidence."

"Tyler Benson is a blowhard with a terrible temper who is used to getting his way. In this case, he clearly didn't. Yet you didn't even consider the possibility that he got angry at Ms. Carson, lost his temper, followed her outside the club, and stabbed her?"

"We found no evidence, Ms. Fernandez."

"That's because you didn't look."

"Move to strike."

"Sustained."

Rolanda moved to the next name. "You also interviewed an attorney named John Foreman, who was at the club that night. Did he mention that Ms. Carson also rejected his advances?"

"He told us that he knew Ms. Carson."

"He's a power player at a big law firm who makes millions of dollars and is used to getting whatever he wants, isn't he? Surely, he would have been very unhappy about the fact that a young woman rejected him."

"Objection," O'Neal said. "This is pure fantasy."

"He was at the club that night," Rolanda said. "He admitted that he had a relationship with Ms. Carson."

"You have provided no evidence that Mr. Foreman or anybody else that you've mentioned had anything to do with Ms. Carson's death."

"We might have such evidence if Inspector Wong had done her job and engaged in a thorough investigation instead of jumping to the conclusion that my client is guilty."

"There was a knife in the Dumpster with Ms. Carson's blood and your client's fingerprints."

"Somebody else could have used the same knife to stab Ms. Carson."

Judge McDaniel had heard enough. "The objection is sustained. Move along, Ms. Fernandez."

Rolanda pointed at the next photo. "You also spoke to Mr. F.X. Quinn?"

Wong pushed out a melodramatic sigh. "Yes, Ms. Fernandez. Cutting to the chase, while it is true that Mr. Quinn knew Ms. Carson from his union organizing activities at the club and a couple of social encounters, we found no evidence that he was involved in her death."

"Come on, Inspector."

O'Neal's tone turned caustic. "Perhaps Ms. Fernandez should provide a list of everybody she intends to accuse of Ms. Carson's murder."

Rolanda pointed at the screen. "There it is."

"Your list isn't evidence."

No, it isn't.

Judge McDaniel stopped them with an upraised hand. "The objection is sustained, Ms. Fernandez. I understand what you're doing, and I know why you're doing it. Do you have any more questions for this witness?"

"No, Your Honor."

"Do you wish to call any additional witnesses?"

"One moment, Your Honor." Rolanda walked over to the defense table and spoke to me in a whisper. "Should we put César on the stand and have him issue a full denial?"

My heart was tempted, but my head prevailed. "Not at a prelim."

César's voice filled with desperation. "Please, Mike."

"It could hurt our case at trial. If we need you to testify, we'll do it then."

Rolanda turned around and addressed the judge. "We have no further witnesses, Your Honor. The defense rests."

Judge McDaniel looked at her watch. "I'm going to call a brief recess. We'll hear closing arguments after the break. For now, we're adjourned."

58

"WE'RE GOING TO TRIAL"

César's voice filled with resignation. "We're going to trial."

"The judge hasn't decided yet," I said.

"She will."

Rolanda's voice remained steady. "Let's not jump to conclusions, César. Judge McDaniel said that she wanted to think it over. If she had made up her mind already, she would have made the decision in court."

He wasn't convinced.

At two-forty-five on Thursday afternoon, the mood was somber in the consultation room in the Glamour Slammer. Rolanda and O'Neal had presented compelling closing arguments. Judge McDaniel listened intently to the carefully-crafted presentations by two excellent attorneys. At the end of the day, it seemed likely that O'Neal would prevail. If this was a college debate, Rolanda might have squeaked out a victory on points. Out here in the real world, the prosecutors always have the upper hand at a prelim.

"What happens next?" César asked.

"We wait for Judge McDaniel to rule," I said. *And we start preparing for trial.*

"If she rules against us, is there any chance that you can get me pretrial release?"

Unlikely. "We'll try."

His voice filled with resignation. "I didn't kill her, Mike."

"We're doing everything we can." As I recited the defense lawyer's standard line, I realized that it wasn't remotely satisfying for our client.

Rosie knocked on the open door of my office. "Did you send Rolanda home?"

I looked up from my laptop. "Yes."

"Good." She smiled. "Mama thinks you're working her too hard."

I returned her smile. "Rolanda will forgive us. Your mother won't."

Rosie and I were the only people in the PD's Office at ten-thirty on Thursday night. Rolanda had gone home to play with her kids. Dazzle was performing at the Gold Club. Terrence "The Terminator" had departed twenty minutes earlier.

I looked over at Rosie. "Seems like it's just the two of us again."

"Just like old times."

I took a moment to admire the magical smile that I first saw almost three decades earlier. "When we decided to come back to the PD's Office, we figured that there would be an army of young people who would work late so that we wouldn't have to."

"That's not how we're drawn, Mike."

"That's true, I suppose. You ever wonder what it might be like to have a job where we could work from nine to five?"

"Every day."

"That would make your mother happy."

"She talks a good game, but she's just like us. If she'd had the opportunity, she would have gone to law school and become the Public Defender. Then she would have run for mayor."

"You're probably right," I said.

"You know that I am."

I took a sip of Diet Dr Pepper. "How did it go tonight?"

She rolled her eyes. "You know how much I enjoy meeting with my campaign team."

"Whatever they're doing seems to be working. Are you getting tired of politics?"

"Comes with the job, Mike. Besides, I like the strategizing and the battle."

"I'd go out of my mind."

"That's why I'm the PD, and you're the head of the Felony Division." Her expression turned serious. "I heard that things didn't go so well in court today."

"Rolanda made an excellent closing argument. You know how hard it is to get the charges dropped at a prelim."

"I understand that Betsy hasn't ruled yet."

"She'll wait a day or two, but I think we're heading to trial. We had no solid rebuttal for the bloody knife with César's prints. We tried to foist the blame onto Jerry Henderson and some of the others who were at the club that night, but I don't think Betsy was buying it."

"You'll have another chance at trial, and you only have to convince one juror of reasonable doubt."

"Hopefully, Pete will find some new evidence between now and then."

"Hopefully." Her voice softened. "Why are you here so late?"

"I'm catching up on some other cases and paperwork."

"You're second-guessing yourself about César's prelim, aren't you?"

"Maybe a little."

"Let it go. You and Rolanda did everything that you could. You need a ride?"

"I have my car."

"I'll see you at home."

Twenty minutes later, Pete's name appeared on my phone.

"Are you still at the office?" he asked.

"Yes."

"Good. I need you to meet me in a parking lot on Boardman Place just north of Brannan."

It was a block from the PD's Office.

"What's going on?" I asked.

"I told you that I was going to look for some of Chloe Carson's blood."

"So?"

"I may have found some."

59

"I WANT TO FILE A POLICE REPORT"

Pete emerged from behind a Corolla. "Over here, Mick."

Boardman Place was quiet at eleven-ten PM. The alley ran one block south from the Hall of Justice to Brannan. Its two- and three-story buildings included Earthquake-era apartments, light manufacturing businesses, a bail bondsman, a Vietnamese sandwich shop, a Korean restaurant, and three law offices. There were also a couple of parking lots where some of the older buildings had been leveled. Eventually, they will be redeveloped for tech and AI firms as San Francisco's once seedy South of Market neighborhood continues to gentrify.

"This is Kelly Ryan's car," he said. "She reported it as stolen a couple of days ago."

"I'm sure she'll be happy to get it back." I eyed him. "How did you find it?"

"I got a tip from a reliable source."

"Does he have a name?"

"That's not important, Mick."

It might be, but you aren't going to tell me.

He opened the driver's-side door, which was unlocked. He took out his phone, turned on the flashlight, and illuminated the steering wheel. "There are traces of blood."

I couldn't tell. "How can you be sure?"

"I tested it with Luminol."

It's a chemical used by law enforcement to test for minute traces of blood.

"You happened to have Luminol with you when you happened to find this car?"

"Yes."

"And you tested the steering wheel?"

"Just a tiny spot."

"And you're sure there was blood?"

"One hundred percent."

"I take it you're prepared to tell the police that you tested this car for blood?"

"Absolutely, Mick." He added, with a grin, "I have nothing to hide."

"Do you know whose blood it is?"

"Afraid not. But if I were a betting man, I would guess it's Chloe Carson's. Ryan was one of the last people who saw her. She was coy when we asked her about their relationship. I had a feeling that there was more to the story."

"Do you have any evidence?"

He pointed at the car. "There's blood where it shouldn't be."

For all we knew, the blood could have been Ryan's. Maybe she cut herself. However, we had nothing to lose by reporting it.

Pete eyed me. "We'll want to report it to somebody with SFPD that we trust."

"You have somebody in mind?"

"Of course." He pulled out his phone and punched in Tim Volpe's number. "It's Pete Daley. I need you to meet me on Boardman Place between Bryant and Brannan. I want to file a police report. I may have located a stolen vehicle."

60
"IT WAS A MATCH"

Assistant District Attorney Catherine O'Neal sat behind her desk at two-forty the following afternoon, expression somber. "Thank you for coming in on short notice."

Rolanda and I were sitting in the uncomfortable chairs on the opposite side of her desk. "You're welcome," I said.

Inspector Wong sat in the chair next to O'Neal's desk, eyes looking down. The door was closed. An untouched Cobb salad in a plastic container sat on the corner of the desk.

O'Neal cleared her throat. "Late last night, Sergeant Tim Volpe informed Inspector Wong that a stolen car belonging to Ms. Kelly Ryan was recovered on Boardman Place. Given the fact that Ms. Ryan worked at the same club as Chloe Carson, Inspector Wong asked Lieutenant Kathleen Jacobsen to perform an analysis of the car. Lieutenant Jacobsen found no fingerprints other than those belonging to Ms. Ryan."

Uh-oh.

O'Neal's eyes darted over to Wong, then back to us. "In addition, Lieutenant Jacobsen found traces of blood on the steering wheel and the driver's seat. The blood type matched Ms. Ryan's. Coincidentally, it also matched the blood type of the decedent, Chloe Carson."

My heart beat faster, but I forced myself not to change my expression.

O'Neal turned to Wong, who picked up the story.

"I asked George Romero of the Criminalistics Lab to compare the blood found in the car to the DNA obtained from Chloe Carson's corpse. It was a match."

Bingo! "I trust that you asked Ms. Ryan to explain how traces of Ms. Carson's blood found their way into her car?"

"I did. She admitted that she picked up a knife from the table where your client was sitting shortly before she left For Gentlemen Only. She and Ms. Carson had argued earlier that night in a dispute over a client. Evidently, it wasn't the first time that Ms. Carson had attempted to steal a customer from Ms. Ryan. The argument continued in the alley and grew more intense. Ms. Ryan alleged that Ms. Carson lunged at her. She said that she stabbed Ms. Carson in self-defense."

"Do you believe her?"

"About the stabbing, yes. About the claim of self-defense, we'll see."

Her explanation doesn't matter for César's case. I turned back to O'Neal. "We will be filing a motion to dismiss the charges against César."

"That won't be necessary. Later this afternoon, I will be filing a motion to dismiss. I have already informed Judge McDaniel."

"Are you going to charge Kelly Ryan with murder?"

"I haven't decided. Inspector Wong has taken her into custody. Her arraignment will be tomorrow. She has asked to talk to a Public Defender. You'll want to notify your office that you will be getting a request to represent the new defendant in connection with Chloe Carson's death."

61

"WE GOT THE RIGHT RESULT"

César's voice was filled with relief. "I don't know how to thank you."

"You're welcome," I said.

He turned to Rolanda. "Thank you, too."

"Just doing our jobs, César," she said. "We got the right result."

At four-forty-five on Friday afternoon, a warm breeze was blowing through the Sheriff's Department parking lot between the Glamour Slammer and the Hall. Rolanda and I had just helped César collect his belongings. He was a free man.

He took a breath of the evening air, which smelled of a combination of exhaust from the nearby freeway and urine from the homeless encampment around the corner. "Where's Pete?"

"He's already working on another case. Something about a cheating husband."

"Please tell him that I said thanks. I'll buy him dinner at Dunleavy's next week."

"I'll let him know."

"How did he find Kelly's car? And how did he know that he would find Chloe's blood?"

"He's very resourceful." *I know better than to ask my brother too many questions.* "Can we give you a ride somewhere?"

"No, thanks. Selena is going to pick me up."

"That's nice. Maybe you and Selena could spend a little more time together."

"Maybe." He shrugged. "It's probably better for her to keep a little distance. Trouble seems to follow me everywhere."

That it does.

Rolanda spoke up again. "Are you going back to work at For Gentlemen Only?"

"I think it might be better if I look for a job in an industry that isn't so complicated."

"Probably a good idea," I said.

He glanced over my shoulder. "Selena is here. Thanks again for everything."

Rolanda and I watched as he walked through the parking lot to Selena's car.

"You think he'll be able to stay out of trouble?" I asked her.

"Doubtful." She gave me a sad smile. "Trouble seems to follow him everywhere."

Dazzle was sitting at her cubicle when Rolanda and I returned to the office at five-fifteen. Most of our colleagues had left for the weekend.

"You working at the club tonight?" I asked her.

"I'm taking the night off. It's been a busy week."

"Is Terrence around?"

"He went home early. I heard you got a good result for César."

"We did."

"I heard that they arrested Kelly Ryan."

"They did."

Rolanda looked at her and grinned. "You were right, Dazz. If you want to know what's going on at a club, you should talk to the dancers."

Dazzle pointed at the open door to Rosie's office. "The boss wants to see both of you about a new case."

It never ends.

We headed into Rosie's office, where she smiled broadly. "Congratulations on resolving César's case. You got a great result, and it will look nice on our statistics."

"Thanks," I said.

Her eyes twinkled. "Kelly Ryan has requested a Public Defender. Since you two are already familiar with the case and you now have some free time, I thought it would be good if you handled it. The arraignment is tomorrow morning."

"I'll take care of it," I said.

"You sure?" Rolanda asked.

"Yes. Go home and see your kids. I'm already in hot water with your grandmother."

"I'll talk to her."

Rosie grinned. "You aren't going to win that argument, Rolanda. I've tried."

"Nady will be back on Monday," I said. "I think I'll ask her to handle Ryan's case."

"It's really no trouble," Rolanda insisted.

I smiled. "I'm pretty sure that there will be some additional criminal activity here in San Francisco over the next few days. I'll hit you up for the next one."

62

"NOW WE'RE EVEN"

Joey flashed his best bartender's smile. "Last call, Mike. You need anything else?"

"We're good, Joe."

He pointed at Rosie's empty glass and Pete's coffee cup. "Either of you?"

"All set," Pete said.

"I'm fine," Rosie said.

We were the only people in the backroom of Dunleavy's at nine-forty-five on Saturday night. A few regulars were watching ESPN at the bar. A young couple stared at their phones and nursed their beers at a table near the window. The jukebox was playing a Sinatra song. The playlist at Dunleavy's hadn't changed much over the years.

Joey spoke to Rosie. "I heard your worthy opponent dropped out of the race."

"She finally exercised some good judgment."

"What made her change her mind?"

"We filed our latest financial disclosure. My war chest was twenty times bigger than hers. You know how it goes in politics. Donors lose interest if they think they're backing a loser."

"Is anybody else going to run against you?"

"It's a free country. If somebody can collect enough signatures and file the paperwork, there is still time to get their name on the ballot. Hopefully, the result will be the same."

"Well played."

"Thank you."

He turned to me. "I heard you got a good result for César."

"We did."

"This seems like a pretty low-key victory celebration."

"We try to take things in stride."

"No Rolanda tonight?"

"She's home with the kids."

"I heard that one of the other dancers at For Gentlemen Only confessed to killing Chloe Carson."

"It's true. She and Chloe got into an argument about a customer. She picked up a knife that César had used and followed Chloe outside. They argued again, and she stabbed Chloe."

"That's terrible. How did you figure it out?"

Rosie pointed at Pete. "Your cousin found some new evidence that the DA found very compelling."

"Well done. Is the PD's Office going to represent the murderer?"

"Alleged murderer," Rosie corrected him. "And yes, we are."

Joey looked my way. "You going to handle the case?"

"I made the appearance at the arraignment this morning. I'm going to let Nady take over on Monday."

Rosie changed the subject. "Everything good with Margarita?"

"Fine." Joey's smile broadened. "We're moving in together. Please thank your mother again for introducing us."

"I will." Rosie's eyes sparkled. "Mama will be pleased."

Joey headed back to the bar to count up the day's receipts.

"He looks happy," Rosie said.

"He and Margarita make a nice couple."

"Mama has good instincts."

That she does.

Pete put on his bomber jacket. "I should head home."

I stopped him. "Are you going to tell us how you found Ryan's car?"

"Good detective work."

I eyed my brother. "Did you steal it?"

"I found it. Nothing else matters."

"Did you steal anybody else's car and test it for traces of blood?"

"That would be illegal."

"Did you break into anybody else's car to see if there was blood?"

"No comment."

"And you just happened to have Luminol on hand when you 'found' Ryan's car?"

"A fortuitous coincidence."

Fortuitous, indeed.

Rosie's expression turned serious. "How did you know that Ryan killed Chloe Carson?"

"I didn't." Pete shrugged. "I played a hunch."

"You don't believe in hunches."

"That's all that we had left. Ryan was evasive when we talked to her. Several of the other suspects had issues with Carson, but none of them had a compelling motive to kill her."

"Did you steal her car?"

"I *found* her car."

It's your story, and you're sticking to it.

Pete's expression turned thoughtful. "I know César. For all of his issues, he isn't a killer."

Rosie leaned forward. "Does this have anything to do with what happened twenty years ago?"

"In part."

"You and César didn't mean to fracture that kid's skull," I said. "It was an accident."

"Not entirely. I didn't mean to hurt him, but I definitely meant to hit him."

"You told me that César hit him."

Pete lowered his voice. "He didn't. I did."

Oh. "You told me that the kid hit his head after he fell."

"That's what César and I told our superiors. The truth is that I hit the kid with my nightstick. I don't know if I cracked his skull, or if it cracked when he hit the ground. Either way, it was my fault."

"It was an accident," I insisted.

"The kid was high on speed. I thought he was going to take a swing at me. So I reacted. It happened very fast. I lost my composure and hit him too hard. A witness saw me hit the kid. The board believed him—in part, I suppose, because he was telling the truth. This was before police wore body cams. The kid's family filed the lawsuit, the City caved, and César and I got fired."

"It wasn't your fault."

"Actually, it was."

"What does that have to do with César's case?"

"Off the record?"

"Of course."

"The investigative panel gave César a chance to tell the truth and save his job. He never changed his story. He could have pointed a finger at me, but he didn't. He took the hit for me." He shook his head. "Everything worked out okay for me, but he blew up his marriage and his life to protect me."

Rosie scowled. "That's why you've been so gung ho to help him?"

"Not just to help him, Rosie. To prove his innocence."

"You did."

"Now we're even."

Rosie exhaled heavily. "For the record, I'm not ecstatic about your methods, but I think that justice was served."

"So do I."

"Don't steal any more cars, Pete."

"I won't."

"And we'll never talk about this again."

63
"THE SYSTEM ISN'T PERFECT"

"That's good news about Joey and Margarita," Rosie said.

"Yes, it is."

We were sitting on her back porch and sipping Pride Mountain Cab Franc at eleven-forty-five on Saturday night. The evening fog had rolled in, but the winds were calm. The embers were burning in the firepit. A lamp from the house behind Rosie's provided a little illumination.

Her eyes gleamed. "Do you think they'll get married?"

"Let's not get ahead of ourselves."

"We'll throw them an engagement party at Dunleavy's just like Big John threw for us. They can get married at St. Peter's just like we did."

So did my parents. And Grace and Chuck. "Sounds like a fine plan."

She arched an eyebrow. "Mama gave me some edibles. Are you interested?"

"Not tonight, Rosie."

"You got the charges against César dropped. You should celebrate a little."

"I'll stick to wine, thanks. Have you heard from the kids?"

"All fine. Tommy is heading up to the Lair next week to get ready for camp. He's looking forward to his second year on staff."

The Lair of the Golden Bear is the Cal Alumni Association's family camp at Pinecrest Lake about an hour east of Sonora. Rosie and I took the kids there every summer until they were teenagers. The tent cabins are rudimentary, the food is more hearty than gourmet, and the facilities are far from luxurious. And people keep coming back for decades.

"I'm jealous," I said.

"So am I, although I'm not sure that I could deal with the dust anymore. Grace and Chuck are meeting us for Mass at St. Peter's. So is Tommy. Mama promised to take them to the St. Francis for burgers after church. We're invited to join them."

"Excellent." I took a sip of wine. "You think your mom is slowing down?"

"We're all slowing down, Mike. And just like Mama, we're doing our best to avoid admitting it. How much did you know about Pete and César?"

"Some of it."

"Did you know that Pete hit the kid?"

"I had suspicions."

"Does our discussion with Pete earlier tonight change anything for you?"

"Not really. I wish that he had told me the whole story when it happened."

"He's an excellent PI, but I don't always approve of his methods."

"Neither do I." I grinned. "I would prefer that he didn't steal any more cars. Then again, the fact that he took a few, uh, liberties with the law kept César from going to trial and possibly getting convicted for a crime that he didn't commit."

"I saw Betsy McDaniel at Pilates this morning. She said that she was going to bind César over for trial if Ryan hadn't confessed to killing Chloe."

"I'm not surprised. I probably would have made the same decision based on the evidence."

"She said that you and Rolanda did a nice job."

"Good to know."

"You're good lawyers. You would have gotten an acquittal at trial."

"Maybe. You never know what's going to happen in front of a jury. Besides, the system isn't perfect."

"Neither are we."

That's for sure.

She took a sip of wine. "I believe in the system as much as anybody, but I'm willing to live with some imperfections as long as we get to the truth and justice is served." She eyed me. "Are you pretty sure that justice was served in this case?"

"Yes."

"Good." Her voice softened. "Is Pete going to be okay?"

"He'll be fine. He just keeps plugging away."

"So do we. Are *you* going to be okay?"

"I just keep plugging away, too."

"Are you going to ask Nady to handle Kelly Ryan's case?"

"Yes."

"Good. You should take a few days off."

"Too busy."

"At the very least, you should walk the steps with Zvi tomorrow."

"I will. What about you? You should take some time off, too."

"Too busy. And the campaign is starting to heat up."

"You've already vanquished your only challenger."

"I've been through enough campaigns to know that it's important to avoid complacency."

"It's okay to be confident."

"It isn't okay to be overconfident."

I'm not going to win this argument. "It'll be nice to see Grace and Chuck and Tommy."

"We don't spend enough time with the kids."

"They're busy, Rosie. So are we. We're doing the best that we can."

"I suppose." She finished her wine. "I promised Rolanda that we would take her kids to the park after we get back from lunch with Mama."

"I'd like that."

"We should do more of that, too." Her expression turned serious. "Do you think it's time for you and Wilma to move over here permanently? You already spend most nights here."

It's tempting. "We've talked about this, Rosie. I think it might be good to keep the apartment in case we need a little space."

"You'll think about it?"

"I will."

She picked up her wine glass and stood up. "It's getting cold. We should go inside."

"Right behind you. Do you want to watch a movie?"

"I had something in mind that would require a little more energy." She added, "If you aren't too tired."

"I can make myself available."

"Good to hear." She grabbed my hand, pulled me close, and kissed me. "I love you, Mike."

"I love you, too, Rosie."

A Note to the Reader

San Francisco is a city of wonderful neighborhoods, and North Beach is one of my favorites. It's among the oldest parts of the city, and you always know that you're in North Beach by the glorious aroma of garlic, tomato sauce, mozzarella, shrimp scampi, and veal parmigiana. After setting fifteen books in other parts of the city, I decided that it was finally time to set a story in North Beach. It was also a fortuitous choice because North Beach has many wonderful restaurants. Since Linda and I didn't get out much during Covid, it seemed like a fine place to "do research."

As for the plotline (you need one of those, too), I decided that it should reflect North Beach's tawdry past. Mike and Rosie represent the doorman of a strip club who is accused of stabbing one of the dancers in the alley after last dance. I figured that if the story included murder, sex, drugs, infidelity, etc., there would be something for everybody. And since there's always a personal connection, the accused is a former police officer -- and the former partner of Mike's younger brother, Pete, the tenacious cop-turned-private investigator.

North Beach is also the lifelong stomping grounds of the ageless Nick "The Dick" Hanson, the nonagenarian private investigator, mystery writer, real estate tycoon, TV star, and bon vivant. It was inevitable that Nick would make an appearance in **LAST DANCE**.

I like spending time with Mike and Rosie, and I hope that you do, too. I hope you enjoyed **LAST DANCE**. If you like my stories, please consider posting an honest review on Amazon or Goodreads. Your words matter and are a great guide to help my stories find future readers.

If you have a chance and would like to chat, please feel free to e-mail me at sheldon@sheldonsiegel.com. We lawyers don't get a lot of fan mail, but it's always nice to hear from my readers. Please bear with me if I don't respond immediately. I answer all of my e-mail myself, so sometimes it takes a little extra time.

Many people have asked to know more about Mike and Rosie's early history. As a thank you to my readers, I wrote **FIRST TRIAL**. It's a short story describing how they met years ago when they were just starting out at the P.D.'s Office. I've included the first chapter below and the full story is available at: www.sheldonsiegel.com.

Also on the website, you can read more about how I came to write my stories, excerpts and behind-the-scenes from the other Mike & Rosie novels and a few other goodies! Let's stay connected. Thanks for reading my story!

Regards,
Sheldon

Acknowledgements

As I have noted in the past, I am extraordinarily fortunate to have a very supportive and generous "board of advisors" who graciously provide their time and expertise to help me write these stories. As always, I have a lot of thank yous!

Thanks to my beautiful wife, Linda, who reads my manuscripts, designs the covers, is my online marketing guru, and takes care of all things technological. I couldn't imagine trying to navigate the chaos of the publishing world without you.

Thanks to our son, Alan, for your endless support, editorial suggestions, thoughtful observations, and excellent cover art and formatting work. I will look forward to seeing your first novel on the shelves in bookstores in the near future

Thanks to our son, Stephen, and our daughter-in-law, Lauren, for being kind, generous, and immensely talented people.

Thanks to my teachers, Katherine Forrest and Michael Nava, who encouraged me to finish my first book. Thanks to the Every Other Thursday Night Writers Group: Bonnie DeClark, Meg Stiefvater, Anne Maczulak, Liz Hartka, Janet Wallace, and Priscilla Royal. Thanks to Bill and Elaine Petrocelli, Kathryn Petrocelli, Karen West, and Luisa Smith at Book Passag

A huge thanks to Jane Gorsi for your excellent editing skills. A huge thanks to Linda Hall for your excellent editing skills, too.

Another huge thanks to Vilaska Nguyen of the San Francisco Public Defender's Office for your thoughtful comments an d terrific support. If you ever get into serious trouble, he's your g

Thanks to Joan Lubamersky for providing the invaluable "Lubamersky Comments" for the sixteenth time.

Thanks to Tim Campbell for your stellar narration of the audio version of this book (and many others in the series). You are the voice of Mike Daley, and you bring these stories to life!

Thanks to my friends and former colleagues at Sheppard, Mullin, Richter & Hampton (and your spouses and significant others). I can't mention everybody, but I'd like to note those of you with whom I worked the longest: Randy and Mary Short, Chris and Debbie Neils, Joan Story and Robert Kidd, Donna Andrews, Phil and Wendy Atkins-Pattenson, Julie and Jim Ebert, Geri Freeman and David Nickerson, Bill and Barbara Manierre, Betsy McDaniel, Ron and Rita Ryland, Bob Stumpf, Mike Wilmar, Mathilde Kapuano, Susan Sabath, Guy Halgren, Ed Graziani, Julie Penney, Christa Carter, Doug Bacon, Lorna Tanner, Larry Braun, Nady Nikonova, Joy Siu, and DeAnna Ouderkirk.

Thanks to Jerry and Dena Wald, Gary and Marla Goldstein, Ron and Betsy Rooth, Jay Flaherty, Debbie and Seth Tanenbaum, Jill Hutchinson and Chuck Odenthal, Tom Bearrows and Holly Hirst, Julie Hart, Burt Rosenberg, Ted George, Phil Dito, Chuck and Nora Koslosky, Jack Goldthorpe, Char Saper, Flo and Dan Hoffenberg, Lori Gilbert, Paul Sanner, Stewart Baird, Mike Raddie, Peter and Cathy Busch, Steve Murphy, Bob Dugoni, and John Lescroart. Thanks to Gary and Debbie Fields

Sadly, we recently had to say goodbye to the wonderful Rabbi Neil Brief who, together with his wife, Erica, were always there when we needed them for many years. We also had to bid farewell to my longtime reader, Sister Karen Marie Franks, of St. Dominic's Convent in San Francisco. We miss you.

Thanks to Tim and Kandi Durst, and Bob and Cheryl Easter, at the University of Illinois. Thanks to Kathleen

Vanden Heuvel, Bob and Leslie Berring, Jesse Choper, and Mel Eisenberg at Berkeley Law.

Thanks to the incomparable Zvi Danenberg, who motivates me to walk the Larkspur steps.

Thanks as always to Ben, Michelle, and Andy Siegel, Margie and Joe Benak, Joe, Jan, and Julia Garber, Roger and Sharon Fineberg, Scott, Michelle, Kim, and Sophie Harris, Stephanie, Stanley, Will, and Sam Coventry, Cathy, Richard, and Matthew Falco, Sofia Arnell, and Oliver Falco, and Julie Harris and Matthew, Aiden, and Ari Stewart. A huge thanks once again to our mothers, Charlotte Siegel (1928-2016) and Jan Harris (1934-2018), whom we miss every day.

Excerpt from FIRST TRIAL

Readers have asked to know more about Mike and Rosie's early history. As a thank you to all of you, I wrote this short story about how Mike & Rosie met years ago as they were just starting out at the P.D.'s Office. Here's the first chapter and you can download the full story (for FREE) at: www.sheldonsiegel.com. Enjoy!

1
"DO EXACTLY WHAT I DO"

The woman with the striking cobalt eyes walked up to me and stopped abruptly. "Are you the new file clerk?"

"Uh, no." My lungs filled with the stale air in the musty file room of the San Francisco Public Defender's Office on the third floor of the Stalinesque Hall of Justice on Bryant Street. "I'm the new lawyer."

The corner of her mouth turned up. "The priest?"

"Ex-priest."

"I thought you'd be older."

"I was a priest for only three years."

"You understand that we aren't in the business of saving souls here, right?"

"Right."

Her full lips transformed into a radiant smile as she extended a hand. "Rosie Fernandez."

"Mike Daley."

"You haven't been working here for six months, have you?"

"This is my second day."

"Welcome aboard. You passed the bar, right?"

"Right."

"That's expected."

I met Rosita Carmela Fernandez on the Wednesday after Thanksgiving in 1983. The Summer of Love was a fading memory, and we were five years removed from the Jonestown massacre and the assassinations of Mayor George Moscone and Supervisor Harvey Milk. Dianne Feinstein became the mayor and was governing with a steady hand in Room 200 at City Hall. The biggest movie of the year was *Return of the Jedi*, and the highest-rated TV show was *M*A*S*H*. People still communicated by phone and U.S. mail because e-mail wouldn't become widespread for another decade. We listened to music on LPs and cassettes, but CD players were starting to gain traction. It was still unclear whether VHS or Beta would be the predominant video platform. The Internet was a localized technology used for academic purposes on a few college campuses. Amazon and Google wouldn't be formed for another decade. Mark Zuckerberg hadn't been born.

Rosie's hoop-style earrings sparkled as she leaned against the metal bookcases crammed with dusty case files for long-forgotten defendants. "You local?"

"St. Ignatius, Cal, and Boalt. You?"

"Mercy, State, and Hastings." She tugged at her denim work shirt, which seemed out-of-place in a button-down era where men still wore suits and ties and women wore dresses to the office. "When I was at Mercy, the sisters taught us to beware of boys from S.I."

"When I was at S.I., the brothers taught us to beware of girls from Mercy."

"Did you follow their advice?"

"Most of the time."

The Bay Area was transitioning from the chaos of the sixties and the malaise of the seventies into the early stages of the tech boom. Apple had recently gone public and was still being run by Steve Jobs and Steve Wozniak. George Lucas was making Star Wars movies in a new state-of-the-art facility in Marin County. Construction cranes dotted downtown as new office towers were changing the skyline. Union Square was beginning a makeover after Nieman-Marcus bought out the City of Paris and built a flashy new store at the corner of Geary and Stockton, across from I. Magnin. The upstart 49ers had won their first Super Bowl behind a charismatic quarterback named Joe Montana and an innovative coach named Bill Walsh.

Her straight black hair shimmered as she let out a throaty laugh. "What parish?"

"Originally St. Peter's. We moved to St. Anne's when I was a kid. You?"

"St. Peter's. My parents still live on Garfield Square."

"Mine grew up on the same block."

St. Peter's Catholic Church had been the anchor of the Mission District since 1867. In the fifties and sixties, the working-class Irish and Italian families had relocated to the outer reaches of the City and to the suburbs. When they moved out, the Latino community moved in. St. Peter's was still filled every Sunday morning, but four of the five masses were celebrated in Spanish.

"I was baptized at St. Peter's," I said. "My parents were married there."

"Small world."

"How long have you worked here?" I asked.

"Two years. I was just promoted to the Felony Division."

"Congratulations."

"Thank you. I need to transition about six dozen active misdemeanor cases to somebody else. I trust that you have time?"

"I do."

"Where do you sit?"

"In the corner of the library near the bathrooms."

"I'll find you."

Twenty minutes later, I was sitting in my metal cubicle when I was startled by the voice from the file room. "Ever tried a case?" Rosie asked.

"It's only my second day."

"I'm going to take that as a no. Ever been inside a courtroom?"

"Once or twice."

"To work?"

"To watch."

"You took Criminal Law at Boalt, right?"

"Right."

"And you've watched Perry Mason on TV?"

"Yes."

"Then you know the basics. The courtrooms are upstairs." She handed me a file. "Your first client is Terrence Love."

"The boxer?"

"The retired boxer."

Terrence "The Terminator" Love was a six-foot-six-inch, three-hundred-pound small-time prizefighter who had grown up in the projects near Candlestick Park. His lifetime record was two wins and nine losses. The highlight of his career was when he was hired to be a sparring partner for George Foreman, who was training to fight Muhammad Ali at the time. Foreman knocked out The Terminator with the first punch that he threw—effectively ending The Terminator's careers as a boxer and a sparring partner.

"What's he doing these days?" I asked.

"He takes stuff that doesn't belong to him."

"Last time I checked, stealing was against the law."

"Your Criminal Law professor would be proud."

"What does he do when he isn't stealing?"

"He drinks copious amounts of King Cobra."

It was cheap malt liquor.

She added, "He's one of our most reliable customers."

Got it. "How often does he get arrested?"

"At least once or twice a month."

"How often does he get convicted?"

"Usually once or twice a month." She flashed a knowing smile. "You and Terrence are going to get to know each other very well."

I got the impression that it was a rite of passage for baby P.D.'s to cut their teeth representing The Terminator. "What did he do this time?"

She held up a finger. "Rule number one: a client hasn't 'done' anything unless he admits it as part of a plea bargain, or he's convicted by a jury. Until then, all charges are 'alleged.'"

"What is the D.A. *alleging* that Terrence did?"

"He *allegedly* broke into a car that didn't belong to him."

"Did he *allegedly* take anything?"

"He didn't have time. A police officer was standing next to him when he *allegedly* broke into the car. The cop arrested him on the spot."

"Sounds like Terrence isn't the sharpest instrument in the operating room."

"We don't ask our clients to pass an intelligence test before we represent them. For a guy who used to make a living trying to beat the daylights out of his opponents, Terrence is reasonably intelligent and a nice person who has never hurt anybody. The D.A. charged him with auto burglary."

"Can we plead it out?"

"*We* aren't going to do anything. *You* are going to handle this case. And contrary to what you've seen on TV, our job is to try cases, not to cut quick deals. Understood?"

"Yes."

"I had a brief discussion about a plea bargain with Bill McNulty, who is the Deputy D.A. handling this case. No deal unless Terrence pleads guilty to a felony."

"Seems a bit harsh."

"It is. That's why McNulty's nickname is 'McNasty.' You'll be seeing a lot of him, too. He's a hardass who is trying to impress his boss. He's also very smart and tired of seeing Terrence every couple of weeks. In fairness, I can't blame him."

"So you want me to take this case to trial?"

"That's what we do. Trial starts Monday at nine a.m. before Judge Stumpf." She handed me a manila case file. "Rule number two: know the record. You need to memorize everything inside. Then you should go upstairs to the jail and introduce yourself to your new client."

I could feel my heart pounding. "Could I buy you a cup of coffee and pick your brain about how you think it's best for me to prepare?"

"I haven't decided whether you're coffee-worthy yet."

"Excuse me?"

"I'm dealing with six dozen active cases. By the end of the week, so will you. If you want to be successful, you need to figure stuff out on your own."

I liked her directness. "Any initial hints that you might be willing to pass along?"

"Yes. Watch me. Do exactly what I do."

"Sounds like good advice."

She grinned. "It is."

There's more to this story and it's yours for FREE!

Get the rest of **FIRST TRIAL** at:
www.sheldonsiegel.com/first-trial

About the Author

Sheldon Siegel is the New York Times best-selling author of the critically acclaimed legal thrillers featuring San Francisco criminal defense attorneys Mike Daley and Rosie Fernandez, two of the most beloved characters in contemporary crime fiction. He is also the author of the thriller novel The Terrorist Next Door featuring Chicago homicide detectives David Gold and A.C. Battle. His books have been translated into a dozen languages and sold millions of copies. A native of Chicago, Sheldon earned his undergraduate degree from the University of Illinois in Champaign in 1980, and his law degree from Berkeley Law in 1983. He specialized in corporate law with several large San Francisco law firms for forty years.

Sheldon began writing his first book, Special Circumstances, on a laptop computer during his daily commute on the ferry from Marin County to San Francisco. Sheldon is a San Francisco Library Literary Laureate, a former member of the Board of Directors and former President of the Northern California chapter of the Mystery Writers of America, and an active member of the International Thriller Writers and Sisters in Crime. His work has been displayed at the Bancroft Library at the University of California at

Berkeley, and he has been recognized as a Distinguished Alumnus of the University of Illinois and a Northern California Super Lawyer.

Sheldon lives in the San Francisco area with his wife, Linda. Sheldon and Linda are the proud parents of twin sons named Alan and Stephen. Sheldon is a lifelong fan of the Chicago Bears, White Sox, Bulls and Blackhawks. He is currently working on his next novel.

Sheldon welcomes your comments and feedback. Please email him at sheldon@sheldonsiegel.com. For more information on Sheldon, book signings, the "making of" his books, and more, please visit his website at www.sheldonsiegel.com.

Connect with Sheldon
Email: sheldon@sheldonsiegel.com
Website: www.sheldonsiegel.com
Amazon: amazon.com/author/sheldonsiegel
Facebook: www.facebook.com/sheldonsiegelauthor
Goodreads: www.goodreads.com/sheldonsiegel
Bookbub: bookbub.com/authors/sheldon-siegel
Twitter: @SheldonSiegel

Also By Sheldon Siegel

Mike Daley/Rosie Fernandez Novels
Special Circumstances
Incriminating Evidence
Criminal Intent
Final Verdict
The Confession
Judgment Day
Perfect Alibi
Felony Murder Rule
Serve and Protect
Hot Shot
The Dreamer
Final Out
Last Call
Double Jeopardy
Dead Coin
Last Dance

Short Stories
(available at sheldonsiegel.com)
First Trial
The Maltese Pigeon - A Nick "the Dick" Story

David Gold/A.C. Battle Novels
The Terrorist Next Door

Made in the USA
Las Vegas, NV
19 April 2024